V.P. NIGHTSHADE

Now, Always, Forever

A Dark Paranormal Vampire Romance (Vampiris Bloodline – A Paranormal Vampire Romance Series Book 2)

Now, Always, Forever: Notes from the Author:

1: This work contains coarse language, explicit violence, and mature sexual content.

2: Trigger Warnings: This book features a serial killer/rapist (villain).

3: Vampires do not exist (that's our story and we are sticking to it)!

Paranormal Vampire Romance, MA 18+ Content, Dub Con/NC/Rape Scenes and Language, Violence, Blood, Gore, Angst – if any of this bothers you, do not read this book!

This is the second book in a series! It is a True Sequel! If you have not read Book 1, The Choice, you will not understand the character motivations or enjoy this book. Please read The Choice first!

Cover Design Images used under license from Canva.com

EPUB ISBN: 978-1-7374885-5-2 Paperback ISBN: 978-1-7374885-6-9 Hardback ISBN: 978-1-7374885-7-6

First edition

This book was professionally typeset on Reedsy. Find out more at reedsy.com

This book is dedicated to everyone who ever gave me inspiration and who will never read it!

For My Readers - This sequel would not have been written or published at this time without your desires! I hope it is everything that you wanted it to be!

"The only word to describe you is mine and the only word to describe us is forever." ~ Jon Kortajarena

"I will love you with all my heart, To have forever – never to part. This is a promise engrained in me, Take my hand and let it be." ~ Diana Lynn

"Forever I love you, for there is nothing in this world I want to do but love you and to be with you, now and forever. Till the oceans dry, till the sun dims, I'll still be loving you forever and for eternity."

Contents

Preface

Writing for me is almost a compulsion. To me, the best thing about being a writer is creating your own worlds and charting your own course. Don't get me wrong, sometimes your characters take over a manuscript, all of the sudden you're typing as fast as you can and you're crying your eyes out at the same time and you end up at the end of a project emotionally exhausted and not realizing that's where you were going - but that is writing! It's always an adventure!

I always imagined something more than the real world! I would read and watch paranormal based books and movies and think to myself, well this wouldn't work – they would be found out right away. So, basically, I am a realist that fits my paranormal characters into real world settings. I always try to keep an eye out to how these otherworldly creatures would truly function and more importantly survive in the 'real world'. How would they adapt to the human world around them so that they are able to not only survive, but to use their powers to thrive?

So, where do I get my ideas? I get my ideas from life itself, the people around me, the things that happen in my day-to-day life – the way my mind works is that everything can be turned into a story.

In 1995, the idea of The Choice came to me in a dream. Basically, the whole prologue was my dream, that's where it started. In a weekend, I had the prologue written, and the rest of the book outlined out, it was like it was flowing out of my mind. Of course, as I always say, LIFE HAPPENS, so after moving all over the U.S. for 25 years, I found myself in 2020, along with half the country asking myself, "If I died today, what would I regret?" My answer was not getting published.

You see, I have more than 30 manuscripts in my office that are in various stages of development (and various genres), that I have carried all over the country. I read through them all, dusted them off, grabbed The Choice and said, "Let's get you finished." Then made the decision that LIFE wasn't going to HAPPEN to me anymore and that finishing this project would take priority over the little things in my life!

So for the budding writer out there: Don't let anything stop you. Life will stop you if you let it. What I am talking about is the little mundane things that happen to us like: job, kids, television, cleaning the house, laundry! While these things are important, they can suck the creativity out of your mind! Don't let them. If you have people in your life that are not supportive of you - ignore them. MAKE TIME TO WRITE. WRITE ABOUT WHAT'S IMPORTANT TO YOU!

If you don't make time to write in your life, you will not write. It is really that simple!

Thanks so much for reading the sequel: Now, Always, Forever - A Dark Paranormal Vampire Romance (Vampiris Bloodline - A Paranormal Vampire Romance Series, Book 2)! I hope that you are enjoying this modern world where my vampires live!

In this novel, I wrote about some pretty dark subjects that bother me and that I care about, that make me angry, make me cry, and then when I was getting too dark my characters took over and made me laugh. Believe me, I did all of it while writing this novel. Which is good, because not everything is dark and not everything is light, life is a mixture of both; and so it is with my characters.

To use the words of a reviewer, I hope that that this book makes you "laugh, cry, get mad," and after all of that emotional roller coaster ~ fills your heart with love!

V. P. Nightshade - January 29, 2022

Acknowledgement

The completion of this sequel would not have been possible if not for the persistence of the readers of The Choice! Thank you for pushing me to the finish line! Knowing that some of you wanted this so badly was a huge motivator.

Thank you so much to Robyn Nagle, a wonderful artist who helped me with some color issues with the cover art. You can see Robyn's art at: https://www.facebook.com/RobynsDigitalArt/

Specifically a HUGE Thank You to my friend and partner in crime, Romana Disrud. In this book I delved into some really dark areas and you were always there to pull me out of the darkness and back into the light!

As always, thank you to my family and specifically my extremely grumpy husband, who though I know he hates the time I spend in my office writing, still allows me to do so by paying the bills and taking care of the really hard parts of everyday life! Thank you, honey, you are my rock!

Prologue: August 2021

I was reading a prospectus when I heard Mansuetus's smartphone ring, causing me to close my eyes in irritation; he'd just recently installed the *Uptown Funk* ring tone, which he had received from one of Leila's children, and I had not gotten used to it, so it still grated on my nerves.

"Kyría! What are you up to?" I heard Mansuetus's pleased deep voice come from the other room and then pause as he listened. "We are in Peru for the season." He said obviously replying to a question.

This was not their day to be speaking! If I had known that she would be calling today, I would have made myself scarce so I wouldn't have to listen to a one-sided conversation of hers. I've been harboring a deep-seated resentment toward her for more than a year; ever since the death of her human husband.

I expected her to come to me upon his death; instead, I received no call, no communication whatsoever. Thank God that communication from her wasn't my sustenance, or I would have starved to death! Obviously, she didn't need or want me in her life and as far as I was concerned, I was just fine with that! I felt a pang in the general vicinity of my heart as I thought this, belying the lie that I continued to tell myself as my anger grew.

I attempted to focus my whole attention on the prospectus in front of me and closed my hearing to Mansuetus's voice. The worldwide pandemic had caused my businesses to take some initial decreases, but I was highly

1

diversified, and it wasn't the first pandemic I had experienced in my long life. As such, I was able to quickly adapt to both the needs and fears of the human populace. My manufacturing lines of designer masks and hand sanitizer were making more than healthy profits and had more than compensated for the initial financial decreases of some of my portfolio.

Movement in front of my desk caused me to look up to find Mansuetus looking down on me. I met his concerned look questioningly.

"She wants to speak with you." He said softly, extending his phone.

I paused to look at the phone briefly before I took it from him, only to feel my heart lurch painfully in my chest, creating a shame and anger that the thought of a simple telephone conversation with her could affect me so.

"Hello?" My voice unfortunately was not as strong as I would have liked. "Hello?" I repeated louder, quickly, coldly.

"Nichola." Her sweet voice caressed the syllables of my name and my frozen heart melted and started pounding erratically within my chest. "It's Devin. Nichola, I need you."

The part of my soul that was hurt and furious urged me to tell her to go straight to hell! But the part that worshipped and ached for her battled it into submission and then locked that part away in an iron box and whispered into the void, "Finally!"

San Antonio International Airport

I nervously paced back and forth just outside of a private hanger looking at the sinking sun over the San Antonio International Airport; shaking my head in thought, I realized that it never failed to amaze me at the speed in which Nichola was able to just make things happen: a fact, I had depended on.

I guess having more money than God was a powerful advantage in accomplishing any goal that you had in mind. Still, being able to arrange for transportation and documentation to leave the country in the span of twenty-four hours was no mean achievement, especially with COVID restrictions. Both Devin and I had gotten vaccinated early on, though I knew it was unnecessary at least on my part, because it made operating and traveling in the human world simpler. We both had passports so that part was taken care of, but I knew from my research last night that we were supposed to provide a negative test result before leaving the airport to travel to Peru. Neither one of us had the time to even take a test, nor did I plan for it as I had no idea where they had been staying before speaking to Mansuetus yesterday. It made no difference in any case, because according to Mansuetus this morning, that requirement for us was waived. I guess money talks and bullshit test results walk.

I wondered how much money and influence Nichola had to lay down to make it happen and how much of it was preplanned? He always had the uncanny knack to be about a dozen steps ahead of everyone else. I also understood that he used many resources in addition to Mansuetus to track me and the boys. Stalker was not a term that I would use loosely with anyone. But it is what it is.

I glanced back into the hanger looking at Devin's tired-looking body seated in a chair next to where Zachary stood. Having been in his position myself years ago, I could sympathize. Devin's eyes closed in exhaustion, and Zachary had a supporting hand on his shoulder, his shiny new detective's badge attached to his belt.

Looking at their handsome faces, I realized that I was so proud of both of them! Zachary was one of the youngest Detectives ever on the San Antonio police force and Devin, up until his illness started a few days ago, was highly courted by several powerful law firms in the city.

They both had moved in with me after Michael had died last year and were a huge help. Of course, free rent and board worked to offset the fact that they lived with their mom again. Since Michael's death had left me very well-off, both financially and property-wise, living in a four thousand square foot home where all of the bedrooms were ensuite, meant that we didn't overrun each other too much. It worked for me because I was able to observe them to see if they were experiencing any symptoms of transformation into what we all truly were. It worked for them because they felt they were keeping me company. Still, the fact that they both felt they needed to be there to protect and comfort me made me feel very guilty.

Pride and guilt wrapped up into one neat little package; yeah, that was me.

"Mom, how much longer do you think?" Zachary asked, suddenly checking his cellphone, and reading a text message. As a hotshot detective he always was on-call. He had a nose for it. Reading people, delving into their minds and actions to sense both guilt and innocence. His successes had quickly placed him in the homicide department, and he loved his job; but, like me, nothing came before his love for his family.

"I don't know, honey. I know that they were flying out of Cusco. It is a straight flight to here. It should take them about seven to seven and a half hours according to Mansuetus. It's the same time zone as here. So, if they left around noon like they were planning, it should be anytime." I replied and walked back into the hanger to lay my hand against Devin's forehead. He wasn't burning up, but he wasn't cool to the touch either.

"I'm okay, Mom!" He said sharply pulling away, then took my hand to give it a kiss to take the sting from his words. "I'm just tired."

"I know, baby." I murmured looking into Zachary's worried blue eyes over Devin's head. "It shouldn't be too much longer." I heard a plane on the tarmac, then looked out to see a large private jet taxiing toward the hanger. Hmmm. Well, that's new.

Soon, the door was folding down and out of the plane. Mansuetus walked down the stairs, tweed nondescript sports coat over a mahogany brown t-shirt, jeans, and soft brown boots on his tall frame. Even though I hadn't seen him since Michael's death, I knew for certain that he carried at least three deadly weapons on his person at all times and just attempted to look innocuous. He looked around the area outside the hanger with interest, and only knowing him as well as I did now convinced me that he was in 'scout' mode and searching out any danger. He shortly looked at me with a smile on his face and held his arms out wide. I couldn't help it, smiling myself, I ran to him for a hug. I looked in surprise around him to see Dr. Dene Lambert descend the plane's stairs. He gave me a bashful look and one of his sweet sexy smiles as I walked into his arms to hold him tightly. Sometimes being partners in a major crime will make you fast friends; and Dene and I were. I looked up into his still sexy blue eyes and realized that he hadn't aged a day over the last twenty-six years.

"God, Dene!" I said softly. "How are you doing?"

"Better than ever, Leila." He gave me another tight squeeze before releasing me. "I hear I have a new patient? I am sure that you will be glad to know that I have an idea of what I am dealing with now." He looked at me, blessing me with one of his boyish, movie-star smiles.

I looked into the hanger to see Mansuetus embracing the boys. "God, Uncle Man. You never change." Zachary told him smiling as he received pats on the back from the big man.

"You do!" Mansuetus said in return. "You are a man that sports a beard now, eh?"He patted Zachary's short, trimmed, reddish-brown beard then looked down at Devin who looked up at him with clove-colored eyes, tired and annoyed. "How are you feeling, Imp?" He asked giving him a concerned look as he ruffled his hair.

"You are still going to call me Imp, Uncle Man? I am twenty-seven years old!" Devin said with a tired growl to his voice as he smoothed his silky dark locks back into place.

Mansuetus gave a short laugh. "You will always be my Imp! Answer my question, counselor, how are you feeling?"

"Generally, crappy." Devin murmured.

I decided to step in, "Devin, this is Dr. Dene Lambert, an old friend of mine. You met him a few times when you were just a baby."

Dene stepped forward his hand outstretched, "Just let me know if you are going to start screaming at me!" He chuckled.

Devin responded, "Huh?" shaking his hand.

"An inside joke." He told him glancing at me and I returned his smile in remembrance.

"Come." Mansuetus said helping Devin to stand, then bracing an arm around him. "We have a schedule to keep."

"Aren't you going to refuel?" I inquired.

"Not with this!" Mansuetus told me smiling, gesturing towards the plane.

"So, it is new! I thought so!"

"Yes, this is the Global 8000. Just came out. We will refuel when we land back at Cusco." He said excitedly. "Wait until you see the inside!"

I just shook my head at his fascination with new toys. Looking at Zachary through the tears in my eyes, he stepped forward and gave me a hard hug.

"I love you, Mom." He said to me quietly, kissing me on top of the head.

"Take care of my house and my dog." I told him swallowing my tears hard.

"I will. Take care of my brother," he whispered, "and yourself too." Zachary adjusted his detective's shield attached to his belt, looking down to try to hide the bright sheen in his own eyes.

"I will call you tomorrow night and give you an update." I told him looking into his sad, robin-egg blue eyes as I pulled his face to look at me and ran my hand over his short silky beard. "This is not forever, son. We will see each other soon. I promise."

* * * * *

I sat at the table in the cabin across from Dene and looked around with interest. This plane was so much larger and more luxurious than the last private jet that Nichola had owned. This one easily would comfortably hold twelve, most likely more, and had two main compartments. I glanced toward the back compartment to where Mansuetus had led Devin and watched as he got him settled on a sofa, somehow buckling him in, though he was basically prone. I watched as he spoke softly to him, turned on a television, popped in a DVD, adjusted the volume, and then covered him with a blanket. He walked toward the front of the plane, closed an accordion door across the compartment where he had left Devin and then continued to walk to where Dene and I were seated at a four-person table in comfortable, and luxurious berthable seats. He took the outside seat next to mine and buckled himself in, prompting us to do the same.

A human cabin steward came through and introduced himself. "Lady Tsoukalous, it is a pleasure to have you aboard the Dragonfly. My name is Jared, and I will be taking care of you during this flight. Once we are airborne I will return with drinks and something to eat." He bowed his head as I tentatively thanked him, surprised. It had been a long time since anyone had referred to me as 'Lady Tsoukalous' and the title had caught me off guard.

I settled back into the extraordinary comfort of my seat and looked out the window with a trepidation that I didn't feel before. I was so caught up in getting packed and worrying over Devin and what he was going through that I hadn't had the capacity to worry over seeing my lover and soulmate again after more than a quarter of a century. That trepidation now came full force.

I felt Mansuetus enfold my hand in his large warm one as we started to taxi down the runway for takeoff. I glanced over at him in question.

"If the gods had meant us to fly they would have given us wings!" He murmured to me.

"He's just happy to have you here as I wouldn't hold his hand on the way over!" Dene told me with a smirk in his ice-blue eyes as they glittered in humor.

"Why make the trip if you are a nervous flier?" I asked Mansuetus.

"Because we do what we must for those we love, Kyría." He said closing his eyes and leaning his head back on the seat still holding my hand as the Dragonfly took flight into the night sky.

There Will Be More of Your Children Dead Tomorrow

"Hey, Zach!" I heard coming from behind me.

I nodded to my partner, Sammy 'The Salsa' Garcia, as I knelt next to the cold body of a young girl in the second level of the Houston Street Parking Garage next to the Majestic Theatre. In life, this girl had been a pretty little thing, no more than fifteen or sixteen, but she had obviously been dead a while by the look of her glazed over pansy brown eyes. The deep, intentional cuts crisscrossing her half naked body lacked blood, the flesh exposed by the wounds an off-pink instead of a blood-red, and as I looked around, I saw no traces of blood around the area telling me that she had been killed elsewhere and dumped here next to a dumpster like so much trash. Fury took hold of my chest as I gazed at her poor broken body.

"This cocksucker is fucking with us!" I snarled and Salsa nodded his head.

"No shit, partner! What do you think?" He knelt next to me putting on gloves and carefully, gently lifted her hand from the pavement no more than six inches. "Broken nails and what might be defensive wounds." He stated.

"I'd bet money that she was killed 48 hours or more ago and that she has little to no blood left. Just like the others." I ground my teeth, scratching my beard. "Has anyone looked at the security video? Hamilton is playing

9

next door. There is no way that she laid here for two days without being discovered, this had to be a recent dump. If we can get this fucker on camera we can nail his ass!"

"Johnson is getting us a warrant. They won't release them to us without one."

"That's bullshit! We have a dead girl here!" I snapped at him, the fury in my chest growing.

"You know how these rich downtown fuckers are." Salsa muttered to me. "The parking garage is probably worried we might see one of their 'upstanding citizens' getting blown in their car!"

"It would be a different story if they thought she was one of theirs!" I looked at this girl, obviously she was Latino, and what little clothing she had on made it look like she could possibly be a hooker. If that was the case, she probably was a runaway or an illegal immigrant just trying to make her way. San Antonio's dark criminal underbelly was just as dark as any other big city. Either way she was somebody's little girl, along with the ten others that this sick fucker had left for us all over the downtown area in the last eleven months. Looking down at the dead girl's body I felt helplessness start to overtake me, and with supreme effort I shook it off, preferring to deal with rage.

"I don't give a shit who Johnson has to blow, but I want that fucking warrant tonight!" I told Salsa standing up to head over to the uniformed officer who was speaking with the lot security attendant who had reported the body, looking up at the several security cameras in the garage as I made my way. "This fucker's finally made a mistake." I murmured to Salsa as he stepped up beside me.

Cusco, Peru: 3:00 am

As we landed in Cusco and taxied down the runway, the pilot turned the plane toward a large private hanger. Mansuetus had plied us with Coca Tea and his blood building foods throughout the seven-hour flight.

Devin had decided to join us at the table after about an hour. Our eyes met as he sat next to Dene across from Mansuetus and I, and we smelled the tea that kind of smelled like freshly cut grass. After steeping for a while in the hot water the smell transformed into a strong herbal scent. Sipping it, I found it to be unlike both black tea or green tea, without any citrus or tangy flavor. Overall, it had a strong herbal, slightly sweet flavor, that soon had me feeling a numbing at the back of my throat that covered the strong scent. I realized that the tea would be great if you had a sore throat, so knew it must be medicinal.

I had long ago learned to just eat or drink whatever Mansuetus put in front of me. Of course, Devin had to question everything.

"This smells weird." Devin told Mansuetus.

"Just drink it. You will like it." Mansuetus replied.

"Why? What makes it so special? Coca leaves? As in cocaine? Are you trying to make us high? Will I fail a drug test if I drink this?" His voice had been sharp and distinct.

I smiled at Devin's questions. It was too bad that he had decided to specialize in contractual law instead of criminal. He would have made a hell of a trial attorney!

"Like that matters now." Mansuetus said giving him a stern look. "Just drink it, Imp. It will help with any possible elevation sickness that you may experience while we are in Peru."

"Elevation sickness?" I asked sipping the tea. "Just drink it, Devin! It's not half-bad."

Devin brought the tea to his lips wrinkling his nose at the odor.

Mansuetus replied to my question. "Yes, elevation sickness is always a concern for humans. You are coming from 650 feet above sea level, to over 11,000 feet above sea level. It's a concern. This helps."

* * * * *

We had made good time due to a prevailing tail wind. I found that I couldn't relax at all during the flight, though my companions and son seemed to enjoy themselves, even with Devin experiencing some weakness and laying back down a couple of hours ago. By the time we had landed I was as nervous as a cat in a room full of rocking chairs, thinking about what I would say to Nichola when we arrived at Temuco de Wila Tatitu, his newest vampire resort located just outside the Temple of the Sun near Machu Pichu. Well, newest for Nichola, in any case, as I realized that he had finally completed construction of the hotel just nineteen years ago, five years past his original construction schedule which Mansuetus had told me irritated him to no end.

The geography was tough to say the least and according to Mansuetus, they had to lay out a ton of bribes as well as deal with construction issues to finally get it completed. The mountainous region was difficult to navigate in a vehicle, and when we finally taxied to a stop I knew we had to endure at least another hour and a half by helicopter to reach the place.

I followed Mansuetus who was assisting Devin down the stairs of the jet and shivered in the 30-degree temperatures of the Peruvian darkness under my lightweight, long-sleeved sweater I had luckily thought to bring with me on the plane, as my coat was packed in my luggage. I had the strangest sensation, an ache in my chest and a shortness of breath. I started to panic

12

thinking I was having a bout of elevation sickness. I walked a few steps clutching my sweater over my chest and my pounding heart, wondering if I would pass out when I realized with a shock that for the first time in 26 years I was feeling *his* presence. I watched as Mansuetus walked Devin to a large helicopter to help him climb up. Dene followed closely behind them hovering like a mother hen over his new patient, assisting Mansuetus in securing Devin into the back seat of the helicopter. I followed them slowly, the ache almost sucking the air from my lungs.

He approached me from the front of the helicopter, materializing out of the darkness. He was dressed in a long, dark-colored canvas duster against the thin chilly Peruvian air, his white shirt underneath opened at the throat, a glimpse of his tight jeans and soft brown boots finished out his attire as he steadily walked toward me. His burnished gold hair was slightly longer and more tawny-brown than I remembered, but his mesmerizing eyes were the same light-amber color that they had always been, and they glowed hotly at me as he strode toward me. I stopped in my tracks, turning toward him, and just stared in fear. I was so not ready for this!

* * * * *

I felt her fear and the pounding of her blood through the veins in her body as I walked towards her. Her fear was the last thing I thought to find, and it was the last thing that I wanted. She was different. Older, but not as aged as I had expected. Less of the thin fragile girl of transition remained, and I beheld a womanlier version with curves that I suddenly found I was aching to explore. Her hair was longer, heavily streaked in silver. It framed her beautiful face and set off the teal of her mysterious eyes. I slowed my approach towards her and ignored the machinations of the three men inside the helicopter and the plane's steward who was handing them luggage, as I focused my attention solely on her. Despite the fear that I knew she felt, she met my gaze bravely, lifting her chin in defiance and her teal eyes glowed into mine. There's my girl.

I removed my coat as I reached her and wrapped it around her shivering shoulders pulling her to me by the lapels as I bent my head to run my lips and my nose against the side of her throat to breathe her in. I breathed deep

13

of the licorice, jasmine and peppermint that was the scent of my Leila. There she is: my soul rejoiced.

Still holding her tightly by the lapels of my jacket with one hand, I smiled down into her defiant eyes as I wrapped one long, thick, silky, silver bang around my finger, enjoying the feel of it against my skin, and of her against me, then said, "You've changed your hair." Which was not what I had planned to say to her at this momentous time, but the fierce look in her eyes told me it was exactly the right thing to say to wipe away her fear.

"I see you've changed yours also," she quipped. "I guess that's what happens to all of us, when we get old." The side of her full lipped mouth lifted in a small deprecating smile.

I chuckled softly returning both of my hands to grip the lapels of my jacket and pulled her even tighter against my body. "I am never going to let you leave my side again, i psychí mou." I glared down into her wide teal eyes. It was a statement; a promise; a threat. "Never again."

"I know." She said simply as she gazed up at me and I did the only thing that I had wanted to do since I heard her voice on the phone yesterday. I wrapped my arms tightly around her, pulling her softness against me as I engulfed her lush lips with mine.

* * * * *

"Mom! What the fuck!" Devin's harsh, shocked voice came from the helicopter.

Nichola raised his head from the deliciousness of her lips and looked down into Leila's eyes. "Obviously, one of yours." He said softly. It wasn't a question and Leila raised her arched eyebrows. "O Theé mou! I do not have the patience for *two* stubborn, foul-mouthed transitioning vampires!"

"I have confidence in you, Nichola." She said sweetly with an angelic smile.

He pulled her by the hand towards the helicopter, getting her fully situated into his duster and got her up and secured into the front passenger's seat. She looked at him in surprise. "Where is the pilot?"

"You are looking at him!" Nichola told her as he secured her door walking around the front to climb up into the pilot's seat. He handed her some headphones, "You'll need those." Then he turned to make sure that

14

Mansuetus, Dean, and Devin had their headphones on.

"Since when do you know how to fly a helicopter?!" Leila asked incredulously as he started to buckle himself in and secure his headphones.

"Since before I met you. As always you are safe in my hands." He smiled at her, and she felt happiness radiating from him throughout her body. Happiness that she was finally with him.

He began flipping switches and the machine shuddered as the blades above them rotated. "Everyone ready?" Nichola's voice came through her headphones, and she heard everyone else's tinny reply as she nodded to him, and he smoothly maneuvered them into the air.

The night was pitch black, the only lights from the gauges of the helicopter panels, and she didn't know how he navigated, but she trusted him with every part of her soul. Exhaustion overtook her as she leaned back in her seat finally able to relax and she felt sleep overtake her.

* * * * *

"Wake up, i allagí mou, I would have you see Temuco de Wila Tatitu from the sky." I heard Nichola's voice through my headset waking me from my light slumber.

I looked over a mountain top curious to see his newest hotel, especially after sensing the pride in his voice. The compound was enormous, and he must have had them turn on all of the lights for us as the multiple acre estate was brightly lit on our approach, shining like a beacon in the night. Multi-leveled, it looked like it was carved into the mountainside with at least two-levels running under the ground to exit into open balconies looking out onto a forested, jungle infested valley.

There were several buildings on top of the mountain which looked like it had also been sheared into several flat levels. The main building was mostly stone, three stories high with tile and thatch roof-lines and encompassed several acres. I could see a row of several off-facing, small private stone villas attached to one side of the main hotel via a long, open, covered walkway. The front courtyard of the hotel looked out upon miles of the forested jungle below and the centerpiece was a large fountain sculpture that lit up the front of the hotel, it was in the center of a large round stone-paved drive which had only a very few of what looked like rugged utility vehicles parked, a couple of black hummers and jeeps. It looked like the hotel was sparsely populated, which was a bit of a surprise.I could see the splashes of water rising from the fountain as we approached and slowly flew over the main building of the hotel to see a flat area that looked like it was some large recreational area consisting of several open acres of green grass.

I could see on a higher level to the right of the main hotel that there was a section of acreage devoted to small stone houses, where I could see some small wisps of smoke rising from a few chimneys, this looked like a small village. I knew from past experience from my time at Château les Ténèbres, that this section housed the hotel's human and the odd vampire staff that worked at the hotel and housed them in more luxury than they would ever have been able to afford in any of the nearby local villages that may have existed. There was always a method to Nichola's thinking when in development of one of his 'vampire sanctuaries'; though, I knew, he would take issue with that term.

Further to the left of the small village sat a larger passenger helicopter next to some sort of outbuilding. Nichola gently maneuvered our smaller helicopter into position onto the helipad next to it and proceeded to shut the machine down. From the outbuilding ran three men, two vampires and one human, one of the vampires wheeled a wheelchair, the human wheeling a luggage wagon, to our helicopter as the blades slowed. The other vampire was smartly dressed in a dark suit, and obviously the majordomo of the hotel. I was more surprised to know him. He ran to my side and opened my door to assist me with getting out of the helicopter.

"Nelson! It is nice to see you again! What are you doing here? Why aren't you in Florida?" I asked with a smile.

"Lady Tsoukalous, it is wonderful to see you again! I have been promoted!" He exclaimed returning my smile.

"Well, I am not surprised! What a beautiful hotel! What does Temuco de Wila Tatitu mean? I don't think that it is Spanish?" I asked. Having lived in Texas for nearly a decade, I had an ear for the language, but couldn't speak it as I butchered rolling my 'r's'. I could usually keep up with a conversation if two other people were speaking it in my presence and had found the skill useful in the past.

"Oh, no, my lady! It is Quechua, the surviving language of the Incan Empire. It is loosely translated as Temple of the Blood God." Nelson told me helping me out of the helicopter to smile down at me.

I looked over at Nichola as he rounded the front of the helicopter and raised my eyebrow at him. "Your sense of humor never ceases to amaze me!"

"Well, there was some debate over the subject. But I thought Temple of the Blood King sounded a little self-important!" He said with a mischievous smile and a small chuckle, his eyes twinkling down at me as he took my hand.

"Oh!" I exclaimed. "So, you are saying that my giving you the title of 'The Vampire King', gave you the idea?"

"Well, after some time, I decided I kind of liked your nickname. I missed it at least." Nichola held me to him loosely.

"Where will we be, Nichola, if you decide to adopt all of the nicknames that I give you that are designed to irritate you?" I asked with a small laugh.

"Perfectly happy?" He questioned softly in return.

"I am capable of walking!" Devin exclaimed harshly as he descended from the helicopter. "I am not an invalid!"

"Master Devin," Mansuetus said sternly. "Follow the doctor's order! It is not good to wear yourself out during this time of transition. It only makes the process more difficult for you."

I looked at Devin and said, "Just do as they ask, honey. You will find that following their advice is the right thing to do. Besides, I am tired and want to get into the hotel."

"But Mom!" Devin started to protest.

"Do as your mother asks!" Nichola looked at him in command and his voice held an essence of power.

Devin fixed him with a look of resentment but did as he was told, and Dene quickly wheeled him toward the outbuilding as Nelson, Nichola and I followed. I soon saw the building was larger than I had first thought and housed a separate workshop and an elevator. The five of us rode down first and let Mansuetus, the vampire and the human, handle getting our luggage off of the helicopter.

I could see that the elevator descended at least three levels: B1, B2, and a level marked G, which I thought might be an underground garage of some sort. The doors opened to a dimly lit underground concrete passage, and we had quite a walk to end in glass double doors. Nelson opened them and I could see a spread-out area, with polished concrete floors, which housed a few shops, several seating areas in the large open-area and some of the spa facilities that I had come to expect; a large section of the floor was open to a long glass wall which had several glass double doors that led to the balconies that I had seen from the air. I realized that in the daylight it would be an absolutely impressive view of the valley below the hotel.

"How much did you spend on this facility?" I asked Nichola in awe, to which he laughed heartily.

"I have missed your directness, Glykó! You are the only person to dare ask me that directly!" He smiled in pleasure. I looked at him and he continued, "I am far wealthier now than I was when I met you." He murmured seductively to me, the smile remaining on his face.

Well, in Nichola-speak, that could *mean* almost anything. "Still not an answer." I stated.

"I am aware." The pleased smile never left his face as we walked hand-in-hand following Nelson, Dene and Devin to another elevator and ascended into the main hotel.

My mouth literally dropped open as we left the elevator. The lobby of the hotel was breathtakingly beautiful! The granite of the stone floors shone grey with hints of blue, the walls were white-washed plaster, and the ceilings were high and crisscrossed with dark-stained mahogany beams. Native art and pictures of Incan temples, the jungle valley, and portraits of what I thought must be Incan gods lined the walls. The main desk was a dark stained mahogany, covered by a polished grayish-blue veined granite counter. The trim and base-boards were all dark-stained mahogany and shone in the soft light. Comfortable-looking grouped couches and over-sized chairs for gathering and relaxing were arranged around a massive stone fireplace that burned brightly to ward off the chilly Peruvian air.

I could feel Nichola's eyes on me gaging my reaction as I turned to him. "It's stunning!" I told him in awe.

"I am happy that you find it so, Glykó. We spend most of your summers here as we get about twelve hours of darkness most days." He said smiling softly. I started to head into the lobby and through a large opening across from the desk and he pulled me back and down a wide private hallway behind the desk area. "Explore after you have a chance to rest. The elevation here is not as high as Cusco, but we are still at around 8000 feet above sea level. You will find that you may need some time to acclimate to avoid elevation sickness. I am sure in a few days that Nelson would love to take you on an extended tour of his domain."

Nelson smiled back at me. "Nothing would please me more, my lady."

Devin looked up at him grumpily from the wheelchair as we passed several offices to end at a large heavy-looking mahogany door. Nelson punched in a security-code on the keypad next to the door, and they followed him into a large, high beamed ceiling, open living area with another large stone fireplace burning brightly in the far-left corner. A large, flat-screen television was mounted above the mahogany mantle.

The same comfortable-looking cushioned furniture that was found in the lobby was arranged around it and a dining table was set in front of a small bar in the far-right corner. The far wall was mostly made of glass, had double glass and mahogany French-doors, and looked out into a small private yard, encased by a stone wall, which had a stone pool and garden area. The far-left wall was lined with three sets of mahogany double doors. The far-right had one set of mahogany double doors set in between the bar and a large dark mahogany spiral staircase in the front right-corner of the large room.

"This is our family suite." Nichola said simply. "Mine and Mansuetus's private offices are upstairs as well as the doctor's lab and a small library."

"It's nice." Devin finally spoke in a tone less than grouchy.

"Where's Aunt Iris?" I asked, expecting the flamboyant vampire to be here.

"She's been living with Aleksei for a while now." Nichola spoke softly moving into the living room and heading to the table which looked like it had a tea service set up. I cast a surreptitious look towards Dene as I moved to sit on one of the sofas.

"Oh, I didn't realize. She never told me."

"I am sure that she didn't." Dene said bitterly helping Devin from the wheelchair.

"Well, she will definitely be here in December as the large council and small council will be meeting this year here. Knowing her she might arrive sooner unexpectedly when she finds out that you are in residence." Nichola stated flatly, and Dene grimaced.

Devin came to sit next to me on the sofa and put an arm around me. Which I found to be out of character and intentional. Nichola handed me a cup of tea and took a seat in the cushioned chair to my left, next to the end table beside and facing me, proceeding to stretch his long legs out behind mine so that my legs rested against his shins, as he met my gaze with a smile. I smelled the strong herbal scent of the Coca as I sipped it. Nelson handed Devin a cup also, to which he wrinkled his nose in distaste.

"Drink it." Nichola told him. "You will find that it helps."

"Just exactly who are you?" Devin asked testily, as he sipped the tea.

Nichola's answer was interrupted by Mansuetus's arrival, as he started directing the vampire and human porters and two human maids. "Those go there." Directing Devin's bags into the first set of double doors on the left. "Kyría's bags in Kýrios' rooms." He pointed to the double doors on the right.

"What are you to my mother?" Devin continued in his testy voice.

Overhearing both his question and his tone, Mansuetus pointed a finger at him, looking sharply at him for silence, during which both Devin and Nichola glared at each other. After several minutes of this stilted silence, the other vampire and the humans were ushered out by Nelson, he then bowed to me and said softly with a smile, "I am so pleased to have you in residence, my lady, I will see you tomorrow and we will schedule your tour," and he too left closing the door behind him.

"I am Nikolaos Tsoukalous..." Nichola began.

Devin cut him off rudely, "That means nothing to me. I repeat, who and what, are you to my mother?"

"Devin!" I exclaimed angrily at his tone.

"I will tell you who he is, Master Devin." Mansuetus said harshly before anyone else could speak. "He is your mother's mate, and the man who wanted to be and should have been your father! But, most importantly, he is your family's elder who will help you through this transition into the next stage of your existence and you will listen to and respect him!"

Nichola and I looked at Mansuetus in surprise. To my knowledge, he had never spoken sharply to the boys in his life and had always loved, coddled, and instructed them when he came to visit. As such they worshiped him like some sort of hero.

Devin looked down in silence for a brief moment and then said softly, "Okay."

* * * * *

Dene had bundled Devin off to his room telling him that he wanted to take some blood samples, and he wanted him to get some rest. Mansuetus left with them to make sure that Devin had everything that he needed and that he could find everything that the maid had unpacked for him. More likely to insure that Devin wouldn't give Dene any trouble.

"How odd!" Leila speculated to Nichola as he stood and offered her his hand to stand also. He looked at her in question. "Devin must be exhausted, or he respects Mansuetus's opinion more than I ever thought." She told him as she started heading into the room where they had taken her things.

Nichola remained silent but when he closed the door to the suite behind them he burst out laughing, and she turned to him with a questioning look.

"He's just like you are!" Nichola said still laughing and his eyes danced in glee.

"What do you mean by that?" She questioned him incredulously.

"Oh, please! That conversation is far from settled! He's choosing his battlefield is all. Just like you do!" Nichola moved past her into the walk-in closet.

"I do not!" She replied hotly, feeling his mirth throughout her body even though he was no longer in her sight.

21

"You do too! I have been in more than enough conversations with you to know your strategies. He just employs them better than you!" His voice floated from the closet.

She gasped in outrage at his words. "That is not true!"

He walked out of the closet shirtless and barefoot, his jeans sans belt rode low on his hips, revealing the pronounced cut of his Adonis belt. She stopped speaking to gaze at his sculpted chest and abdomen in sudden nervousness. She had forgotten how physically beautiful he was.

"It is wholly true, i psychí mou. Your lígo vampír is very like his mother and as such he is going to be a definite handful! I am warning you right now, I don't want to hear from either one of you a request to delay his or your transitions. I will not agree to it." He looked at her with sharp, knowing eyes.

"But Nichola…" Leila began in confusion.

"No." His voice stopped her. "I will never do that again, and you will be experiencing why, when you are further along than you are right now in transition. Or did you think that I couldn't feel your awareness of me? I have always been able to feel you. My venom coursing through your veins never arrested *my* senses; *only your own.* I have always been able to feel you, mikró." He looked at her tenderly for a moment as she met his look with shock, suddenly remembering why he was so dangerous. "You need to get some sleep." He told her offhandedly and walked back into the closet.

She quickly started opening drawers looking for her nightgowns, grabbed one when she discovered them in the dresser and then rushed into the bathroom.

* * * * *

When she returned to the bedroom he was in bed waiting for her and as she looked at him he flipped the top sheet and blanket back, not exposing himself below the waist, to pat the bed beside him. She paused realizing that the light from the partially closed closet was still on. "I am not doing this with the light on!" She told him primly.

"Doing what, mikró? Sleeping? Did you forget that I have excellent night vision? I can see you quite well whether the light is on or not. I left the light on because you are unfamiliar with this room and if you get up while still dark, I do not want you running into anything." He smiled innocently at her, patting the mattress softly again.

She got into bed beside him, and he covered her suddenly chilled body with the blankets. He rubbed her arms with his slightly calloused hands. "You are cold. I will instruct Nelson to make sure that the fireplace is lit in here from now on." He murmured as he pulled her gently against his warmer, and she realized naked, muscled body, to kiss her lips softly.

"Nichola," she whispered. "There are things that I must tell you."

"I already know." He turned her to spoon against her body, holding her tightly, lacing his fingers with her own, crossing her arms over her chest. He kissed the back of her bare shoulder gently, next to the strap of her silk nightgown, as he settled against her. "Go to sleep. You need to rest. We will talk later."

With only the silkiness of her nightgown separating his hard body from hers, her heart pounded in nervousness for several minutes. She wasn't foolish enough to think that he was asleep. She knew he needed very little if any sleep at all. But, after a while, wrapped in the comfort of his arms and feeling his warm steady breath against the nape of her neck, she realized that he wasn't going to make any demands of her. Either of sex or blood. At least not tonight. She eventually relaxed her exhausted body against him to descend into a much-needed deep slumber.

The Sunlight at Temuco de Wila Tatitu

Leila slowly opened her eyes against the late morning sunshine streaming across the bed from the opened doors of the master suite patio. She held up her hand to shade her eyes, feeling the harshness of the sun against her skin. The feeling hadn't been truly painful in over a quarter of a century, but it hadn't ever been pleasant either. In fact, she had come to notice over the last couple of years, that the feeling was growing even less pleasant daily to where she stayed mostly indoors only venturing out during the day when she really had to.

She was astonished that someone had left the doors open, thinking that it must have been a maid who hadn't secured them properly and they had come open from a sharp breeze. She quickly got up to close them before Nichola returned to the bedroom, knowing that he would need their UV protection.

As she approached the doors, she gasped when she saw him sitting at a small patio table and chairs amongst the plants of the garden, in the sunshine, drinking what she assumed was coffee and reading the business section of what looked to be the New York Times on a wireless laptop. She stopped inside the doorway and stared at him. He turned toward her with a smile. She saw that he was wearing black sunglasses that wrapped around even the sides of his eyes, preventing even the slightest bit of sunshine from entering. He looked at her and said "Surprise!"

She felt tremors of shock throughout her body and knew that she had to sit down before she fell down. She turned to make her way back to the edge of the bed to sit heavily. She heard him close the doors as her world started to spin and her empty stomach lurched. He quickly sat down next to her to force her to bend over with her head between her knees.

"Breathe, i psychí mou," he told her gently as he massaged the back of her neck, "just breathe."

After several seconds, the dizziness dissipated, and she slowly sat up to look at him. "You were in the sun." A statement that needed no answer and he supplied none. "How is this possible?" She asked weakly. "Are you becoming human?"

He laughed lowly and without humor. "We were never 'human' to begin with." He told her as he pulled her back to lay on the bed beside him. "As to how? Well, let's just say that your aunt gave me an unexpected gift when she decided to orphan her companion and leave him on my proverbial doorstep; and to think I actually considered killing him to put him out of his misery. Instead, I tasked him to look at our weaknesses to see how he could mitigate them. I must say that he is doing an excellent job, even though myself, Nelson, and a few others have had to be occasional guinea pigs for him. He has been working very hard on this process that allows us to tolerate direct sunlight."

She rolled to her side and looked at him. He had taken his sunglasses off to lay them beside him on the bed, was shirtless and had on a pair of grey cotton shorts. "What are you wearing?"

"I am told that they are called 'gym' trunks. I refuse to sit around in the sun exposing myself fully until I totally trust the process." He asserted.

"Well, I can understand why." Leila giggled. "It would not do to be sunburned on your..."

"No, it would not!" He agreed quickly, smiling at her.

"Does he do this by injection?" She inquired.

"No, it is a topical treatment. You have heard of spray-tanning, yes?" As she nodded he continued. "It is actually applied using the same equipment. You step into a booth, spread-eagled, with your eyes closed, and are sprayed from head to toe, in a round circular motion, all exposed parts are treated.

Then a fan system is turned on until the solution dries."

"What would happen if you were to breathe the solution in?" She wondered. "Is it truly safe?"

"Well, due to my vampire state, I have the ability to hold my breath the whole time, but the doctor has developed nostril plugs that fit up the nostrils to prevent that from occurring." Nichola explained to her.

"Your skin doesn't look darker." She said examining his normal light tanned chest with her fingers and her eyes.

"It shouldn't be as the 'sun block' isn't designed to change skin color at this time, I am sure that will be a later iteration when this product is fully assessed." Nichola told her gently rubbing his fingertips over her arm as she examined him. "But, it has made my hair a slightly different shade than what it has been for centuries." He murmured as her fingers ran through the waves of his longish locks.

"I saw it was a different color last night, but I thought it was something that you had done intentionally to fit with one of your many aliases." Her voice was laced with curiosity as she examined him, and she ran her fingers over his scalp around his hairline. "It doesn't seem to have changed the texture much, just the color. It is tawnier than before. Not really the roots, more so the ends."

She felt him rub his fingertips over the top of one of her nipples through her nightgown, as he answered her, "The doctor believes that may be because the hair follicle itself is fed by tiny blood vessels at the base to keep it growing, but the cells within the strand that is beyond the skin's surface, the ends that you refer to, aren't alive anymore, and as such are susceptible to the chemicals within the block itself. There by the change in color is possible."

"I like it." She murmured as he ran his hand down her side over the silk of her nightgown.

"Good." He murmured in return, rolling toward her to breathe in her scent along her throat. "Mmmmm."

"So do you have to be sprayed every day?" Pushing him back down to bring his attention back to their conversation.

"The initial treatment lasted between seven to ten days before the effects of the sun were felt, the next formula held steady between ten to fourteen days. The timeframe has been improving with what the doctor calls 'tweaks' to his formula. Nelson and I had a treatment yesterday with the new formula and have hopes to surpass fourteen days. We shall see." He quickly rolled her onto her back, sliding her nightgown up, and settled himself in between her legs. "But overall, I am quite pleased with the doctor. He has developed a far stronger sunblock than any human in history. Your aunt was an idiotic fool to give him to me, she didn't realize what she had. He's going to make me a fortune!" His eyes twinkled with both avarice and a kind of evil glee as he said this.

"Nichola, you are being unkind!" Leila told him sharply.

"Please! She tortured the poor man for sixteen years as she whored her way through vampire society, and he miserably dealt with it. When she finally left my household to live permanently with Aleksei she had almost broken him and left him here for me to deal with, probably thinking that I would put him out of his misery for her, and I almost did! Instead, I picked him up, shook him off and challenged him to use that big, beautiful intellect of his to create some good for the society around him.

I also gave him permission to fuck whoever he wanted to without reserve. Something that your aunt refused to do; with her attitude of 'only for me, but not for thee'. She does not play those types of games with Aleksei, as indulgent as he is with her, this is something that he will not tolerate. So, I have the doctor who is highly productive, and she must live with Aleksei and his more stringent rules. From all accounts, everyone seems to be happy; at the very least the doctor is and since he is now a permanent member of my household this is all I truly care about." He kissed her softly and then ran his lips across her collarbone as he ran a hand along the outside of her thigh to her hip, hooking his fingers in her panties.

"Nichola, we need to talk." Her voice came out a nervous croak as her breath caught in her throat and desire spiked through her veins.

"I am done talking right now, Glykó. I have other things on my mind." He murmured as he rolled his hips and his erection against her, and even through her panties and his shorts it caused her to gasp in desire.

27

"That's what we need to talk about." She told him desperately trying to make him listen to her. "It's been a very long time."

"I told you last night, that I know." He said sliding from her body to stand next to the bed, taking her panties down her legs with him as he did so. He quickly untied his gym shorts and let them fall.

As she took in the sight of his rampant cock, which rose to his belly button, and his hard, tanned, muscled body with the sun streaming through the glass of the French doors haloing around him, she knew there was no way she would be able to take him this quickly. "It's been a lot longer than you think and this body is older than you remember." She gasped aloud when he grabbed her arms to lift her to her knees before him to quickly strip the silk nightgown up and over her body. "I don't want you to see me." She said self-consciously covering her breasts with her arms.

"I think it has been at least five years for you, your body is not as old as I expected, and I am glad that you are no longer a skinny little girl and hope that your womanly curves remain after your transition. I like them very much." He pulled her against his body and his erection, as his hands ran over her ass. "You fit me better this way. You keep forgetting I come from a time where men actually liked their women to be women and I have been aching to touch you since I saw you last night. I was a gentlemen, you are rested now, and I do not want to wait anymore." He kissed her lips hard, thrusting his tongue deeply, and then proceeded to pull her up his body to shower her throat and the tops of her breasts with kisses and small nips of his teeth. Gasping against the pleasure of his mouth, she wrapped her arms about his shoulders to steady herself.

"But it's going to hurt..." She whispered with a tremor in her voice despite the desire that ran through her body.

He stopped his kisses, grabbed his sunglasses from the bed, tossed them onto a chair across the room, and simultaneously pulled the blankets to the foot of the bed as he laid her down on the sheets. Over the years, she had forgotten both his speed and his strength, and her breath caught for a moment in her throat. He looked at her body with his hot amber eyes and she felt herself flush under his gaze. He reached over to the nightstand next to him, opened the drawer, and pulled out a tube of lubricant. "I took care of my own immediate needs this morning while you slept," he told her as he lay down next to her, running a fingertip around her nipple as it hardened under his touch. "I am under complete control. I will go slow and make sure that your body remembers me. Any pain that you feel will soon be followed by such pleasure it will quickly be forgotten."

She met his eyes to whisper, "I guess you have thought of everything."

"I usually do." He whispered in return with a small smile and lowered his lips to hers as his fingers moved down her body to gently stroke the lips of her pussy as she wrapped her arms around him and raised her hips to meet his hand, thrilling to his touch.

He moved to cover her body with his own, ignoring her when she stiffened in response to his movements. He took her nipple into his mouth to suckle and tongue it into a stiff peak, then took the other to do the same, eliciting sharp gasps and small moans from her lips. His hand had never stopped his soft stroking of her pussy and finally he could feel her moisture on his fingertips and spreading her thighs wide with his hips he spread her moisture along her crease and over her hard bud, rubbing her gently, bringing a moan from her lips.

He had told her that he was in complete control but was starting to doubt his own words as she started responding to him and running her hands over his shoulders and chest causing his cock to jump against her in response, begging for her attention. She reached between them to hold him firmly in her small soft hand, then started to stroke him and he groaned in return. He knew that he couldn't wait any more as she bent one of her legs and wrapped it around his thigh. He quickly slid down her body to taste her, pulling himself from her hands, causing her to groan in disappointment, and pulling her leg over his shoulder to rest along the muscles of his back.

He ran his tongue between her folds to gently encircle her clitoris. "Mmmmm. So sweet." He sighed against her thigh, feeling a thrill climb up his spine when she made a small cry of ecstasy; how he had missed these sounds from her lips. As he gently entered her tight channel with one of his fingers, he suckled at her clit and he could feel her muscles contract in response and she lifted her hips seeking out both his touch and his mouth, with a surprised 'oh'. "Don't hold back on me, moró." He murmured as he worked his finger deeper. He suckled her pussy, licking and feasting on her clit and he finger-fucked his way into her tight body.

Soon, she was panting in response, and he slid his other hand up her body to pluck and pull sharply on her pebble hard nipple, never slowing or altering the rhythm he was playing out between her legs. She could feel her orgasm building in her stomach, causing her muscles to bunch and tremble, as she arched her back and clutched his head against her. He growled in his throat in response and sucked her clit into his mouth to flick her with his tongue. As her orgasm crashed over her shores she tried to control it, and he didn't let her, holding her in place he continued to suck upon her clit forcing her to ride it out screaming out his name to the end.

He knelt in between her limp legs, and she felt so weak she couldn't move. He had wanted to drink her juice in, but contented himself with licking his fingers clean, breathing deeply of her intoxicating scent.Her breath came in short gasps, and he reached for the lubricant.

Her eyes widened as they met his and he stroked the lubricant over his hard cock. "It's too big, I can't take it right now. I can't." She whispered.

"You will." His whisper a promise, and his eyes never left hers.

* * * * *

Mansuetus, Dene, and a wheelchair bound Devin, who was just past the point of grumpy and on his way to really angry about being wheeled around by Dene, were coming down the private hallway toward the family suite from having lunch in the hotel dining room, when Mansuetus suddenly stopped, and Dene narrowly avoided a collision with him.

"We need to turn around." Mansuetus turned around telling Dene over Devin's head. Dene met his eyes then started to back down the hallway.

"What the hell, Uncle Man!" Devin said in irritation.

"I forgot; you have an appointment with the tailor." Mansuetus quickly said.

"What? I do?" Devin asked bewildered.

"Yes. Kýrios wants you to be fitted for several suits." Devin gave him a look. "Think of it like this, he has not given you a budget limit yet. Until he remembers to institute a budget, you can spend as much of his money as you want."

"Really? I can get into that!" Devin said with an evil smile.

Mansuetus had no idea what he had just done, but his extraordinary almost vampiric hearing told him there was no way he could take Devin into the suite with all of that moaning, groaning, and screaming coming from Kýrios bedroom. Devin would throw a fit, when he realized that his mother was being debauched in such a way and it would cause a huge fight, which after 26 years of Kýrios waiting for her, could get the hell beat out of all of them if he were interrupted right now.

* * * * *

Leila and Nichola laid side by side, both breathing heavily. Nichola reached over and held her hand tightly. "How are you feeling?" He panted slightly.

"Thoroughly ravished," she panted back with a small laugh.

"Any pain?" He asked.

"Not anymore."

"Great, that's what I was going for." He chuckled, grinning widely, and breathing deeply as if he had run a marathon, pulled her against his side kissing her temple, to feel her heart pound in her chest against him. She smiled softly as his happiness washed over her.

* * * * *

After showering and throwing on a pair of black yoga pants, sandals, and a tight neon teal-colored sport tank top I left the bedroom to find a spread of food on the table in front of the bar, and Mansuetus, Dene and Devin, lounging in the living area playing a video game.

"Really?" I asked them.

"We are bored! Besides, Dene needs to get his ass kicked, he's been bragging all day about how great he is at Halo." Devin answered, never taking his eyes from the television. "Ha! That's what you get!" He yelled.

Mansuetus never took his eyes from the screen as he said. "I know you haven't eaten today. Get something to eat now. Stop it, Imp! We are supposed to be a team! Don't forget to drink some tea. Kýrios is upstairs if you are looking for him."

I wandered over to the table to nibble at the cold meats, cheeses, and vegetables. Though neither hungry nor thirsty, I even took a couple of sips of Coca tea. Then asked, "Hey, Dene? Where is the sun-block booth that Nichola was telling me about? Could I be part of your experiment?" Dene hit the pause button on his handset.

"Hey!" Both Mansuetus and Devin yelled.

Dene ignored them. "Yes, Leila, that would be great! There aren't a lot of vampires here at the moment, I would love to get your feedback on it. It is already a part of the spa, and the personnel know how to operate the equipment. Do you want me to show you?"

"Oh, no. I have done spray tanning before. As long as they can tell me where it is. Where are all the vampires anyway? I am surprised that there aren't more here. This should be the perfect season for them."

"Travel issues basically. Most of them don't travel in style the way Nick does. They usually use a combination of train, ship, and air. Even though vampires aren't susceptible to it, the damned COVID restrictions are playing havoc with transportation services. It is taking most a lot longer to get from point A to point B. We are expecting more to arrive over the next few weeks. If they can get themselves to Cusco, Nick goes and picks them up. We have one guy that has lived here for the season every year since Nick opened the place up. He is here right now and am helping to evaluate it too. But you will be the first woman to do so. There is also a booth at Rom's home that just was completed, but I just shipped their first batch of solution to them, so Esmerelda hasn't tried it yet. Though according to Rom she may not do so as she is extremely nervous about the whole thing."

"Wow! I am special?" She teased him. He always got so serious when it came to science.

"Oh, my gosh, yes! Despite thought trends, men and women are totally different in all areas of physicality, and not just reproductive organs. You see on average, a man's skin is about 20 to 25% thicker than a woman's, has a tougher texture, and contains more collagen. That is why it has a tighter, firmer appearance than a woman's does. Also, the collagen level determines the appearance of the skin as they age. So, a man's skin ages slower than a woman's skin. In fact, a woman's skin is about fifteen years 'older' than a man's skin of the same biological age. But a man's oil production is about double that of a woman, and they have more, and larger pores so have more acne issues. So, I guess that offsets it." He paused for breath.

"Basically, you can't wait for me to try your sun-block on my old-ass skin?" My tone was slightly snarky, as I raised an eyebrow at him in inquiry.

"Well, I wouldn't put it that way…" he started to answer.

"That's exactly what he is saying, Mom!" Devin laughed with a smirk.

I gave Devin a look. "I will let you know how it works out," I told Dene as I walked out of the suite heading for the spa.

The Burke Effect

eila made her way to the B1 level wandering over and checking out the view from the open balconies; it did not disappoint and was absolutely breathtaking. Leila noticed that despite the few guests in attendance, that the shops were now all open. She returned a wave to a seamstress who was arranging a lovely gown on a mannequin in the window as she passed. Walking into the hair salon, she picked up a new hairbrush and comb set, charging it to Nichola's suite. Everywhere she stopped in, she was greeted with a small bow and respectful murmurs of "Lady Tsoukalous." Obviously, Nelson had put out the word that she was at the hotel. She always smiled kindly in return to these greetings. She was neutral about the title, as she realized that it was a sign of respect, but she wasn't quite used to it or having everyone know who she was. That made her feel a little self-conscious.

She finally made it into the spa area, and they were very excited to see her there, offering her their array of services of facials, pedicures, manicures waxing and massages. The mostly human staff seemed a little disappointed that she was only there for the spray booth. Leila figured that they were bored without any clientele to serve.

"Would you like me to take you and walk you through the machine, my lady?" The male vampire manager said quickly grabbing a soft terry cloth red robe for her from behind the counter.

"Oh, no, that's okay. Dr. Lambert told me that it is just like any other spray booth. I have done that many times in the past. But, I have been told that you have some sort of nose plug to use to prevent the spray from being inhaled?"

"Oh, yes, my lady! Here you go. You just put one in each nostril. There is a fabric mesh across both the top and bottom of each one that will still enable you to breathe through your nose, but you will not be able to breathe in the solution. Dr. Lambert designed them, and they are quite ingenious in their own way. They are disposable, so when you are done with them just toss them in the waste basket. If I were you, I would wear one of these, and not let the solution get into my hair." The manager handed Leila what looked to be a plastic shower cap of some sort. "Your hair is streaked such a beautiful silver, and we know that at least once the hair color has changed. The only difference is that you will need to wear a hat outside."

"Thank you! I wouldn't want my hair color to change, and I am used to wearing hats anyway." Leila told him taking the shower cap.

"Now remember, everything is automatic. So, once you press the button, you will have fifteen seconds to adjust your body in accordance with the drawings in the room. Close your eyes and stay still throughout the process. Once the spray stops, the fan system will automatically come on, and you just hold still until you are dry. I wouldn't put my tighter clothes back on for at least a half hour just in case you aren't totally dry. But you can wear this robe back upstairs. Just follow the sign through the dressing room." The manager told her happily.

"Thank you so much." Leila responded pleasantly.

* * * * *

In the dressing room, Leila struggled to pull her tight sport tank up and over her head. She paused shaking her long-layered hair out around her shoulders. She opened her eyes to see a handsome, stark-naked, obviously well-endowed, male vampire standing in the doorway to the spray booth room. He had a towel to his dark wet hair and, though surprised, was regarding her bare breasts with interest in his dark-eyes. Her mouth dropped open in embarrassment and she quickly turned around putting her shirt up to her face and her chest.

35

"Oh, my God, oh, my God, oh, my God!" She exclaimed in mortification. "I am so embarrassed, I apologize! I didn't know that anyone was in here!" She could feel herself blush deeply in awkwardness. "Oh, please don't tell me that I went into the men's dressing room by mistake!"

"No, ma'am! It is entirely my fault! This is the lady's dressing room. I just wandered in here looking for an extra towel." Came a deep drawl that sounded vaguely familiar, which at any other time would have intrigued her. "I thought you were a staff member."

"No, I am not!" She said to him hotly, not turning around and quickly grabbed one of the two towels that the manager had given her. "Here take one of mine!" She tossed it over her shoulder behind her.

"Much obliged, ma'am." He said to her, and she could hear the humor in his voice, deepening her blush and irritation, and just when she was going to peek over her shoulder to check if he was gone, his voice continued, "and from where I am standing, I am here to tell you, that you don't have anything to be embarrassed about!"

"Go!" She ordered him out without turning around.

"Yes, ma'am." He replied with a small good-natured chuckle.

She heard a door close and risked a look over her shoulder to find the vampire gone. She trotted into the spray-room, looked around quickly, and noticed a door labeled Men's Dressing Room. She quickly locked the door.

Cheeky damned vampires! She thought, shaking her head, going back to the dressing room to grab her towel and get this spray-block process over as quickly as possible.

* * * * *

After being sprayed with the solution, the whole drying process took her about twenty minutes and afterwards, Leila donned her robe, peeked out into the dressing room to find it empty and basically speed-walked to the elevator, her clothing bundled in her arms, to make her way back to the suite.

The guys were still playing their video game and Dene hit the pause button again ignoring Devin's yell of 'what the hell!' to ask her, "Well, what did you think?"

"It's seems like a very simple process. How long do I have to wait to test it out?" She replied asking.

"You should be able to go out into the sun right now. You didn't treat your hair? You will have to wear a hat outside." Dene cautioned.

"No, I didn't want to take the chance of it changing my hair color, like it did Nichola's.I have lots of hats that I brought with me, so no problem." She headed into the bedroom changed into a loose short and tank top outfit, grabbed her sunglasses and hat, and walked out the master suite's French doors. She was very tentative at first, as she didn't know if it would work as well for her as it did for Nichola, and she hadn't entered the sun in a short outfit in years. She stretched her hands from the shade of the patio out into the sunshine.She could feel the heat of the sun, but no pain or discomfort whatsoever.

"Oh, this is cool." She whispered to herself walking barefoot into the grass of the garden and out into the sunshine slowly.

"It's really quite extraordinary, isn't it?" Nichola's whispered voice came from the French doors as he leaned against the door jamb, sunglasses in place, to watch her hold out her arms in the sunshine in wonder.

"Oh, yes, but it must be even more so for you. I mean, I could venture into the sun in my current condition, yes, I had to be covered up, but still, I could do it. For you it must have been amazing!" Leila told him in awe of what he must have experienced after almost 1000 years of being imprisoned by the night.

"I never thought to ever see you in the sunlight." He said approaching her and touching her bare shoulder in wonder. "I want to make love to you in the sunshine." He whispered pulling her close to kiss her hungrily for a moment.

"I thought you weren't exposing yourself for fear of sunburning sensitive areas?" She smiled up at him, wrapping her arms around his neck.

"I think that I will mostly be buried inside of you, I feel very safe there." He whispered huskily into her ear, nibbling lightly on her earlobe.

"Mom! Knock it off!" Devin's angry voice came from the adjoining living room patio.

"I don't remember him being such a pain when he was a small child." Nichola began, throwing Devin a glare.

"It is a little chilly out here anyway," Leila told Nichola, as it was barely 62 degrees. "I just wanted to test it out." She took him by the hand, and hand-in-hand, they walked to the living room patio to enter the living room area.

"Mom, you need to know. It looks like you are creeping on some young guy! It's really messed up!" Devin told her angrily.

Nichola started to step toward him, and she instinctively knew that he was going straight to a physical confrontation, which in no way would end well for Devin. She stepped in between them and faced Devin. "Devin, we are all adults here. What I choose to do and who I choose to do it with is none of your business! Transitioning and the fact that he is our elder aside, you're being deliberately rude toward my mate, I will not have that."

"I am telling you, Mom. It is weird and creepy looking! He barely looks older than me and I don't like it!" Devin said bluntly.

"Well, deal with it, son! I have not seen him in more than 25 years and frankly I have missed him!" Leila said heatedly.

"Well, you never did this with Dad!" He replied furiously, then marched into his room to slam the door behind him.

"I will go speak with him," Mansuetus murmured standing.

"No. Leave him be and let him calm down. I will speak with him later." Nichola stated and Leila looked at him in concern. "Just speak, I promise." He tipped her chin up to give her a soft reassuring kiss. "I have to go back to work." Smiling, he headed up the stairs with Mansuetus following.

Dene looked at her eagerly. "Well, tell me! How was it? Did you feel any discomfort?"

She smiled sitting next to him on the couch and proceeded to answer all of his questions.

* * * * *

Leila had finished dressing for dinner, wearing a long-sleeved, V-necked, forest green silk blouse with her pearl necklace and pearl and diamond earrings, a pair of rayon, belted, black, cropped, flyaway, tulip pants that were slit in front from mid-calf to just above her knees, which showed off her still trim waist despite the curve of her hips, and a pair of short black heels. She had piled her silver-streaked hair on top of her head in a riotous top-knot, leaving some of her long bangs to showcase her high cheekbones and the still smooth skin of her long neck. She felt that she had attained the relaxed, but classy look that she had been working toward in her attire.

Though she would never admit it to herself, Devin's earlier words had hurt her feelings. Despite her 56 years, and Devin's thoughts on the matter, she knew that she looked at least fifteen years younger. Even with the silver streaks in her hair, which she knew many of her friends had paid a lot of money to their beauticians to try to copy, she still had retained some semblance of youth especially in the skin of her face and throat.

Creeping on Nichola, indeed! She thought as she made up her still bright, teal-colored eyes, liking the way her eyes were picking up the forest green of her blouse.

She opened the door to the suite a few minutes past six as she was absolutely starving not having had much to eat all day. Calling out in general, "I can't believe it is taking you all so long to get ready! I am going to the dining room. Nichola, are you coming?" She called to him specifically.

"I have to make a phone call to my Tokyo offices, which just opened, you go ahead, and I will catch up with you." Came his reply from upstairs.

She closed the door behind her and headed for the dining room. As expected, it was open and beautiful, decorated with Incan art, just like the lobby. Every area that she had seen that day was open and inviting. She waved off a couple of the staff who were working to place tablecloths on the tables. "Don't bother, please." She told them with a smile as they headed toward her, not wanting to interrupt them. "I am just going to sit over here at this large table," which already had a tablecloth and condiments on it.

She knew that there were only a few guests at the hotel so didn't expect to really see anyone else. As she sat down at the table, she picked up a drink menu and started perusing it. Noticing movement from the bar area she looked up into the smiling, interested eyes of the vampire that she had encountered in the dressing room earlier, and with a blush, she quickly and pointedly looked down at the menu again.

Noticing movement to her right, she gave a mental groan, and looked at a pair of highly polished, black, knee-length boots, that just cried out for spurs, and housed tight fawn-colored pants, moving in her direction. She looked up to take in his trim waist, black belt, a crisp white shirt, which was thankfully, buttoned up to his throat, with smooth black buttons.She noticed that his broad, muscled shoulders set off a plain black blazer as she looked into mahogany brown eyes that crinkled slightly at the corners in mirth; eyes that were housed under dark brown, bordering on black, slightly arched, full brows. His straight, deep brown hair was short, with sideburns that ran to just the top of his ear lobes; he had longish bangs that he had attempted to comb back but had willfully fallen to rest in a slightly messy style against his intelligent forehead, just above those arched brows. His handsome face was weathered, slightly tanned, with a day's growth of dark beard. If he had been human, she would have placed him in his late thirties, forty at the maximum; in his vampire state, there was no telling how old he was.

She coolly arched her brows in inquiry, preferring that he speak first. After all he had been the one to stroll stark-naked into the ladies dressing room!

"Ma'am." He began, and she knew that drawl was from Texas! "I thought I should come over and *formally*," here he paused just slightly with a small, charming smile, "introduce myself after our encounter earlier. My name is William Lionel Burke." His voice was smooth and deep. He bent slightly at the waist extending his hand, to which she formally extended hers.

"Leila Sutton." She replied simply, not encouraging him.

"Ah, Ms. Sutton, please accept my apologies for earlier." He held her hand in expectation in his warm and calloused one. She nodded her head at him, not liking to be at odds over something so trivial, just embarrassing. After all, it was just between the two of them and he was being so polite.

She nodded her head again, this time giving him a small gracious smile, murmuring, "Of course."

"Might I join you? I have no idea where my companion has gotten to, and I hate to eat alone." He asked politely.

She looked around at the large round table mentally counting the chairs. Plenty of room for one or even three more people. "Of course."

He took a chair, one chair away from her, with a smile. Placing his glass down in front of him, he crossed his legs and relaxed back in an open and friendly manner. She curiously looked at his glass. It suspiciously looked like bourbon. He noticed her looking at it and said, "Elijah Craig Straight Bourbon Whiskey. Nothing like Kentucky whiskey." He smiled charmingly at her.

"So, I have been told." She smiled at him in return.

"So, you are an American." It was a statement.

"And you are a Texan." She declared with a smile, knowing that true Texans considered themselves Texans and not *just* Americans. Having lived in Texas for a number of years now, she knew that there was always a portion of the population who still wanted to secede from the Union. Real Texans considered Texas as a country unto itself.

"Well, yes, ma'am! I sure am!" He said flashing straight, strong, white teeth at her. "What gave me away?" He held out his hands looking down at his outfit.

She gave him a small laugh at his antics. "Nothing physically, I recognize the accent. I have lived in Texas for almost a decade now."

"Whereabouts?" He asked.

"Outside of San Antonio in Boerne." She pronounced it Bur-knee.

"We are almost neighbors!" He exclaimed pleased. "I have a ranch in Brownsboro."

"I don't know..." Leila thought with a furrowed brow, not recognizing the town.

"You probably know it as Kerrville." He said with a smile.

"Really?" She asked incredulously.

"Yes, ma'am. It's my family homestead."

"Small world." She declared.

"Even in Texas!" He raised his glass in acknowledgement at her and took a small sip. "So, what brings a *human*," stressing the word "to the Peruvian Vampire Palace?" He asked with a mocking little laugh.

41

"What makes you think I'm human?" She questioned smiling.

"Well, actually, I don't. But you aren't a vampire either." His look was direct and being fairly direct herself she appreciated that. But as she didn't know him she hedged her bets.

"I could be a companion." She looked at him in challenge.

"No, ma'am! You have too much independence, too much spirit, hiding behind those eyes of yours. My maman, would refer to you as a pouliche fougueuse." He stated emphatically, with a sharp discerning eye..

"What's that?"Leila asked.

"A spirited filly! Much too much spirit to be anybody's companion!"

"I am transitioning. Both myself and my son are transitioning." She supplied.

"So, you are here with family?" He asked as a waiter approached.

"Lady Tsoukalous, may I get something for you from the bar?" The young human asked.

"I will take a frozen strawberry margarita."

"Would you like another, Mr. Burke?" He inquired.

"I believe I will." Burke told him looking at her in speculation as the waiter left. "Lady Tsoukalous? I've heard of you." He revealed to her softly.

"You don't seem to be the type of man who traffics in rumor." She stated, unsure if she should be offended.

"Most rumors have at least a grain of truth." He disclosed looking at her intently. "So, you are Klaus's mate?"

"Klaus?"

"He was going by Klaus when I first met him a long time ago. So, that's what I continue to call him." The smile he gave her was impish; and she was distinctly reminded of Devin when he was hatching a scheme, who just then was walking in with Dene and Mansuetus.

"Sorry, Mom!" He called out as he came through the doors. "Uncle Man insisted that I wear this jacket, something about 'dressing for dinner', and Dene won't leave me alone about that damn wheelchair!"

"But you really need to conserve..." Dene started.

"I am not doing it anymore. I'm not." He told him emphatically.

As he approached the chair in between he and Leila, Burke stood up and held out his hand to him, "William Lionel Burke."

Devin gripped his hand firmly, smiling and replying, "Pleasure to meet you Mr. Burke, I'm Devin Sutton."

Burke looked at Leila with a smile as if to acknowledge the way she had brought up her son. Despite their occasional outbursts with her, both her sons, were sociable, stood straight and tall, were very respectful to women, and usually very well-behaved and well-spoken in public and around strangers. Burke looked at the other two men, nodding at them in acknowledgement. "Doc, Mansuetus."

They nodded to him in return as Devin took the seat in between Burke and his mother. Mansuetus left the chair to Leila's left, vacant, to sit one seat away, where he was able to keep an eye on the door, and Dene sat next to him to his left, leaving a vacant seat in between him and Burke.

"I hear from your mother, Mr. Sutton, that we are neighbors." Burke said engaging Devin.

"We are? Do you live in Texas?" Devin asked.

"Yessir. I have a ranch in the Kerrville area."

"I have several good friends that live in Kerrville! What kind of ranch do you have? Cattle, hunting, dude?" Devin asked with interest.

"Well, I don't have it opened to the public, but I have a nice herd of beef cattle, some longhorns, and a few years ago I imported some Axis deer, some zebras, and of course the native wild hogs, wild turkey and white tail deer are everywhere." He said with a grin.

"Wow. So, you don't allow public hunting?" Devin inquired but was interrupted by the waiter returning.

"Sir, what would you like to drink?" The waiter inquired.

Devin looked at what Burke was drinking with a raised eyebrow. "Is that bourbon?"

"Yes, the selection here is quite good. This is Elijah Craig." Burke told him.

"I will try that, thank you." Devin told the waiter starting to focus on Burke again when Dene interrupted.

"Master Devin, you probably shouldn't imbibe during this time."

"Doc, while I appreciate your concern and assistance, I am not going to let this thing change me. I am going to walk on my own like a man and drink on my own like a man." Devin told him with a direct look, reminding Dene very much of his mother.

"Well, good for you, son!" Burke slapped him on the back. "Get Mr. Sutton some Elijah Craig." Burke told the waiter.

* * * * *

By the time Nichola walked into the dining room, Leila was on her second margarita, and with an empty stomach feeling a little tipsy. Devin and Burke were becoming fast friends as they discussed aspects about Burke's 8000-acre ranch complex. Leila noticed him take in the scene and a scowl settled on his handsome face that didn't bode well.

"I apologize, agápi mou, that took me longer than expected." Nichola murmured to her giving her a kiss on the side of her mouth when he sat next to her. This caused Burke to give them a little smirk, and Devin to glare in their direction, though he refrained from making any snide comments in front of Burke.

Burke was a sharp-eyed individual though and noticed the glare.

"Klaus, how are you doing this evening!" He greeted Nichola with a smile that held very little warmth.

"I am doing extremely well, Burke. How are you finding your accommodations this season?" Nichola returned in a chilly voice.

"Just as nice as ever, thank you!" Burke returned.

Devin also was a sharp-eyed individual and noticed the cold exchange between the two vampires. "Mr. Burke is going to have dinner with us, Nick!" He exclaimed happily. "Did you know he has a ranch in Texas very close to where my mom lives? He's practically our neighbor!"

"Yes. I was aware. Mr. Burke and I have been…acquainted for a number of years." Nichola returned smoothly as Burke grinned at him beyond Devin's shoulder.

Devin intentionally ignored him and turned back to Burke. "Well, if you don't allow public hunting, how do you cull the deer and wild hogs? They are a horrible nuisance where we live in Boerne! They would be even worse if they weren't hunted, not to mention they can get diseased."

"When I am in residence, Fred and I will occasionally hunt the land. My ranch manager, hands, and their families all live on the ranch, and they do the majority of the hunting. They keep the coyote population from exploding as well as prevent any big predators from preying on the cattle."

A waiter came, placed a glass of red wine in front of Nichola, and took their food orders, asking if he could get them another round of drinks. To which Burke, Devin and Leila all replied yes. Neither Mansuetus nor Dene were drinking anything other than water and lemon and had been receiving the occasional refill as the waiters passed the table.

"What are you drinking?" Nichola asked Leila looking at her almost empty glass in front of her.

"Strawberry margarita." She replied.

He raised his eyebrows at her in inquiry. She could feel a little fluttering around the edges of her brain. Suddenly she realized that she could not hear his voice at all in her thoughts and hadn't since she had been there. She reached over placing her hand over his that rested on the table and leaned in close to him to whisper. "I am not quite there yet. You will have to speak to me." She pulled back to look at him with sad eyes, realizing that she actually missed his voice in her mind now that she understood that she hadn't been hearing it since she had reunited with him.

He reached up to tenderly stroke her jawline with his other hand and smiled gently in return, "I will start working on that tonight." He murmured quietly.

"So, who's Fred?" Devin loudly asked Burke but glared in their direction, irritated that Nichola kept touching his mother.

Burke smiled widely as Nichola gave Devin a quelling glance, enjoying the fact that Devin obviously objected to his mother and Nichola's connection. "Fred is my companion. But the good Lord knows where he has gotten to, usually he is rarely late for feeding time." His tone loud like Devin's had been.

"You could always call him to you, William." Nichola told him crossly.

"Why? He's not my slave you know! I detest slavery!" Burke replied as if

Nichola didn't.

"But companions aren't slaves are they?" Devin asked appalled. "Uncle Man, you aren't a slave are you?"

"Of course, I am not! I have always been a freeman, even when I was fully human!" Mansuetus replied as if the question was ridiculous.

Devin looked at Dene in inquiry. "Absolutely not!" The doctor replied with a roll of his eyes.

"Wouldn't either of you die for Klaus?" Burke asked sharply.

"Of course, we would..." Dene started loudly.

Mansuetus put a restraining hand on Dene's arm. "That's a ridiculous question, Burke," and Leila realized that he had intentionally dropped the respect of calling him 'mister', "and you know it. Both of us would die for Kýrios, Kyría, and the boy." He indicated Devin with his head, making Devin's eyes widen. "That doesn't mean that we are slaves, it means that we are family. Our life for theirs, it is our way. Both the good doctor and I have free will, as does everyone who works for Kýrios. He employs no slaves."

Devin turned to Burke asking bluntly, "If you believe companions to be like slaves, why do you have one of your own?"

"Because sometimes when we are young vampires we often do things unintentionally. I didn't intend to make Fred my companion. It happened though." Burke smiled grimly to himself, explaining. "But, because of our laws, if I abandoned him, free him to his own devices, or I die, our society would put him down like a rabid dog because they consider companions to be property. Don't they Klaus." He looked in Nichola's direction who had settled back to rest his arm along the back of Leila's chair watching the argument between Mansuetus and Burke.

"Yes, unfortunately, that is the case, William." Nichola said softly in acknowledgement. "In the case of my family, I long ago made legal provisions for all companions of my line, as well as all of my assets to belong to my mate, if I were to perish; thereby insuring their survival." This soft statement made Leila look at him in amazement.

"What about those of us who are a family of one?" Burke asked sharply.

"I am working on that Mr. Burke." Dene told him softly.

"Well, I suppose I will have to survive until you figure it out, Doc!" Burke said bitterly.

"Mr. Burke, if you feel so strongly about the subject," Leila ventured tentatively, "why don't you address the large council and put forth a resolution in December to change these archaic practices?"

"I fully intend to ma'am. I also fully expect it to crash and burn." He gave her a bitter smile. "But, I won't be deterred, I already fought one war over slavery, I will see this one through also." This time he smiled at her with a determined look.

Just then, a scruffy looking man who could be anywhere from 35 to 45, with dirty-blond colored straw-like hair came walking up to their table.

"You cur! Where have you been?" Burke said to him, but his tone wasn't harsh, instead it was teasing.

"Sorry, boss! I was in a game and time got away from me." His voice wasn't as educated and his clothes looked a little less pressed and polished than Burke's, but he was clean, and his drawl was just as Texan.

"Well, your ears must have been burnin' because we were talking about you!" Fred looked at him in inquiry in a worshipful way. "Mr. Devin Sutton, this is Cross-eyed Fred, my wayward, card-cheating, companion."

"Boss!" Fred protested.

"I better not hear about it Fred." Burke warned good-naturedly.

Devin stood up, walked to him, and held out his hand, and Fred looked at it in amazement to be shown such a respect from someone that he could sense was a vampire. After a few seconds, he reached out his hand in return. Devin grasped his firmly, shaking it and said, "An immense pleasure to meet you Mr. Fred."

"You too, Mr. Sutton." Fred told him in awe. "You too." He smiled at him gratefully, taking the seat in-between Burke and Dene. "Doc," he nodded.

As Devin sat back down, he looked at him curiously. "Mr. Fred, why did Mr. Burke call you Cross-eyed Fred? Your eyes aren't crossed."

Burke burst out laughing, and Fred blushed furiously. "Well, now mind you I didn't give him that nickname." Burke said after a moment with a cheeky smile. "The saloon gals gave him that nickname because he crosses his eyes when he comes!"

Leila choked on her margarita quickly putting her napkin to her mouth.

"Burke!" Nichola admonished. "Remember, you are in mixed company!"

"Oh, beg your pardon, ma'am. You were so quiet I completely forgot you were sitting there!" Burke looked at her apologetically but there was a gleam in his eyes, and she knew he was lying through his teeth.

She couldn't help it; she burst out laughing as Devin joined her. Nichola looked at them both shaking his head in irritation and told the waiter, who was bringing out their plates, sternly. "No more liquor for these two." To which they laughed even more, and Burke joined them in laughter.

* * * * *

Halfway through their meal, musicians set up to softly start playing a classical melody. Nichola glanced at Nelson in inquiry, who had taken a stance by the hostess at the door to the dining room. Nelson quickly walked to the table to tell Nichola softly, "Yes, sir, I know that you said it wasn't necessary, but they were so eager to play for her ladyship! Frankly, they haven't been getting much exhibition time due to the travel difficulties."

"Oh, Nichola! They do play beautifully." Leila whispered.

"Come on, Nick!" Devin said just to be irritating.

"Come on, Klaus! It's been dull around here; besides, you pay them either way." Burke said taking a bite of his rare steak.

Nichola, who had really wanted to spend a quiet evening speaking with Leila, relented with a sigh, nodding to Nelson, who smiled gratefully at him in return.

Devin asked Burke, "So, Mr. Burke, you spend the 'season', I have heard, here every year. Why is that? What do you do here every day with the hotel being so deserted?"

"Well, I explore the ruins in these parts." Burke said glancing at Nichola. "When there are other guests in attendance, I play poker, or shoot at the gun range. Klaus put one in oh, about ten or fifteen years ago."

"You enjoy the Incan culture?" Leila inquired.

"I find it absolutely fascinating, ma'am. I have been studying it, and the culture that preceded them, the Wari, for many years. That's how Klaus,

48

Aleksei, and I originally met." Burke said looking directly at Nichola who seemingly ignored him, as he took a sip of his wine.

"Oh, you know, Aleksei Ostrovsky?" Leila asked and Burke nodded his head. "Then you must know my Aunt Iris." Leila stated, then felt bad about mentioning her name as Dene looked pointedly at his plate.

"I do, but not very well." Burke replied. "She seems to be a very vivacious lady."

"That's one word for it." Dene muttered, but Leila heard him none the less and felt sorry for him.

"So, there is a gun range? That's great! I will have to get some practice time in." Devin said.

"Do you rent out guns here, Nichola?" She asked him, and Nichola nodded at her starting to speak but Devin cut him off.

"I don't need to rent any, Mom! I brought my guns and a bunch of ammo with me."

"On an airplane?" Leila asked shocked.

"It's a private plane, Mom! You didn't really think I was leaving my guns behind, did you?" Devin asked incredulously. "I brought your Walther PK also."

Nichola raised his head to focus his full attention on her.

"So, you shoot ma'am?" Burke asked with interest.

"A bit." She deflected, unable to detect Nichola's emotions as she looked at him out of the corner of her eyes.

"Don't let her fool you, Mr. Burke. She's a hell of a shot! She's the one who taught me how to shoot. I am a pretty decent shot, and she's much better than I am. Downright deadly!" Devin said, enjoying his mother's discomfort, and Nichola's bewilderment about this revelation. Obviously, Nick, didn't know as much about his mother as he thought he did.

"Is this a recent activity, i psychí mou?" Nichola asked surprised.

"No, and I fail to understand why you are so very surprised about it." Leila told him slightly put out. "My father is from Wyoming. I have shot most of my life. I also live in Texas; it would be strange if I didn't know how to shoot."

"Ma'am, it is very strange amongst vampire women." Burke broke in. "They pretend to be so very delicate, and helpless, when we all know that in reality they have fangs and claws just like the rest of us, and as such are just as dangerous." Burke said. "I for one find it refreshing! I would love to practice with you, and of course, your son at any time."

Nichola looked at Burke in warning.

"Oh, are you very skilled, Mr. Burke?" Leila asked with interest.

"I'm a fair shot." He said mimicking her earlier tone of 'a bit', giving some attention to his food and sipping his bourbon.

Nichola snorted in humor sipping his wine.

"What?" Leila asked.

"William here was considered a 'shootist' in his time." Nichola said with a smile, and it was Burke's turn to glare at him.

"You were a gunslinger?" Devin asked in awe.

"Gunslinger is a modern term." Burke said repressively.

"Devin, you will have to ask him about his time in Tombstone." Nichola encouraged, strangely gleeful.

"You were in Tombstone, Arizona? During the OK Corral incident?" Devin's voice was astonished and interested.

"Before, during and after." Burke murmured.

"Wow! Did you know Wyatt Earp?" Devin asked.

"He was a right pompous prick!" Burke said vehemently.

"William, your language!" Nichola murmured, actually smiling.

"Pardon', ma'am!" Burke apologized, nodding to Leila. "But Doc Holliday was a good man." He said to Devin sincerely. "How history got that incident so wrong is only due to propaganda!"

"Doc was a damn fine poker player." Fred said nodding his head.

"Fine enough that he knew you were cheating all of the time!" Burke said with a laugh. "If he didn't like you so damn much he would have killed you half a dozen times." He nudged him with his elbow, causing Fred to give a wide grin in remembrance.

"The Doc sure knew how to have a good time! That Wyatt Earp though! That man had a stick so far up his," here Nichola cleared his throat, and Fred nodded toward Leila, "beggin' pardon, ma'am, his...backside that he couldn't bend at the waist. It's no wonder people rebelled against him. Course then his brother got hisself killed, then Earp went mad, and people felt sorry for him. Never knew what the Doc saw in him, myself."

"There's no accounting for love." Burke said to no one in particular.

"Are you saying that Doc Holliday and Wyatt Earp..." Leila let her sentence hang raising her eyebrows.

"I don't know nothing for sure." Burke said.

"Please," Fred scoffed. "Josie was a beard!" Causing Devin to laugh at him uproariously.

* * * * *

Leila giggled as the waiter served her coffee, "Thank you so much for joining us for dinner tonight, Mr. Burke and Mr. Fred, it's been highly entertaining, and rather educational!"

Nichola slid her a small glance and gave her a neutral smile.

"Oh, Mom! You sound like you are going to bed!" Devin said incredulously.

"Well..." Leila started.

"It's early. Come dance with me, Mom!" He demanded, holding his hand out to her, and startling Nichola. "You made me go to lessons with you! You might as well put them to good use."

Leila smiled at him good-naturedly.

"Do you two-step, ma'am?" Burke asked with interest.

"Yes! She learned how to do that one also." Devin told him.

"I get next dance then!" Burke declared and Nichola glowered at him, which he ignored.

Devin pulled her up and out onto the dance floor in front of the musicians, who looked overjoyed to have someone dancing. "Hey, guys, could you play us a waltz?" Devin asked them and they nodded enthusiastically.

Devin stood straight and tall, looking down at his mother with a sassy grin as he took her hand in his and placing his other hand behind her shoulder blade, she put her hand on his shoulder resting her arm across the top of his.

Nichola turned his chair to observe Devin move his mother gracefully across the floor and as he caught Leila's eye he smiled gently at her. Burke came up next to him turning Leila's chair around and sat down next to him watching them also.

"What are you up to, William?" Nichola's question was low.

"What ever could you mean, Klaus?" He returned, not taking his eyes from the couple, then continued not waiting for a reply. "The boy gets his good looks from his mother. Despite his darker coloring I can see her around his eyes, mouth and jawline." Nichola nodded watching them dance and not replying. "Your lady is charming and graceful. You are a lucky man." His voice this time was sincere.

"She's also very naïve and her heart is innocent of many things." This time Nichola faced him fully. "I would hate to think that you would seek your revenge against me through her or her son." Nichola's tone was dangerous, and his eyes glittered at Burke in warning.

"I am a right bastard sometimes, Tsoukalous, but I know that you have never heard of me abusing either women or children." Burke's quiet, deep voice was just as dangerous as he returned Nichola's look. Then he stood with a smile, as Devin brought his mother to him, murmuring "As the others start to arrive over the next several weeks, you would do well to educate her before she comes across someone who is less benevolent than I."

Nichola studied them in thought as Burke bowed slightly to Leila presenting his hand and took her to dance her around the floor. Devin sat next to him in his mother's chair, surprising him, but he showed no outward sign of that surprise.

"He seems nice." Devin said to Nichola, indicating Burke and his mother, wanting Nichola to be jealous.

"Looks can be deceiving." Nichola murmured in response, and then faced Devin full on. "You understand that I love your mother, don't you?"

"I know that she believes so." Devin told him bluntly.

"She knows that I have given up much for her happiness." Nichola stated holding Devin's pecan-colored eyes, with his amber gaze for a few seconds. "And yours. What we have is not some human weekend fling." Nichola turned to watch Leila smiling as Burke spun her around the dance floor, sometimes leading sometimes walking beside her. "I hope you are not as idealistic and trusting as your mother." He commented softly.

"Believe me, I am not. She sees a goodness in most people. I on the other hand believe the opposite, until proven otherwise." Devin said in a soft voice laced with steel.

"Good." Nichola told him. "That suspicion will keep you out of trouble. Remember, I am not the only vampire in attendance," here he nodded to Burke, "and there are more coming that may be more dangerous to both you and your mother. Some of us are totally without honor. Watch us, including me if it makes you feel better, but never trust us until you can defend yourself against us. Being a part of my house will protect you to a certain extent; but remember, not all of us are to be trusted."

Devin nodded, his eyes shrewd.

"Good. Now, if only I can convince your mother to remember that." He murmured, rising to take Leila's hand from Burke as he led her smiling back to them. "Do you tango, my love?" He asked her.

"Not very well." She replied with a giggle.

"Well, remember, I lead." He pulled her to the middle of the dance floor, pulling her close to his body, to smile and whisper, "It's fairly easy; it's just like sex, except with your clothes on. We both know that you do that very well."

Transitioning Vampires

I glanced at the vampire seated next to me as my mother's 'boyfriend' tangoed her around the dance floor. Burke seemed like he was a decent guy. I have been around Texans for the last ten years and knew how upfront and outspoken the majority of them were. He reminded me of the old timers who I had met during my internship in the county judge's office during college. You could definitely imagine him wearing a hat, spurs, and a six-shooter gun belt.

Nick tangoed Mom past us, looking at her seductively as she tried hard not to laugh playfully at him. Focusing on them, an irritation settled over me surprising me in its intensity.

Usually, I rarely let my emotions control me or effect my actions. I was normally very good at hiding them and maintaining a calm façade to the world. It was something that I had worked on since I was a teenager, when I realized that the more control you had over yourself the more respect others gave you. But over the past month, in addition to the painful sensations I received when I went outside in the Texas sunshine, I found myself behaving unpredictably, and I didn't care for it! Outwardly emotional and quick to anger was not who I tried to be. My mother explained that it was a side effect of transitioning into what we were.

When my mother had told us about her experiences with her vampire family and had told us that she had a vampire soulmate, she had explained that Nick had helped her to maintain her humanity so that she could raise us and remain a part of our lives. Even though I couldn't remember a time that Uncle Man hadn't been a large part of our lives, I had to admit to myself, that when she and he sat Zach and I down for 'the talk' about vampires and companions I only half believed it. For Zach, it seemed to answer questions that I didn't even know that he had.

My brother, luckily or unluckily, had the ability to recall anything that he had ever seen and a large majority of what he had ever heard. I had always envied this ability, knowing I definitely would have had an easier time during law school if I had it too, but Zach always told me that there were things he could never unsee. I never got a straight answer out of him when I asked for details, but he always seemed haunted by something.

Watching them as Nick smiled warmly down at her and seeing the blush on her cheeks in response to something he said, I knew that I was probably being unfair about my mother's boyfriend. He seemed to like her, and she seemed happy. Irrationally, it really irritated me to see them so wrapped up in each other. Nick seemed to be really bossy, like he was actually *somebody* and she was acting like a moonstruck teenager! She never acted like that with my dad, not that I could really blame her. Dad never treated her or Zach and I with much affection, and as we became adults we stopped expecting or even wanting him to.

Though I had to admit the last couple of years of his life he was better about showing that he cared about us, and his sudden death had shocked and hurt both my brother and myself. So much so that when Zach suggested that we move back in with Mom so she wouldn't be alone, I had readily agreed.

Watching Nick twirl her as she laughed, I realized that I didn't understand her. If she really liked this guy Nick, why didn't she leave to be with him after Dad died? It just felt like she was falling for the first guy to show her any attention since she became a widow. I don't like it. I don't like it at all.

Confessions

s she walked out of the bathroom dressed in a long cream-colored silk nightgown, she found Nichola leaning against the backboard of the bed propped up by half a dozen pillows. There was a towel draped across his body, and another draped across one of his shoulders. One of his bare legs was slung over the side of the bed touching the floor, making a space for her in between his legs. She knew instinctively that underneath the towel he was naked.

"Remove your nightgown, Leila." He commanded. She complied slowly with a smile, thinking he was playing some sexual game with her. "Come. Get in between my legs and lie back against me so I may hold you."

It was his tone that alerted her that this wasn't some sexual ploy. "What are you doing, Nichola?" She asked.

"Something that must needs done, of course, always."

"You need to be a little more specific, Nichola." She said sharply crossing her arms over her breasts.

He heaved a sigh, fighting for patience; she was always one to question his commands. "I'm going to start the process of removing this venom from your veins, you're past ready to be what you're supposed to truly be."

"Am I?" She challenged with a raised eyebrow.

"Oh yes. You are."

"So, how exactly is this process going to work?"

"It will be slow." He responded softly.

"And painful?" She asked apprehensively.

"Yes, likely at times, very painful, but I am not positive. I will help you through it in any way that I can." He was being brutally honest with her.

"Alright. Then do something for me if you would."

"I will do anything for you, i psychí mou. You know that I will give my life for you."

"Then tell me, Nichola," she said sadly, sitting down and leaning back against his muscular chest. "Did you help him? Did you help him go as far as he did throughout his life?"

"Who?" He asked, being deliberately obtuse.

"You can read me, Nichola. Just because I can't hear you in my mind, doesn't mean that you can't read me. Isn't that right?"

"You are correct." He whispered into her ear softly as she settled against him.

"Then just tell me." She demanded and she could feel his strong hand just above her shoulder; after a moment the veins in her body felt like they were heating up.

"The answer that you're asking for, is yes, I did everything in my power to help him further his career. But I didn't do it for him. I did it for you and the boys."

"Nichola, I'm not questioning who you did it for."

"How did you find out? Even Mansuetus never knew the full details of our agreement." Nichola's voice was even and flat.

"As he lay dying in the hospital he confessed everything to me. Now I want to hear your side of the story."

"I never expected to love you as much as I do, i psychí mou. I knew how soul mates worked. I've seen it with my own eyes; and I was drawn to you from the very beginning and treasured you as a part of myself. But I never expected to love you the way that I do, nor to ever love your children the way that I do. I never expected to sacrifice my own happiness just to make you happy. I realized that in order to make you truly happy, I would have to give you the time and ability to raise your children in safety.

But I never wanted to leave you Leila, you know this. So, in order to satisfy my own mind, and to insure that you were happiest, I wanted to make sure that you and the children would have something better in your life. I wanted him to be able to take care of you all in a better manner than he had in the past. To give you and the boys opportunities that you didn't have."

"So, what did he ask for?"

"He wanted to know if I could help further his career."

She chuckled to herself, then gasped as she felt a pain flow throughout her body. "In exchange for what?"

"In exchange for him doing the right thing in becoming a better husband and father to his children. Was he?"

"You know the answer to that Nichola, you've always been able to feel me even when I was unable to feel you."

"Well, he wasn't what I had hoped he would be for you, but he provided for you better than he would have ever been able to without my influence. How long did you know about my involvement?"

"Well, I was suspicious after he made senior chief, but I never connected it to you. You see, he didn't even tell me that he had been promoted. I showed up to pick him up from a ceremony and I was late. I ran up the stairs of the Off Crew building and all of the sudden one of the other chiefs grabbed me by the arm. He took me to a platform and Michael was there next to his captain and the captain chuckled at me, *you almost missed this, Mrs. Sutton.* I looked at Michael and he looked away just briefly. I hadn't totally lost my extrasensory abilities at this time, but I couldn't read him. How did you manage to pull that off?"

"I have a long reach in all areas of the world, Leila. I'm not an ancient creature for nothing. Some of my contemporaries may hide in castles all over the world in darkened corners. But I never have." His answer was simple.

"So, you used your influence too push him forward in rank?"

"I did as much as I could possibly do. That was our agreement. But even my influence can only work so far in your military. That's why he never attained a higher rank. When he retired, I helped him attain his various positions. Because of my broad business interests, I have more influence throughout the business world." He was direct.

"I was surprised when he got his first job after retiring from the Navy. Most retiring senior chiefs, even though they have the experience, weren't getting big six figure jobs at that time. I was surprised, pleased and proud."

"It's good. Those are the things I wanted you to feel. I didn't want your life to be unhappy, Leila. You are feeling pain?" Nichola asked abruptly, as she stiffened, suddenly, sharply sucking in her breath.

"I feel...I feel like you're tugging on my soul, Nichola." She groaned.

He quickly pulled her to the side, and with a strong arm pulled her back tightly and securely against him, moving her hair to her other shoulder. She was feeling weak, and her stomach was rolling like she was topside on a ship in a storm. Whatever he was doing to her was causing every part of her body to ache. It was like the mercury of a thermometer was rising, and her body was the thermometer ready to burst. The pressure in her body was building and being pulled to the point where he held his hand above her shoulder.

She felt his long, sharp teeth against the curve of her bared shoulder, and he bit quickly and deeply. Crying out, she felt all four of his teeth, both the upper and lower canines, pierce the flesh on either side of her shoulder and suddenly withdraw, then a pinkish substance ran down her front and she could feel it running over her back.

After the initial eruption, like an abscess bursting, the flow was slow and steady, and he didn't try to stop it, he simply wrapped her in a towel to soak up the liquid and then continued to speak holding her close against his chest, unfazed by what was occurring to her body.

"Yes, I helped him." He confessed.

"Did you always know what was going on with my life?" She asked him in a pained voice, sickened by the liquid that was being slowly absorbed by the towel wrapped around her.

He held her to him tenderly in silence, as the pain throughout her body increased causing her body to shake and shiver.

She suddenly cried out. "Please talk to me, distract me! This hurts so bad." She fought against another spasm of pain, as her muscles clenched so hard she thought her bones would break.

"Hush, my love, I will tell you." Nichola told her in an aching voice, pressing his lips against her temple. "Do not fight it, relax, and let it happen. Yes. I knew much.Mansuetus was there to keep me informed. I sent him to you several times a year."

"I was always grateful for that." Leila sucked in her breath, then panted softly, as another spasm of pain flowed throughout her body.

"I didn't want your gratitude. I wanted him to make sure that you were all right; safe. That you and the boys were happy." His voice was bitter.

"I was never truly happy without you Nichola. Content, glad to be with my children, yes, but never truly happy." Leila admitted.

"I understand, but I wanted you to be as happy as you could be, and I wanted to make sure that Michael was keeping his agreement. I knew when he had the affairs." He told her softly.

"You probably knew before I did." she said trying to chuckle her way through a ripple of pain and failing with a groan. He shushed her and stroked her arm.

"Only for a time. I could feel that you knew something was wrong." He murmured.

"Well, eventually even an idiot had to figure it out. I mean hell the affairs continued on and off for years."

"I realize it was painful for you. When I found out about it myself I wanted to kill him. He stopped, but, not on his own though did he?"

"No, Nichola, definitely not on his own. He stopped because I finally had gathered enough information to take half his stuff, more than, really, as he would have ended up living in a box after child support and alimony. Anyway, he decided that his stuff was more important than she was."

"You sound almost satisfied with that."

"Later, I was. I was hurt, though I realized that I didn't really have a right to be hurt. Not when a large part of me always belonged to you."

"Is that why you stayed with him? Guilt? I'd hoped that he would leave, or you would leave him and then you would call me to you. It hurt me in a way, you'll never understand, when you didn't. Why did you stay?"

"Same reason I left you Nichola, it's always been about them. The boys. Though I wonder if that wasn't one of many mistakes I made over my lifetime." She said weakly and he realized that he needed to keep her speaking. If he didn't, she might pass out and he needed her conscious for the entire process.

"Tell me how you found out?" His voice was emotionless.

"He was stupid." She murmured softly, and her voice was laced with pain. "His behavior was always suspicious. It always was like he was constantly looking for an excuse to storm out of the house. If it wasn't about me, it was about the kids. He threw things in my face that no other woman would tolerate. Yet, I had no solid proof. At least not proof that I could use in court. We hadn't been married quite 20 years when my opportunity came. He went upstairs to work out and left his cell phone downstairs on the kitchen counter. It was on and open. Usually, he had it locked with a password. Since it was unlocked, I just took it. I just decided to take it and look at it. It was 4:45 in the morning. I rarely ever got up so early but couldn't sleep because he had recently been so distant and really cruel toward me and the boys. More so than just ignoring us. I just couldn't take it anymore. He would look at me like he was disgusted, and his looks were boiling over to the boys.

It wasn't just a suspicion by this time, and I knew many details about it. I knew her name, I knew where she lived, you see she was brazen enough to call me to let me know that he and she had been having an affair for more than a year. I confronted him about it and of course he denied everything, said she was mentally unbalanced. She called to cause trouble, because she wanted me to leave him because he wouldn't leave me. Though at the time I didn't know why he just wouldn't leave.

I remember wanting to just call you after she called but when I hung up the phone, the children came home from school. I took one look at them and knew I could escape the pain, but I could not bring them with me and there was no way that I could leave them there with him. If he were going to stay, I could take it. Now I know why he did because he owed his position to your influence. I just continued to ignore them, and he ignored me, and basically conducted this affair in front of our faces.

By the time I gathered solid proof, the boys were teenagers. Zachary was a senior in high school, and it had been going on a number of years. It started shortly after he retired from the military, when he took his new job, and he started to neglect our children. He neglected them. It was like he was someone that lived in the house and provided paychecks. He ignored everything they did; all of their extracurricular activities, all of their interests, it was like they were growing up without a father at all. Worse than when he was in the Navy. Still, being ignored was good in many ways because when he was there he was angry, bitter, and hateful.

Sometimes the abuse in your life doesn't have to be physical. Mental abuse is worse than physical abuse because it lasts longer and hurts more."

Nichola murmured, "That is true."

She could feel the venom flowing from her veins, down her front and down her back, the flow slowed, and she knew Nichola was controlling it with his mind.She could feel the warmth of his hand hovering above the wound he had made on her shoulder and watched the front of the towel getting ever pinker with mixed blood and mixed venom. Her head nodded; she felt weak, disoriented, and wondered how long this process would take.

"Don't pass out on me Leila!" Nichola's voice was sharp in command. "I know this is painful, but this process will not be done in one night. Still, we need to get to a certain point. Continue talking to me. You got into his phone. Then what happened?" He asked. "Focus on my voice, Leila, focus on my voice!" He directed and it wasn't an order that she could disobey.

"So, after I found the emails and the text messages, I forwarded them to my email account. He must have realized what I had done when he got to work; that I had forwarded them, that I had forwarded everything I could find." Leila's words came out high-pitched as she fought the pain and were rushed and jumbled as the pain increased. "He called me when I was at my office, this was in Charlotte, yes this is when we were in Charlotte." She was starting to become disoriented, and she fought against it.

"I need you conscious for this, my love." Nichola murmured apologetically in her ear, and she felt a rush of power from him, which kept her awake but didn't dull the pain.

"He kept calling me over and over. I had to leave my office because I couldn't focus. When I got home, something just took a hold of my heart. So, when he called my cellphone, I just told him that I had had enough. Michael actually thought that he could berate me for being in his phone, in his email, after all of the torture that he had put me and my sons through. What was it for? Revenge because I had spent a few weeks with you?

This was years of neglect, years of moving households every two years because he couldn't find a right 'fit', quitting a job before he got fired. Years of him being gone every weekend doing 'his thing', never spending time with his children. He thought I would take him telling me that I was a horrible bitch for being in his phone! He thought that I would take that from him. After everything? No way. Not anymore. I told him I will take half of everything. Just give me my half and you can walk away.

When he came home that evening. He looked at me and asked *what could you really do to me that you didn't do to me over the years?* Like what he'd been doing wasn't worse than what I did with you. My time with you was very short. I did everything I could to make our family work. With the exception of you, I was a very good wife and mother. I tried to make up for everything that happened." Leila moaned as a burning sensation swept through her.

"You mean I was your guilty pleasure?" he questioned, but there was no laughter in his voice, only neutrality.

"Of course not. You were something that I couldn't help. It is, what it is. Soul mates are not chosen. We are created for each other. I could no longer deny to myself that we were created for each other." Her voice faltered.

"Go on, Leila, don't lose focus now." Nichola whispered against her temple.

"So, he made his decision; his things were more important than she was. He actually became a decent husband after that. The boys in their own way, I think, were bitter towards me for a time. They wanted him to leave because by that time they knew everything that was going on. Children are smart! My two children are exceptionally smart and observant!"

Nichola chuckled softly, "Yes, they are. So, continue."

"You continue, Nichola. I'm so tired." She moaned as another spasm of pain flowed over her body, as if hot needles were pricking her skin.

"Shhhh, it is all right, my love. It's almost over."

"Fine. Did you know, Nichola? Did you know everything at that time?"

"I knew most things. I knew about the affair. And I had Mansuetus finally step in. It wasn't just half his things. It would be everything. Everything he had. Everything he was, the life that he had built, he owed due to his relationship with you. Mansuetus made that very clear. Though I really would have welcomed you, Leila. Even if you had wanted to remain as you were with the venom. I would've welcomed you with open arms, you and the children." He told her sincerely.

"That was the one mistake I couldn't make, Nichola. I couldn't come to you. I could never bring my human children into the vampire world and try to give them a normal life. It would never be safe for them. Not with who and what you are to the community." She murmured her head lagging against his shoulder.

"Yes, you are right." He agreed softly. Then addressed her sharply. "Don't pass out on me Leila!" She felt him shake her as she started to go into a grey area of her mind. "Stay with me!"

"Oh my God this hurts! This hurts so much." His jostling caused her to have another painful spasm and she felt tears flow from her eyes.

"Shhhh, it'll be over soon, see it is slowing down." His voice was soft.

Slowly she looked down to see the towel saturated with thick, viscous, pink liquid. He held her close to him and she could feel that both of their towels were covered in the substance.

Nichola continued. "After he ended the affair, he contacted Mansuetus to speak with me. He told me that in order to keep this other woman from harassing you, he needed to move jobs…again. I told him this would be the last time." His voice was deadly as he remembered.

"So, that's how we got to Texas?"

"Yes, that's how you got to Texas."

"Well, that was a hell of a move!" She chuckled weakly.

"Yes, I thought I did quite well." She could hear the pride in his voice.

"So, what did you have to do to get him his last job?"

"I visited and influenced the decision-makers." He told her like it was nothing. "Why did you stop working when you moved to Texas?" He suddenly asked curiously. "You always liked working."

"I stopped working Nichola, because every time I was doing very well in my career, we would move. Basically, I had to start over with my life and my career, every time. You know how often he moved us. I got tired of starting over, finding new friends, finding a new home, finding a new job and at this point I wasn't sure how long I would remain human; the kids were growing up, Devin was 17, he had graduated high school early, Zachary was taking classes in college." She started to fade away.

"I see." Nichola spoke softly and his tone encouraged her to continue.

"So, when Michael started making so much money, I decided that I would do some good with my time for others."

"Yes, I know you had a lot of charity work; you specialized in children's issues."

"Yes, I did; missing children, shelter children, trafficked children. I joined the Country Club, and various groups. I had likeminded friends. Why? Because there are other things more important than myself. Also, here I was, just existing. I could not feel myself transitioning. I could not feel this venom leaving my veins. I could not see past the horizon." Leila groaned suddenly slightly panting in pain, as if she couldn't catch her breath.

"Breathe my love, almost there, breathe." Nichola whispered, the pain shrinking with his words. "Relax and continue to tell me about your life."

"Whose confession is this Nichola? Yours or mine?" She murmured feeling drugged by the agony.

"Both?" He invited softly in her ear, holding her against his chest. "Maybe it's both of our confessions."

"I decided that I would do something good for society with my time and my life. Something good for the less fortunate amongst us."

"You know I thought after your move; I thought he might be having an affair again. I had determined that if he had followed that path again, if he had done that to you again, Leila, that I would kill him. Even if it would anger and hurt you." Nichola's voice was gruff.

She laughed weakly. "You and me both, Nichola, you and me both." The laugh caused a spasm of pain, and she winced, squeezing her eyes shut as the spasm flowed through her body causing her to tremble around muscles locked in agony.

He held her tight. "It's alright, it's okay, it will pass."

"I think he did have a brief affair. Or was considering it at least. It was not quite a year into the new job and then he started doing his same old bullshit, like disappear without saying he was leaving. He did that once, just once, and I made it very clear to him that it would never happen again. It was one of the few times I felt most like a vampire instead of something just *other* than human."

"What do you mean?" His voice was curious.

"Well, I woke up on a Saturday and he was gone; just gone. It was quite early, barely dawn, I called and texted him, and received nothing in return. So, I waited hours and hours. He finally showed back up, dressed like he'd been off hiking somewhere. Have you ever tried to go hiking in the Texas Hill Country? I wouldn't recommend it. I took one look at him and told him; this will not happen here. You will not mess up our lives again by screwing around with somebody at your job!

He walked past me, and I followed him into our bedroom. He looked at me with a nasty smirk on his face and sat down to take off his hiking boots which were so clean they were pristine. Then he said to me, *what exactly can you do to stop me?* Something in me broke when he said that. It just broke. I turned around and walked into my home office, opened my safe, removed my pistol and started to leave the house."

"Where were you going?" Nichola asked concerned.

"I don't know. I was going to the range I think, it was like my mind had disengaged itself, I was just going to the range and then he came walking out of the bedroom and looked at me. I am not sure what I looked like, but he froze in fear. I looked at him like he was a target, I didn't raise the gun at him, but there was something in me, there was something barely controlled, something cold, something that I didn't fear anymore; that I wanted to embrace. That something wanted to end him." Her voice was gruff and weak.

"Continue, Leila!" Nichola demanded.

"Michael looked at me and he said are you really doing this? And there was true sincere fear on his face. And I relished that feeling of power and I told him: Never again. You'll never hurt us again and I turned around and left the house. I drove, just drove. Driving the Texas countryside is actually therapeutic and relaxing; sometimes it's vastness just has to be experienced and cannot be explained. I wasn't gone very long, not as long as he had been, but when I came back, I put my pistol back into the safe and he was a totally different person after that. Totally different."

"So why in the last five years have you not been having sex? I mean, he's only been dead a little over 16 months."

"He got sick. You know, not cancer sick. It started with typical age things. At first, it was thyroid, then low testosterone, then high blood pressure, then diabetes, and they had him on so much medication that it wasn't physically possible for him to have sex anymore."

She could feel the slow, drip, drip of the venom as he stopped drawing it from her body. He breathed into her ear as she sank into his chest in exhaustion as some of the pain ebbed, "So why didn't you take a lover? You're relatively a young woman. After everything he had put you through," he sighed, "why suffer, if he was unable to fulfill his duty as husband?"

"Because I couldn't imagine ever taking a lover other than you, Nichola. I could never imagine being with anyone else; and I couldn't be with you." Her voice came out in an exhausted whisper.

He kissed her shell-shaped ear, "Don't fall asleep, stay with me."

"After everything, I did what we planned, I raised my boys as humans, which was the main intention after all. Michael and I were better partners, better friends after the sex was done in any case. We actually remembered that we enjoyed each other's company at one time in our lives. He knew that I wasn't unfaithful to him. Though there were times, I think, he expected me to be, it was not easy to become basically a nun. I'm not a nun." She ran her hand up Nichola's thigh, slowly due to the pain, but playfully.

"I know you're not," he chuckled. She flinched as her body spasmed, and another bolt of pain sliced through her veins. "Shhhh, it will shortly stop hurting." He firmly rubbed her muscles, and the action helped slightly, but she felt so weak she could barely hold herself up. Nichola spoke sharply, "Focus. Focus on my voice. Just for a bit longer. You just need to breathe, all right? Relax, and breathe, it'll pass."

"It hurts so much!" She whimpered.

"Tell me. Keep talking." He commanded. "You said he confessed this to you? On his deathbed?"

"Yes, I went to the hospital." Her voice ached with the pain that he couldn't take away.

"Continue," he demanded. "Focus on your words."

"Okay. Remember when they wouldn't allow you to...to visit your loved ones when they were infected in the hospital? Maybe with you being a vampire you don't know what it was like. Well, he was sick with all of these things going on and so when he contracted...contracted the virus, of course he ended up in the hospital. When they tried...they tried to keep me out," she breathed deeply through the pain, exhaling through her nose, slurring her words. "I'd never felt so much like a vampire until that night. I knew he was dying. I knew it the same way you know everything about me. I knew he was dying, and they wouldn't let me in to see him. He was in quarantine. Well, fuck quarantine! I knew that COVID couldn't hurt me; no, we are immune to everything. Hell, they didn't even know how it was spread!

I used my vampire influence for the first time in years the evening that he died. It was quite late, and I just told them I was going to visit my husband. They just stepped aside, like I was parting the red sea. As I sat by his bedside, I held his hand, and he told me that you and he had agreed to give the best possible lives to me and the boys.

I had always suspected something wasn't quite right, I never knew until then Nichola, how deep your treachery could go. I was so angry with you, for interfering, for trying to control me, control the very environment around me. He told me how much he hated knowing that the reason he was so successful was because of me and ultimately because of you. Because of your love for me. For this he resented me and could never really forgive me for being with you.

I held his hand as his life left his body and when it was over, I was lost. It wasn't always unicorns and rainbows, but he'd been in my life longer then I'd lived without him. And I had to go and call my sons to tell them that their father was dead." She fell silent, her pained breathing shallow, and he could feel her anger in her soul.

"I am so angry with you, Leila." Nichola in turn confessed softly and she knew that it was almost over for her. She knew her body was going down into the darkness of the abyss and she fought to escape that darkness. Nichola whispered in her hair, "Why didn't you come to me? Your children were adults, he was dead. Why didn't you come to me, afterwards?"

"I was so angry with you Nichola for interfering. It was almost like I hadn't lived a true life because of everything you did. You were always the one in control. Pulling the strings on me and everything in my life like a master puppeteer."

"I only did what I did to give you the best possible life, Leila, you and the boys."

"I was surprised to find out after the reading of the will and looking over all of the accounts that it was you that paid for the boy's college. But it also confused me." Her statement was met with silence. "So, you helped Michael for what? You still didn't even allow him to spend the money to pay for their college."

"I wanted to be there for them too Leila, I wanted to be their father. It was the least I could do personally; to make sure that their education was the best it could be."

"At least the best that they would decide it to be." She knew that they could have done so many different things and they chose not to.

"We can't control everything that our children choose or choose not to do, Leila." She could hear the bitter smile in his voice, as he read her thoughts, and he held her tight against another spasm of pain as it flowed through her veins. "Almost there love, almost there."

"So, you're angry with me?"

"I am still, yes." He confessed.

"I'm not surprised. I expected you to be. I just couldn't leave them yet, Nichola and I knew if I contacted you that you would force me to do so. I knew, especially after I exercised the power to be with Michael on his deathbed, I knew that Devin was transitioning. I could feel a pull from him, I could feel something from Zachary too, but not, not nearly, what I was feeling from Devin, and I couldn't leave them. I couldn't leave him in case..."

"I understand." He murmured, and he did understand in spite of his anger.

"And I was so angry with you." She continued as if he hadn't spoken. "So, I didn't call you. I didn't cut off ties with Mansuetus though."

"You were considering doing that? I'm not sure he would have obeyed you in that area." Nichola observed quietly.

"I wouldn't have cut the ties with the boys. They're adults and at this point they make their own decisions."

"You've much influence over them, you're their mother. Of course, you know they are their own men, and they do what they want to do. They loved you enough to move-in with you." She felt his kiss against her hair.

"Or they did because I had explained what we are, what we could be, and they were afraid that I would leave. I did not make the same mistakes that my father made. When my sons were old enough to understand, when they were in their late teens, Mansuetus and I explained to them exactly what we were; exactly what we are. As Devin started truly transitioning, experiencing pain, weakness, and sensitivity to the sun, Zachary, Devin, and I, all knew what was happening." She whispered.

"Do you think your revelation changed what they decided to do with their lives? Do you think it interfered with who and what they could have been?" Nichola asked his voice curious, though she knew that he had his reasons for asking. "Zach's almost 30 and he's never been married. Devin's 27 and he's never been married. Most of your friends Leila, and I know who they are..."

"Because you're a stalker, control freak," she interrupted, her voice and laughter weak, feeling numbness throughout her body.

"Maybe, mikró, I am..." he agreed quietly, then continued. "Many of your friends, most of them, are grandmothers. Do you think your revelations kept your children from forming long-term relationships and having children of their own?"

"I truly don't know, but if that is the case then that was their decision. But I did tell them that I knew that you would never do what you had done for both their Grandfather and myself again."

"No. I never will. It is not something to be taken lightly. I'm not sure what this process is going to do to you, Leila." He now confessed to her. "I really don't. I feel fear over the type of vampire you'll be." He said gently, holding her tightly as he felt her stiffen in pain.

"What do you mean?" she asked, slightly frightened.

"What kind of vampire will you be? Will you be horrible? Will you be a monster? Will this affect your powers? Will you be extraordinarily strong and dangerous? Or weak and never develop fully? Will you be simply what you were always meant to be? I truly don't know, and only time will tell." His voice was full of questions and doubts, and she knew these doubts of his worried him more than anything.

"Please, Nichola, please tell me you won't let me be a monster. No matter what. I don't want to be a monster." She said with a sigh, filled with both pain and fear.

"Now my love, i psychí mou, I will do everything in my power to make sure you don't become a monster."

"I love you, Nichola," she whispered weakly. "I think I always have."

"It's done." He told her softly, and she could feel him softly wiping and licking the wounds to seal his bite.

"What will happen now? When I wake up, will I be totally changed?"

"Oh, my love, this was just a part of it. You still have venom in your veins, but I was able to take at least half."

She looked down at the front of herself to see her towel was almost totally wet with venom and blood. "Why is there so much? I don't remember it being so much venom. How could I've held so much?"

"You don't remember the process, Leila? Don't you remember how many days it took us to get you to the point where our connection was so weak it was invisible to you? That you could no longer feel me?"

"Days, yes, it took days and multiple bites." Her voice was exhausted.

"I've taken a great deal tonight and you will be very weak tomorrow, but you will quickly regain your strength. You're more vampire now than you ever were, and I will take care of you, Leila, because you are my mate, and I love you, and I will take care of Devin, because I love him. It's time for us to be a family."

"Are you still very angry with me?" She asked in a small voice, fighting the darkness as numbness spread throughout her body.

"I'm more hurt now, though I understand. I'm just glad to know that even though we've had all of these years of pain apart, that now you are finally back in my life and finally back in my heart."

"So am I, Nichola, so am I." She whispered softly as she felt him lift her into his arms, cradling her against his chest, to take her into the bathroom.

He ran a hot bath while he peeled the venom-soaked towels away from their skin and gently placed her in the tub then joined her there to hold her tenderly against him as the hot water rose around them. As he gently washed her with a sponge, she closed her eyes and drifted to sleep.

* * * * *

Several hours later I woke alone to the feeling that I had not only been hit by a truck, but the driver obviously had intended on doing the most damage because they'd put it in reverse and backed over me; the ache in my body was more than bone deep. The room was black in the night except for a small glow in the corner. I painfully rolled toward the glow to see Nichola, wrapped in a navy-blue plush robe, look up from something he was reading. He stood and walked to the bed, removing his robe, and letting it drop to the floor to reveal his beautiful, muscled body haloed by the glow of the corner lamp, and pulled back the blankets to join me, pulling me gently to him.

"How are you feeling?" He asked me tenderly.

"Weak and achy. How do I look?" I asked.

"Terrible." He said with a slight, teasing, smile.

"Gee, thanks."

"You did ask." He nuzzled the side of my throat. "But you smell wonderful."

"Are you saying that I stank before?" I asked appalled.

72

"Oh, no. Your delicious vampire scent is so much stronger now, is all. I had to leave the bed or ravage you in your unconscious state." His voice was soft, and I could feel his lips trail over my skin.

"You wouldn't do such a thing." I said wanting to laugh at him, but too weak to do so.

He pulled his face from the crook of my neck to look down into my eyes dangerously, "I seriously considered it." I realized that his hands were stroking my body very suggestively.

"So, now that I have regained consciousness, you have returned to...?" I let the sentence hang.

"Oh, yes." He breathed, then kissed me deeply.

When he let me breathe again he was fully on top of me and settled in between my legs. "I can barely move." I complained.

"I can move for both of us." He whispered sliding his cock against my suddenly soaking pussy and entered my tight channel slowly, inch by delicious inch. "Praise be to the gods that makes our ultimate exchange of energy this act." He groaned out, forehead to forehead, and I clutched him to me. "I will never tire of this, pio agapiméni mou."

"Neither will I." I whispered in return, surprised when my whisper came out around small fangs. I spread my legs wider and arched against him giving him more access to me and pulling him closer to my lips as he buried himself to the hilt, rolling his hips, and rubbing his pelvic bone against my clitoris causing me to moan in response.

"That's right, take me into your sweet body." He said softly rolling into me once again and I could feel his balls slap against my ass gently as the muscles of his back and ass flexed under my hands.

My pussy tightened around his cock, as I wrapped my legs around his, and my arms around his shoulders, holding him tight. He was gentle as he wrapped an arm under my back to hold me by the back of the neck, and I could feel his other hand grip me by the hip as he rocked in and out of my body in time with my gasps and moans. I opened my eyes, to see him looking down at me in awe, "There's my lígo vampír."

I could feel the fire in my veins as my orgasm approached. Every muscle in my body tightened and I strained against him as he rolled himself into me, ever driving me toward that ultimate pinnacle. As I headed over the cliff of ecstasy, I felt the power ripple through my veins, and I opened my mouth wide and sank my fangs deep! Nichola cried out in euphoria and continued to drive me through my orgasm with his rolling hips as I feasted on his spicy blood and when he came, I withdrew my fangs arching my body under him and feasted on the power of his release.

As the power ebbed around us, I gently licked the wounds that I had made and held him tightly against me, satiated.

Templo de la Luna

L eila spent the next two days in bed, feeling like she had a bad flu. Her joints hurt, body ached, and everything just throbbed. She had run a slight temperature. Nichola had joyfully insisted on supplying sexual 'energy' treatments a couple of times a day, usually waking her up to do so, until she had unceremoniously ordered him from the bedroom, telling him that it was his fault that she was in such bad shape to begin with. Offended, he had taken himself to his office and not returned, and she had actually gotten a full night's sleep and actual rest on the second night.

Dene was in his element, having two patients to look after, though Devin, who had been introduced to the sun-block spray booth was the most difficult of patients as he was mobile and bored. Early the third morning of her extended lie-in, Devin came dragging her out of bed, forcing her to shower, get dressed, and make herself presentable. He stole Dene's wheelchair and loaded her into it.

"You look different." He commented as he wheeled her through the door to the suite. "Younger."

Leila had dressed herself in fawn riding pants, chestnut brown knee boots, and a white, long-sleeved linen blouse. Both the pants and blouse had been snug on her before she left San Antonio, and now were decidedly looser telling her if nothing else that she had lost a substantial amount of weight over the last couple of days.

"I have just dropped a few pounds." She returned.

"No, it's more than that."

"So, how did you sneak me out of there without them noticing?" She asked looking up at him, ignoring his statement.

He smiled at her like a Cheshire cat, "It's like a prison break isn't it? Or at least it would be if our three jailers hadn't left this morning just before I woke you up. I thought to myself, why not get out while the getting is good?"

She smirked, shaking her head as he wheeled her into the dining room to see William Burke and Cross-eyed Fred sitting at a table having breakfast.

"Hi Billy, hi Fred!" Devin said, moving a chair and wheeling his mother in next to Burke.

"Morning Dev, morning Ms. Sutton." Burke said looking up from his newspaper. His glance became concerned at Leila in the wheelchair. "Ms. Sutton are you doing all right? Your presence has been missed at the supper table the past couple of nights."

"I am better this morning, Mr. Burke." Leila said, repressively.

He studied her intently. "You look different."

Leila looked at him in irritation as Devin grabbed the coffee decanter on the table and poured her some coffee. "That's what I said! Younger!" Devin proceeded to pour himself a cup. Obviously, he and Burke had gotten to know each other better over the past couple of days while she had been ill.

Burke glanced at him with an indulgent smile, then looked at Leila. "You were a very handsome lady when I first met you, Ms. Sutton," Leila glanced at the suave vampire and from his teasing look knew he was remembering their encounter in the ladies dressing room. "but now I must say you are positively lovely." He gave her a captivating smile.

"Thank you, Mr. Burke, you are very charming." Leila replied sipping her coffee with a small smile. She glanced up to see Fred smiling at the vampire. "Good morning, Mr. Fred."

"Ma'am. You do look mighty fetching this morning!" He grinned at her.

"Thank you, Mr. Fred." She smiled at him in return.

"So, transitioning has been rough?" Burke asked, to which Leila just raised her eyebrows. As the waiter approached the table, he asked, "Might I have the honor?" Without waiting for a response, he said to the waiter, "The lady will have two eggs in a basket, over easy, whole grain baskets, a small beefsteak, just flip that critter on the grill, we want it to moo when we stick it and bring her a large tomato juice. Make the same for Mr. Sutton."

Leila and Devin chuckled at him, and Leila asked as the waiter left to do his bidding, "Mr. Burke, what if I have issues with certain foods, such as gluten?"

"Gluten! Ha! A twenty-first century wealthy nation issue. People don't worry about gluten when they are starving." He smirked. "Besides, I transitioned all on my own. Best things for you is protein, and iron."

"You were all alone?" Leila asked sympathetically.

"Yes, ma'am. Back in 1841." He revealed. "I was in Mexican-held California digging for gold in and around the base of mountains that the Indians called Withassa. What is known now as Mount Shasta. Still own a mine and property in the area."

"You own a gold mine?" Devin asked in awe and Leila smiled softly as the waiter brought both of them a large glass of tomato juice. The vampire was certainly interesting she was thinking as she reached for the salt, and Burke covered her hand with his. She looked at him in shock; vampires rarely touched each other unless it was between lovers, greeting or dancing.

"Hold off on the salt, ma'am." He murmured as if he was slightly shocked at his own forwardness, releasing her hand slowly. "The lower your salt intake the easier it is to control your thirst."

"Thank you. I had not heard that before." Leila murmured to him, and he nodded in response.

"Yes, I still own a mine." He replied to Devin.

"Wow! Did you find gold?" Devin asked excitedly.

Burke smiled. "Yessir. Gold, platinum, and diamonds. Not many diamonds to be found in California. But my mine produced a very few."

"That is cool." Devin told him.

"I will tell you a secret, young buck. It's not nearly as impressive as to what I have found here." Burke told him with an air of mystery, then he turned silent as the waiter returned with their breakfasts.

Leila and Devin started eating then looked at Burke expectantly when the waiter left.

"Back in 1853, Klaus, Aleksei Ostrovsky and I found an extensive cave system deep under the Templo de la Luna here in Peru. It is one of the reasons why I come back every year to further explore the cave system." He told them with an air of secrecy.

"Nichola and Aleksei found this with you?" Leila asked surprised.

"Yes, ma'am. You didn't know about it?" He asked.

"No. I didn't."

"It has still not been located by humans to this day, so is unknown to the outside world. The cave system was used for ritual human sacrifice, and the burial of kings and other high officials." Burke whispered.

"Did you find buried treasure?" Devin whispered from Leila's other side.

"In a way." The charismatic vampire's eyes were enthusiastic as he talked leaning into Leila's opposite side to face Devin. "It was originally full of gold, jewels, and other Incan artifacts. We split it, three ways. Fred and I are heading out to walk the cave system after breakfast, we are looking for an entrance into several anti-chambers that we know from seismic testing exist."

"Billy, can we come with you?" Devin whispered.

"Well, now. I don't know. You know how Klaus can be a right stick in the mud and you know he didn't tell your mom nothing about it so…"

"Mr. Burke, how rugged is the interior of the cave? Do we need any special equipment to get in or out?" Leila asked interrupting him and turning to face him. She found herself barely six inches from his face.

"No, and it's pretty clear of debris, ma'am. We aren't planning on doing any excavating today, we are just looking to try to pinpoint the best wall to start taking down." He said softly, looking at her suddenly hot eyes. "But are you in any shape to be walking around?" He asked with a glance at the wheelchair.

"I am feeling better every minute." She told him her voice hard.

* * * * *

Wearing a Bolero hat and wraparound sunglasses, I sat upfront with Burke as he drove the mountainous roads in one of the hotel's black Jeeps, looking out the window at the forested jungle on either side of the road. I listened with half an ear as Devin and Fred sat in the back. They were deep in conversation about the cave system that was our destination beneath the Temple of the Moon. I could feel Burke's eyes on me occasionally, but he didn't try to engage me in conversation. The handsome young vampire was perceptive enough to know that I was furious.

I had asked Nelson before we left the hotel where Nichola, Mansuetus, and Dr. Lambert were and he had informed me that they had taken the helicopter into Cusco; Nichola and Mansuetus to check on the manufacturing plant that he owned that currently manufactured hand sanitizer and expensive designer face masks (another thing I was unaware of), and Dene had medical supplies that he was purchasing and picking up. They were also going to be bringing back some supplies for the hotel.

I had really had it with Nichola and all of his secrecy. Over the years he had taken great lengths to know every aspect of my life, he probably had ordered dossiers on all of my friends, and he even knew that I had never taken another lover out of sexual frustration, with a psychopathic stalkerish determination! But could he have told me he had known Burke for almost two hundred years, and they had been treasure hunters together? Did he bother to tell me that he owned and operated a small manufacturing plant in Cusco?

Oh, no! That would be too much sharing on his part! The only thing that he seemed to want to share with me was his body!

I had wondered why he had chosen such a sparsely populated place to set up one of his vampire resorts. Afterall, it was hard to get to, and hunting wasn't good. Hell, if it had to be Peru for the number of nighttime hours, why not Lima, or at the very least Cusco? Both were large metropolises and tourist destinations. Easy for both entertainment and hunting for his guests. Fairly easy to cover-up any 'accidents' that might happen because one of the guests became 'overzealous'.

But now I knew; those places wouldn't be convenient to him! Because he liked to spend four months a year searching for buried treasure! Probably the only reason he had been hanging at the hotel instead of in this cave system that they had discovered was because currently he liked getting laid more than he liked spelunking for treasure! Who knew how long that would last? Until he decided that he had his fill? Then I would be stuck at the hotel alone while he was off having whatever adventure he decided to have.

No way, no how, would I live forever like that. I wanted my share of adventure too! Devin described sneaking out of the suite this morning as a prison break. How right he had been. If I had to be a vampire, I would not spend any more of forever in a well-appointed prison as some sort of sex slave because I had the misfortune of being mated to a secretive, control freak!

* * * * *

I could tell that the lady sitting beside me was really angry. Outwardly, she was very composed and quiet, but boy, could I feel that anger coming off of her in waves. To say that transitioning was being kind to her was an understatement. She positively glowed with power. I personally had never felt anything like it coming from such a young vampire!

I smiled at Fred and the boy in the back seat in the rearview mirror as they excitedly went over the seismic charts. I really liked the boy. Though he was often like a puppy, following on my heels, he was smart, curious, unafraid, and headstrong; he also treated Fred like a real person. That was a huge plus on the character side for him in my opinion. Most vampires treated their companions as second-class citizens; and despite Mansuetus's and the Doc's championing of him, that included Klaus also.

The more I interacted with her, the more the boy reminded me of his mama. Having been raised by a strong woman, myself, I could appreciate the qualities that the boy had and could see where he got them.

"So, what brought you to Peru initially, Mr. Burke?" She asked me interrupting my thoughts. "Was it always treasure?"

"No, ma'am! In 1850, I met up with a Peruvian miner in California. Now at this time I was the mine owner, and of course was fully transitioned into being a young vampire. I worked alongside of my men in the mine itself during the day. Which made me a different, and popular owner, compared to the owners of the other mines that were cropping up. My men respected me a lot more than just a stuffed suit, of course, it was self-preservation on my part, mining protected me from the sun. At night, the miners would sit around the campfire and trade stories of where they were from. When I spent the evening hours with the miners, I heard these tales. There was a man in my employ, his name was Hasintu, and he was born in Cusco.

Hasintu spun these wild tales of the Incans and before them the Wari, a race of people that worshiped a blood god called Viracocha. Viracocha was nourished by the blood of ritualistic human sacrifice and if you look at some of the depictions today of Viracocha you will see that he sports both extended upper and lower canines.

You see this was all very interesting to me, as up to this time, I thought I was the only vampire in existence as I had never met another like me.Back then, I didn't understand made and born vampires. There was no one that 'made' me. You see when I started my transition in 1841 it had been months since I had even seen another human being! I had been living off of and working the land and mining myself alone. It wasn't even until 1845 that I ran into a group of miners who were mining for gold in the mountains. As you can imagine that didn't go over very well for them." My voice was neutral. I was no longer ashamed for things that I couldn't control or change. After all, there were a lot of vampires that were worse than I was.

"I can imagine." She murmured."So, in 1850, when you first heard about the Inca, you didn't have Mr. Fred with you at this time?" She asked curiously.

"No ma'am, I didn't meet up with Fred until just before the civil war."

"So based on campfire stories, you left California for Peru?" Her voice was incredulous.

"Ma'am, it seems far-fetched, but try to put yourself in my place. I had never set eyes on another vampire in my entire life! I thought I was some sort of monster! If there was a chance of finding out what the hell I was, and maybe other's like myself, I was taking it, even if it was only campfire stories."

"I apologize, Mr. Burke, I didn't mean to judge." She said softly. "I often forget how lucky I am in having a family that looks out for me. Even though

I didn't know that I was a vampire in the beginning of my transformation, my aunt, came to me shortly after it started. I am not sure what would have happened to me if I had totally been on my own." She smiled briefly at me. "So, you said earlier, that you didn't meet Nichola and Aleksei until you arrived here in 1853? Did it take you three years to travel from California to Peru?" She asked, and I could hear the curiosity in her voice.

"No, I traveled first to Texas to see my family. I hadn't seen them since I left in 1837. I wasn't sure that I would make it back you see and figured I better see my family one last time." I swallowed back a painful memory. "I got back to my ranch in early 1851, Texas was now officially a state by this time, to find that my pa had passed away and the ranch being run by my three brothers. My maman was still alive but was doing poorly. She was so happy to see me, even though it was only at night that I could visit her, that I decided to stay with her as long as I could." I glanced at her to see her looking at me with sympathetic eyes and cleared my throat. "She passed a few months after I arrived. But I am glad to have been there with her. Because of my mining operations, I was a rich man. I paid off the outstanding debt on the ranch and set up a ranch account at the bank, and my brothers signed the property over to me. I left them the full running of the place."

"It sounds to me like you were taking care of your family and didn't have any expectation of returning." She commented.

"I guess that's true." I told her not meeting her eyes as I slowed for a rough patch in the road.

"So did you travel through the jungles to get to Peru?"

"I actually took my first sea voyage on that initial trip. I left by ship from Texas and arrived in Havana, Cuba, then took another ship from Havana to Panama City, Panama. My fluency in Spanish held me in good stead during the voyages and kept me from some close run-ins with some unsavory characters." I could feel a smile stretch my face as I remembered my experiences onboard ship, and she must have noticed it too because she suddenly chuckled softly.

"So how many of those 'unsavory characters' survived that experience?"

She asked me.

"Not many." I told her smiling even broader. "From Panama City, I traveled through the jungles of the Amazon to Cusco, finally arriving in early 1853. I met Aleksei first. Then Klaus. They were the first vampires outside of myself I had ever met. They were exploring the ruins of the local Incan cities and looking for the source of vampirism in general. Since I was just looking at that time of discovering others like myself, I guess I succeeded beyond my wildest dreams. Not only did I find others like me, but I had a whole community like me! I had words finally for what I was."

"So, are the Incan and Wari legends the source of vampirism?" Ms. Sutton asked me.

"Depends on who you ask. Klaus will tell you unequivocally 'no'. But both Aleksei and I will answer that question with 'not that we know of…yet'. As far as we are concerned, it has not been proven one way or the other. You see there is no written language of the Incan or Wari peoples that anyone has been able to find. But that doesn't mean that it didn't exist. The Incan people hid much of their wealth and knowledge from the Conquistadors. The Conquistadors destroyed much of the writings of the Mayan people; so, it makes sense that the Incan's written documents could have been destroyed. It also stands to reason that some written documents could have been hidden.

We did find some of their treasures here in this cave beneath the Temple of the Moon. But so far, no written documents. I am hoping to find more than treasure once Fred and I open up the newest sections of the cave system."

"So still even after finding the community, you are still searching for the source of vampirism?" Her voice was curious.

"Well, what else do I have to occupy my time?" I questioned sharply in return, then realized how sharp I had been with her. She continued to look in my direction, and though I couldn't see her eyes behind the dark glasses I knew that she really wanted to know; she really cared about the answer.

I focused again on the road, but after a few seconds found myself telling her, "I am not like you. I don't have any family that I know of. It's just me and Fred. You see, the Doc, has created a Vampire DNA database and he has taken my sample. He's compared it to everyone that has provided him a sample and so far for me, nothing. I am not a match. My brother's died without issue, so I don't even have any human family left. I am alone." I realized that I sounded bitter.

"I am sorry, Mr. Burke." I could hear her sympathy and it wasn't something that I wanted. Not from her.

"Don't you worry about it!" I said trying to sound nonchalant. "The Doc is all excited about the large council calling this special meeting, he is confident that he is going to be able to collect a lot more samples. I am sure I will find any kin folks of mine then. Knowing my luck, they will all be poor as church mice, and I will find myself taking care of a passel of mangy vampires!" I smiled widely at her to which she smiled in return with a small laugh, but I got the distinct feeling that she wasn't fooled one bit.

* * * * *

Burke pulled the Jeep off-road, crossing a dry creek bed, and pulled into a sparse grassy area through the trees. They emerged about 100 meters into a grassy clearing that housed some dilapidated wooden buildings. Burke parked the Jeep and they got out.

"You still feeling okay, Ms. Sutton?" He asked her going around to the back of the Jeep and pulling out a vest, donned it. He also pulled out a brown tooled leather, western, double gun belt and holster which he secured around his hips.

"Yes, I feel fine." Leila said to him as she watched him tie the leather leg straps around his long muscular legs."Are you worried about something, Mr. Burke?"

"Oh, no, ma'am! But you should always be prepared. We have to walk about a quarter mile through these trees to get to the hidden entrance into the cave system and there are all kinds of critters out there. I doubt we will see anything more harmful than a few Llamas, but there are pumas and poisonous snakes. If you see a puma, remember they are probably more scared of you than you are of them. So, just make some noise and they will go on about their business."

"I doubt that Mr. Burke. But don't worry, if I see one I will be screaming very loudly so that should scare them away!" Leila told him and he smiled at her.

"His name is Billy, Mom!" Devin told her as he reached into the back and grabbed his shoulder holster to put it on.

Burke glanced at him as Leila intentionally ignored Devin. "What you carrying there boy?"

"Nine-millimeter Beretta, 15 rounds." Devin told him.

"That's what Mansuetus carries." Burke responded.

"Yep. He gave it to me a few years ago. I see you are carrying Colt Peacemakers. 45's?" Devin asked.

"Yessir."

"But you only have twelve rounds between both guns!" Devin said incredulously.

"Son, if you hit what you are aiming at the first time around how many more rounds do you need?" Burke answered him with a smile.

Devin gave him a little smirk, then said, "Her name is Leila." Turning he jogged to catch up to Fred who was heading on a worn path into the trees.

Leila started to turn to follow after him when Burke stopped her and said, "Here put this on. You might find the cave cold." He helped her into a lightweight canvas jacket, which was a little long in the sleeves for her, and he rolled them up for her so that the sleeves rode at her wrists. "There all set."

"Thank you, Mr. Burke." She gave him a small smile, heading after Devin, and Burke followed sedately after her admiring the view.

* * * * *

William Lionel Burke was not a stupid man by any stretch of the word and was glad that Ms. Sutton was keeping it formal between them. He knew Devin was playing cupid because he didn't like his mother with Klaus. Burke was quite certain that he wouldn't like his mother to be in a relationship with any man that wasn't his father. The pain of his death was still too new.

Still, Burke found he was more than interested in the lady as he watched her swinging hips, and rounded ass cheeks, just below the hem of the blazer he had loaned her, sway back and forth hypnotically in her riding pants and boots as she walked along in front of him. Images of her beautiful, pink-tipped breasts popped into his mind. *She sure was a pretty little thing!*

He suddenly shook his head to clear those images.

He was aware that if Klaus knew he was lusting after his woman and thought he was trying to tempt her to stroll down the primrose path he would murder him without a thought. With their history between them, Klaus most likely would think he was attempting to do so not out of any personal desire for the lady, but out of revenge against himself. Klaus would be wrong, but there you have it.

Besides, he could tell that this lady was nothing like her aunt! Ms. Sutton was keeping it cool between them and that was the way it needed to stay. It obviously had been too long since he had himself a woman, or he wouldn't even be having these thoughts about her! He determined to visit the village to take care of his needs as soon as may be, to shake these thoughts from his mind.

They made good time on the quarter-mile trek, and he was impressed that Ms. Sutton followed Devin and Fred, who seemed on a foot race due to their excitement, steadily through the low undergrowth of the trees without complaint. Burke made sure to keep an eye on her in case she stumbled along the light path. Fred and Devin stopped at a small hill located in the trees that was covered in bamboo trees, Amazonian lilies, and other dense vegetation.

Fred stopped, crossed his arms, and looked at Devin with a smirk on his lips.

"I don't see it." Devin said in confusion.

Leila approached them, glanced between them, and looked at the mound. "I do." She said quietly and to Burke's surprise walked up to the heavy foliage and proceeded to twist in and around it until she was lost to sight. Devin followed her, then Fred and Burke brought up the rear.

"Ms. Sutton, hold on there. Let me go first." Burke told her, stopping her at a dark entrance into the mound that descended into the ground.

Fred turned around to give Burke access to the backpack he was carrying, and Burke pulled out a small torch, lighting it with a lighter. He walked into the narrow entrance and Leila followed him down a flight of stone stairs. As they descended into the cave, Burke reached the torch up to light the torches set into the cave walls.

"Did you create this staircase, Mr. Burke?" Leila asked after a few minutes of traveling down.

"No, whoever created this complex, hundreds of years ago, did. See how the stones are cut and put together without mortar? It's an amazing feat of engineering that a primitive people were able to do this at all." He expressed. "Be careful coming around this corner, one side of the staircase falls away abruptly. We installed handrails, for safety, but it is still a twenty-foot fall to the main cave floor."

As they reached the main floor the cave expanded out, opening on a mostly flat space that would hold at least two hundred people. Burke walked up to one of the walls and held his torch high and showed Leila and Devin a cave painting depicting a humanlike figure and what looked to be a llama.

"The whole place is filled with cave drawings." Burke stated to them lighting more torches.

"What was some of the artifacts that you found here?" Leila asked him noticing that the large open space was bare.

"We found quite a few gold and silver statues. One of the first things that we found was right here beneath this drawing. It was a statue of a silver llama. It weighed at least fifty-five pounds of solid silver. Silver according to the Incans represented tears of the moon, and gold was considered the sweat of the sun."

Burke handed Leila the small torch and she followed the walls looking at the various cave paintings as he and Devin headed over to where Fred had unrolled the seismic charts out on a flat alter stone. The primitive drawings were quite beautiful in their own way. Leila looked up toward the high ceiling of the cave holding the torch high and saw the enormous stalactites attached to the ceiling. They had to have been formed over hundreds and hundreds of years. She noticed as she looked back at the men who were studying the charts that the only debris on the floor of the open portion of the cave seemed to be caused by the occasional stalactite that had fallen from the ceiling here and there.

She continued to follow the cave wall looking at the art until she came to a small, hollowed space that resembled a hallway that was partially blocked by some stalagmites growing from the floor of the cave. She twisted her way around them, ducking down to avoid the stalactites of the lower ceiling and made her way into a smaller anti-chamber. Painted on the wall of the anti-chamber in wonderful life-like colors was the figure of a man in full ceremonial headdress, his eyes were red, and it was obvious that the man's white upper and lower canines were long like fangs.

"Oh," she exclaimed in wonder.

"Yeah, he's interesting, isn't he?" Burke asked behind her startling her causing her to turn in surprise.

She felt something long and heavy land on her back scrabbling with what felt like several claws looking for a purchase hold on the canvas of her jacket. She turned around in a circle yelling in terror reaching and trying to remove whatever it was that had leaped on her, as she felt fangs pierce the side of her neck not once, but twice!

She heard Burke yell, "Son of a bitch!" and pull at whatever it was from the back of her shoulder. Unfortunately, it still had its fangs buried in her throat, and she screamed in fear and pain as she felt them rip the flesh of her neck as he finally dislodged it, throwing it to the floor of the cave, drawing one of his pistols and shot it.

The reverberation of the gunshot along the walls of the small anti-chamber, caused the cave to tremble and the stalactites at the entrance of the anti-chamber to come crashing down in a cave-in. Burke leaped on Leila attempting to protect her as more stalactites came crashing down around them. He pressed her body against the wall next to the painting, covering her head and shoulders with his own body and the sharply pointed formations dropped around them like missiles.

* * * * *

Leila coughed out the cave dust in her lungs in the aftermath and could feel Burke scrabbling around looking for the torch. He found it to light it chasing away the darkness. Blood dripped down the side of his handsome face as he turned toward her. She looked down at herself to see her own blood running down her front and she sank to her knees in shock finally feeling the pain at her throat. Agonizing pain started running down her shoulder and back as she could hear Devin calling out for her through the blocked entrance of the anti-chamber.

"Shit!" Burke exclaimed reaching over and lighting another torch that was set into the wall. He sat the torch in his hand down and examined her wound.

"Mom! Mom!"Devin yelled, his voice panicked.

"Boss!" Fred yelled."Boss! Are you okay?"

"Yeah!" Burke replied loudly. "Get to the Jeep. We need the med-kit. Anti-venom pen and bandages. Hurry! Dev see if you can start moving the debris from the entrance. Work your way from the top."

"Okay. Is my mom okay?" Devin's muffled voice came as they heard movement amongst the rocks.

"She's gonna be just fine, boy. Be careful how you remove those rocks." Burke told him in a steady voice, meeting Leila's pained eyes.

"What was it?" Leila groaned out.

"Giant centipede." His voice was calm, as he removed the bandana from around his throat to dab at the wound on her neck. His calm voice belied his movements, and she could hear the pounding of his heart.

"How bad is it?" She ground out gritting her teeth in pain.

"Looks like he got you a couple of times." Burke pulled her gently into his lap and against his muscular chest, and she was surprised to find that she couldn't move her arm closest to the bite. It was as if her body was becoming slowly paralyzed. "I have to suck this venom out, Ms. Sutton." He told her as she felt his soft mouth and hard fangs against her wound drawing on her. He pulled away and spit to the side, coming back to fasten on her again. She cried out stiffening against him as pain throbbed in her shoulder and her back. He pulled back to spit again, whispering against the side of her face, softly nuzzling her in comfort, "It's okay, darlin', I am almost done." Then fastened his mouth on her wound again, holding her tightly in his arms, drawing hard, pulling back, and spitting a third time. "I don't know if I've got it all, your blood still tastes strange. But you are bleeding hard."

He whispered to her, "I've got to seal it up before you lose too much more blood."

"It's probably Nichola's venom that you are tasting. Just seal it up." She whispered as her eyes started to close and then she felt his soft mouth back on her throat and his tongue lapping against her skin. Her head lolled back on her shoulders to rest against his body behind hers, as he lifted his head.

"No! Wake-up. Here drink this." He said suddenly shaking her slightly. Her eyes fluttered open as he pressed his wrist to her lips, dripping his own blood into her mouth.

"Stop! No!" She protested, but her voice was a whisper as she choked on his blood, trying to move her head away and she found that she could barely move her body.

"Drink! Goddamn it! Don't make me put a boot up your ass!" He warned her with a shake. He held his bloody wrist tighter to her mouth, forcing her to drink his blood while he gripped her body tightly against him with his other arm. "C'mon Leila, baby, drink!" His voice was a coaxing whisper in her ear.

* * * * *

Leila woke up as Burke sliced through her pants with his sharp nails, ripping a hole in them. She flinched as he pushed a needle into her leg muscle.

"She's not going to die is she, Billy?" She heard Devin's fearful voice ask as her eyes closed again.

"She's not dying on my watch, son."

* * * * *

The next time she opened her eyes, she was in the back of the Jeep still cradled tightly in Burke's arms. The Jeep hit a pothole throwing them around causing her to cry out in pain and Burke cussed, "Goddamn it, Fred! Slow the fuck down before you throw us off the side of this mountain!"

Life or Death

⁓⦾⦿⦾⁓

L
eila could feel the Jeep stop and someone open the back door as Burke stepped out adjusting his hold on her. "Get the doors, boy." He ordered and she could feel his quick steps as he carried her.

"Lady Tsoukalous!" She heard Nelson's voice exclaim as they burst through the front of the hotel.

"Where's the Doc, Nelson?" Burke demanded.

"In the suite," Nelson replied worriedly.

"Where's Klaus?" She could feel him carrying her again.

"Same." She opened her eyes to see Nelson quickly open the door to the suite.

"Dene!" Devin yelled.

"Kyría!" She heard Mansuetus's worried voice from above.

"Doc!" Burke shouted. "Bring your bag and a shot of anti-venom. Ms. Sutton's been hurt!"

"What happened? Bring her in here!" She heard Nichola's sharp voice coming down the staircase.

It was like she was in the center of an amphitheater and the voices were floating down to her from a darkness; she tried hard to concentrate and soon their voices were coming from her peripheral vision, yet she couldn't focus her eyes enough to actually see them.

Burke deposited her against the cool sheets of her bed. Then Nichola's hands were on her, removing her filthy, bloody shirt. "Where's her injury?" He asked, his voice cold.

"She was bit twice by a giant centipede. I sucked out the venom, but it gashed her throat before I could get it dislodged and she lost a lot of blood before I could get all the venom out.I had to seal the wound to prevent more blood loss." Burke replied.

"Did you administer an initial shot of anti-venom?" She heard Dene ask, and a weight next to her on the bed as she felt the cold antiseptic feel of a stethoscope against the skin of her chest.

"Yes. About two hours ago. I gave her the shot here." She felt his finger graze her leg where her trousers were torn.

"She should have come around by now. How large was the animal and when did the initial bite occur?" Dene asked.

"Biggest bastard I have ever seen! It was as long as my arm and almost as thick as my wrist. It happened about five hours ago. There was a cave-in, and it took us awhile to dig out. I gave her my blood to try to counteract any remaining venom in her bloodstream until I could get her the anti-venom."

Suddenly, she heard a crash and Nichola screaming, "Did you bite my mate, Burke?!"

Several thumps later and what sounded like fists hitting flesh then she heard, "Get off me, Klaus! Don't make me fucking shoot you!"

"Knock it off, you fucking psycho!" Devin hollered. "She wouldn't be alive if it weren't for him! He saved her life!"

"Take it the fuck out of here!" She heard Dene's angry voice shout at them. Then calmly he said, "Mansuetus hand me that syringe. Nelson hold her shoulders, I am going to administer another dose of anti-venom."

* * * * *

As Devin slumped in a chair at the table burying his face in his hands, Nichola worriedly paced back and forth, and Burke, looking like a wild-man with his hair sticking out in several directions and covered in his own and Leila's blood, walked behind the bar in the corner to open a bottle of whiskey.He tipped it back to drink deeply, polishing off about a third of the bottle, while he ran an agitated hand through his dark locks.

"You will find Devin after you transition to full vampire, that you will never be able to drink enough alcohol fast enough to ever be truly drunk again in your entire existence!" He tipped the bottle back to take another long drink.

"She could be dying, you bastard, and here you are whining about how vampires can't get drunk!" Nichola told him coldly, a growl in his voice.

"If she does die Klaus it's on you!" Burke pointed the bottle at him, telling him just as coldly. "What the hell did you do to her blood? She told me her blood tastes strange because of your venom!"

"That's none of your business! It's between she and I! You probably bit her! That's why you are both covered in her blood!" Nichola looked like he was going to launch himself at Burke again.

"I did not bite her and if you attack me again, Klaus, I swear this time I am putting a bullet in you!"

"Knock it off! Both of you! This isn't helping! Whatever the fuck is going on between you two it doesn't have anything to do with my mom and you two need to shelve that shit right now!" Devin stood up pounding his fists on the table to yell at them.

Nichola walked over to him and pulled him into an embrace, Devin tried to pull away initially, but slumped tiredly in his arms. "I'm sorry, son." Nichola told him softly kissing him on the head as he held him tightly.

"Isn't there anything that you can do, Nick?" Devin asked miserably. "Anything at all?"

* * * * *

I walked into the bedroom. Dene sat on the edge of the bed listening to Leila's heart with his stethoscope, Mansuetus knelt next to the bed holding her small hand between his massive ones with his head bent as if he was praying over her. Nelson stood to the side a worried and terrified look on his face. Except for the doctor, the rest of us were wholly unused to death knocking on our door, at least in the last couple of centuries. Looking down at Leila's pale, small, still form, I knew that death was knocking loudly.

I looked at Nelson, "Bring me a donor." My voice was soft and quiet.

He met my eyes in shock. I didn't need to drink human blood; hadn't even wanted to in more than a century, and unlike my contemporaries I didn't even do so on a whim. I had very little to do with most humans and never engaged them for either food or sex.

"Male or female?" He asked, and I could tell it was a question he must ask out of habit to other vampires when they requested donor services from him.

"Male. Bring me someone young, strong, and beautiful." He left silently to do my bidding.

I looked down at my pale mate. She and I had talked about this. She never intended to feed from humans and had often laughingly said that it was her intention to be the only 'vegan vampire' in existence. Which I found quite strange because neither cows nor pigs would ever be on a vegan menu, but obviously it was some sort of silly modern joke she was making.

Her modern humor often made me laugh and smile even though sometimes I didn't quite understand her. It was one of the things that I loved about her, that she brought laughter and light into my dark and tedious life. Everything that she experienced, she saw with new eyes. Even her rebelliousness pumped blood through my old veins! Every day with her brought new experiences, and she made me look at life afresh. She kept my old soul from wasting away.

I would not lose her!

Mansuetus looked up at me and his eyes were desolate.

I looked at the doctor and he met my eyes grimly, though his voice was calm."It's a waiting game at this point."Dene answered my unspoken question."She will either pull out of it, or she won't."

Nodding at his words, I told them both, "Leave us."

I removed her boots and torn clothes, cleaning the blood from her pale skin, placing fluffy towels around and beneath her limp body. Her wilted body was becoming feverish, driving home the fact that internally she was fighting for her very existence. I removed my own clothing and lay next to her calling forth my venom in her veins; pulling it toward a point in her shoulder as I had a few days ago and then I waited.

* * * * *

94

Nelson entered the room first, then gestured forth with his hand. A beautiful young native man walked into the room. I nodded to Nelson who backed out of the room closing the door behind him. The young man looked at me as I stroked Leila's feverish body with a hand. He met my eyes which I knew were red, without fear. "Awki," he addressed me in Quechuan nodding his head deeply to me. Ah, prince! Nelson had chosen a believer.

Using my *voice*, I answered him in Quechuan, "Come beautiful one and join us."

He walked closer to the bed removing his clothes slowly revealing a body I would have been envious of if she had chosen him for herself or he had been another vampire. He was younger than I first thought, maybe twenty, his skin dark, smooth, and almost hairless.His long dusky hair was straight and soft, falling to his shoulders. As he revealed his semi-erect penis, I read the nervousness in his body, and realized that he was pure, though his chocolate eyes were without fear and held Leila and I in reverence and something like worship.

"Come," I told him in my *voice* as he lay along Leila's other side. I took his hand to run it over her body, up from her belly and up to her lips. "Together we will heal her." I brought his wrist to my mouth and tongued his wrist gently. He murmured "Awki" softly once more in response as I gently pushed my power over his body. I ran my tongue over the small veins in his wrist and he moaned against Leila's other shoulder as he spooned against her, keeping her in between us. I nipped him with my sharp teeth drawing forth a slow flow of blood and placed it over Leila's mouth to drip down her throat. I nodded to him, and he kept his hand in place, then I bit her deeply on the shoulder that I held and started to draw the venom from her body.

* * * * *

The young man moaned with desire as he was encompassed by my power that I forced into Leila's body. For a brief time, there was no movement from her as if she were lifeless, and the only noises was his soft moans. Trying to maintain my composure, fighting the fear that was gripping me, I drove more of my energy harder into her giving her everything that I had, careful not to pull back her energy into myself, when suddenly her body stiffened and gasped in response, clutching his wrist to her mouth. I breathed out slowly in burgeoning relief. The young man gave out a pleased groan that was laced with pain.

"Gently, o ómorfos ángelos mou, be gentle with him. He is here to help heal you and you wouldn't wish to hurt him."I whispered to her, stroking the damp hair from her forehead as her fever broke, washing her in sweat, and the young man moaned louder in response to her drawing on his wrist.

She quickly sealed the small wound that I had made, and whispered, "No."

She opened her eyes to look impassively into the young man's worshipful chocolate brown eyes, as he ran his now uninjured hand down her body to cup her breast causing her to suck in her breath in pleasure.

He whispered to her gently, "Sumag," and I pressed more of my power into her body as I simultaneously drew more of my venom from her veins.

"You must take both his blood and his life essence, glukó mou, it must embrace your heart, your body and your soul. When this dark night delivers the day, your transformation will be complete."I kissed her temple softly, never stopping in drawing the blood mixed venom from her veins and steadily pushed my power, my life essence, into her body; knowing as I did so that I would give everything and anything I had to make her well. With half-lidded eyes, I watched the beautiful young human stroke his slender artists hands over my mate's body.

* * * * *

Leila groaned trying to shake off the intoxicated feeling from her mind.Her body was encompassed by both pleasure and pain. She felt the same painful throbbing in her veins that she had a couple of nights ago when Nichola had taken his venom from her body. She felt soft, full lips against her breasts, a wet tongue lapping at one of her nipples, and soft, long-fingered hands stroking the inside of her thighs.

Opening her eyes, her sight was blurred. It was like she was looking down a tunnel, sharper in the center and hazy around the edges. Trying to breathe deep, the air caught in her lungs as power washed over her like an ocean wave breaking over the sand. She felt full lips trail over her belly, leaving a trail of fire over her skin.She tried to speak, only to have her breath stolen from her by Nichola's lips taking her own as the long-fingered hands parted her legs. As a tongue parted the lips of her pussy, Nichola's tongue plundered her mouth, and she simultaneously felt the waves of pain crash into the waves of power in her body.

There was a euphoric rush that fought against the pain, bringing with it a warm pleasure that centered between her legs. Floating on an ocean of mixed pleasure and pain, sinking in and out of waves of consciousness she tried to move her hands, to push away the restraints on her body. Finally able to move one of her hands she encountered what felt like strands of silk, and she ran her hand through them enjoying the luxurious feel of them against her fingers.

Unable to take a full breath she panted against the pressure building in her body. She felt a beating against her mind, like the massive wings of a bird, or the wind of a great storm blowing against a door, insistent on gaining entrance.

* * * * *

I can feel my power wane as the last of the venom left her. I closed the wound on her shoulder and tried to reach her through our connection. *"I psychi mou. Please, i psychi mou, can you hear me?"* I call weakly into the void reaching for her soul.

I tried to pull the sexual energy from the young man as he moved up her body to suckle at her breasts once more, I noticed his engorged penis as he uncertainly positioned himself between her legs, rubbing the head of his cock against the wet entrance of her pussy. She gave a small moan of both protest and pleasure. *"I am sorry, i psychi mou. I can't let you die on me."* I said to her mind as I pulled his energy to feed into her body. His youth and the desire of his inexperience as he sank into her, feeling the flesh of a woman for the first time, were such strong overwhelming emotions that it was easy to channel them into her body.

"Ah, ah, ah," he moaned. His chocolate eyes were open in wonder to look worshipfully down on her as he moved his cock slowly in and out of her pussy.

I placed a hand on his shoulder slowing his desire, holding back his orgasm.

She needed this energy, and it would not do for him to cum too quickly. "Nichola." I felt her call to me in my mind.

"*Dóxa to theó!*" I responded weakly. I was nearly spent, but I had to see this through. "*I psychí mou, you need to take this young man. You need to feed from both his blood and his energy!*"

"*Nichola! When I am able to move, I swear I am leaving you!*"

"*As long as you are alive to contemplate it, I won't care. I'm not letting you die! Look at him. He is young and beautiful. He is here to heal you and to please you.*" I thought to her as I laid my head on her shoulder in exhaustion. "*Drink from him. Drink in his blood and his energy.*" I coaxed tiredly.

Suddenly, she reached up and pulled the young one to her, wrapping her arms tightly around him and fastening her mouth to him. She was gentle as she kissed him and stroked her long tongue against his shoulder. "*Careful.Don't pierce his artery. The blood will come too quickly, and I am too weak to help you. I know that you do not wish to kill him.*" I whispered in her mind.

I worked to continue to hold back his orgasm. He was aching and thrusting into her harder, giving small cries, as he tried futilely to climax. I could feel her respond in spite of her anger, and she gripped his ass with her hands, guiding his thrusts and grinding herself against him causing him to groan in ecstasy.

I no longer had to channel the young man's energy through my body into her as I felt when she started to take in his energy herself. I ran my hand gently over his back to soothe him as I felt his fear of the unknown start to grow as his ache to cum increased, and his testicles tightened against his body in their need to erupt.

"Oh, oh, oh." He groaned his eyes wide as he felt her pussy tighten sharply around his cock. He sped up his thrusts, his cock twitching, fighting to cum. I couldn't allow him to yet, preventing it once more by holding him on the precipice of orgasm. His sounds got louder and more frantic as he pounded away between her legs, seeking his release.

Through our connection, I felt her on the verge of orgasm. I could also feel her anger and her hunger. Sweet Jesus, her emotions were almost overwhelming, and I almost lost my hold on him allowing him to get even closer to coming.With a cry of frustration, he spread his legs wider moving hers farther apart and thrust his length as deep as he could go, slapping his tightened testicles against her. He lifted his chest off of her, holding himself on trembling arms to look down into her glowing red eyes in wonder, working the muscles of his abdomen, curling in on her as he buried his cock deeply into her pussy over and over, crying out with need as his balls continued to slap against her.

She cried out in delight as he rammed his cock into her, and she gripped his ass tightly urging him on. From where I lay by her side, I could see her fangs descend, they were large, white, fully-developed and oh, so, sharp. The young man looked at them as they glistened with saliva in apprehension, increasing the speed of his hip thrusts, lost to his desire and need for release.

"*Careful, i psychi mou. Careful.*"I whispered my thoughts as I kissed her shoulder gently. "*He is just a young human, time it correctly and you will give him intense pleasure in his sacrifice.*"

"Oh, ah, oh, ah." He panted in need as sweat poured from his body and he drove his cock deeply, straining to reach that magical place that he had only reached using his own hand before.

Finally, I could feel the tremors of her orgasm throughout her body and her pussy pulsated around his twitching cock causing him to give out another sharp cry of need. As her teeth sank into his shoulder, I let go of my control of him and the energy of his pulsating orgasm crashed over us both as he rammed his cock one last time into her and cried out loudly in ecstasy.

* * * * *

Nelson supported the young man's exhausted body, helping me to dress him as Leila slumbered deeply in our bed. "Who was it that gave him to you?" I asked.

"His grandfather. His family has worked for you for decades." Nelson responded quietly.

"They are now our family." I replied."They will want for nothing." Nelson nodded as I pulled the young man close, resting my forehead against his, gripping him gently by the back of the neck.

"Awki." He murmured softly.

"Sulpayki." I murmured in response, thanking him.

I walked with them to the door of the suite as Nelson pulled his arm over his shoulders and supported him with an arm around his waist. I closed the door after them and turned to see Devin sleeping on the sofa, and Burke sitting in a barstool, with his head laying on his arms across the top of the bar.

The American is so like a human. I thought as I moved to the sofa intending to pick up Devin and take him to his room. Suddenly, Mansuetus was there next to me.

"I have him, Kýrios. How is Kyría?" He whispered.

"She will live." I responded quietly.

"Thank the gods!" He murmured easily picking up Devin to cradle him gently in his arms and taking him into his bedroom.

I turned to walk back into my bedroom and noticed Burke was sitting up watching me. "I am surprised that you are still here." I stated walking behind the bar and taking another bottle of whiskey opened it to pour us two drinks.

"Well, you know me, I have an insatiable curiosity." He said, picking up the glass to salute me and drinking it.

"Uh-huh." I responded.

"So, she is going to be okay?" He asked gazing into the amber liquid.

"Yes. She should be fully transformed by morning."

"Thank God for that! Scared the blazes out of me that she reacted the way she did to the bite to begin with. You or I would have shook it right off." His voice was quiet and contemplative. "I need to tell you something."

"Burke, if you are going to tell me that you bit my mate, know this; I am too exhausted to fight you tonight, but soon I will hunt you down." I said to him, drinking the rest of the whiskey in my glass.

"I did not! Why do you keep saying that? I like her and her son; I would never do anything to harm them! Why would you even think that?" He asked exasperated.

"Because I bit, fucked and indirectly killed Killari. I know that you loved her, and I know that you hate me for taking her from you." I told him bluntly and tiredly. It needed to be laid out in the open between us, there had been too many years where I had to watch my back where the other vampire was concerned.

"That's what I want to talk to you about." He said taking the bottle from me and pouring us two more drinks. "I have wanted to tell you for a long time that that is bullshit. You are not responsible for Killari's death. Never were."

"What are you talking about? I was here. I know what happened. You left in 1859 to go back to the states after I took her from you. After you left, I tossed her aside. I never really wanted her to begin with, I just wanted to prove to you how unreliable humans really were! But know this, I never wished harm upon her. I never thought that the shame of what happened would cause her to kill herself! I have had to live with that guilt for more than a century. I learned my lesson from it, Burke. Until Leila, I never took another human as a lover. Never." I said bitterly and drank down the whiskey that he had poured for me. He immediately refilled my glass.

"I did love her. It hurt me to find out that she was fucking you too. That's why I left. I thought we were friends. I came back here after the war to find you gone and Aleksei still here. He was the one that told me that she had committed suicide, and that you thought it was because of you.

I admit, I initially blamed you, then I blamed myself for leaving. But then a few months after I had returned I ran into her brother. He told me the truth. She didn't kill herself over you or me. She killed herself because she was sleeping with a third man, a human, the son of the mayor; she got herself in the family way and he wouldn't marry her. She couldn't live with the shame of being an unwed mother. Her family had tried to get the mayor to force his son to wed her, but you see, he was betrothed to an Ecuadorean heiress and there was no way that he nor his father would allow some native woman to ruin that, pregnant or not.

I took my revenge on her behalf. I killed her lover and his father." He stopped suddenly to sip the whiskey in his glass fixing me with a direct look. "I went to London to find you, to tell you that her death wasn't your fault.

To tell you that I had forgiven you. That it didn't matter."

"I remember you coming to London. I thought you wanted revenge."

"I guess that's why you were such a huge prick. Well, that's the reason I never told you the truth. I figured if you were going to be such a colossal bastard, you could just torture yourself." Burke told me matter-of-factly.

"I was ashamed. I was ashamed of my behavior towards her and you, and too proud to admit it.Afterall, what did I really care about humans for anyway? I had no reason to pursue her, other than the fact that you loved her. As young as you were you had found someone to love. When I had been alive over 800 years and never had.I was jealous of you. I am sorry." I confessed, then sipped my whiskey, not meeting his eyes.

"I am sorry too, Klaus. I am sorry for allowing you to torture yourself needlessly." Burke replied softly.

I finally looked up at him. "So, she was fucking three of us? And a human on top of that?" I asked surprised, with a slight shake of my head.

"I guess our vampire cocks aren't as fabulous as we thought!" Burke smirked at me, then gave a small chuckle, downing his whiskey, reminding me of why I use to enjoy his crass company over a drink at the end of a long night of looking for treasure.

A Child With No Name, A Man Without a Face

I hung up the phone, rubbing my eyes in tiredness and frustration, thankful to disconnect another crazy call from the so-called 'helpful' citizenry of this town. Asking the public to call in with any information about our latest victim was a call of last resort. The dead girl from the garage was still unidentified, just like the other ten girls that had come before her, and according to the last call, was a victim of death from the hands of a ghost-like alien capable of leaping multiple stories and disappearing into the thin night air. I loathed phone duty with these nowhere leads and delusional callers!

Salsa walked over and flopped down in the seat across from my desk in disgust, his black hair liberally laced with silver, and his round belly flopping over his belt.

"What's up?" I asked.

"The security feed for the parking garage is corrupted." His voice was disheartened.

"What are you talking about?" I asked feeling the fury of helplessness start to envelop my chest again.

"Come on. I'll show you." He got up and I followed him back to Johnson's desk. Johnson was sitting there looking at a computer screen and I could tell he was pissed. "Show Sutton." Salsa said to him, crossing his arms over his chest.

Johnson rewound the grainy video that he was viewing. "See this," he pointed to the monitor. "One minute, no body, the next poof! There's her leg visible from behind the dumpster!"

I watched the video intently. Sure enough, it was as if the girl's body just appeared on the video.

"Spliced? Modified?"I asked him.

"Not according to IT. It is fully intact, it doesn't appear to be screwed with in any way."

I had a sinking feeling in my gut. "Pan it out. I want to see it from the different cameras pointing in the same general vicinity.Can you slow it down? Frame by frame?"

Johnson worked the keyboard and the monitor displayed four different camera views. One pointing directly at the dumpster, one pointing from a distance down the lane in front of the dumpster, one pointing at the elevator with just a portion of the dumpster showing, and one pointing at the stairwell with the opposite side of the dumpster in view.

Johnson turned the knob on the video viewer slowly and we all saw a fuzzy muted form suddenly appear on the ledge of the second floor of the open parking garage, perched for half a frame.

"Stop!" I exclaimed."Go back one frame and freeze it."

It was evident that the human shaped form, though blurry and distorted was male and he had the body of our victim clutched in his arms as he knelt on the ledge.

"I'll be a son-of-a-bitch!" Salsa exclaimed.

"What the fuck is this?" Johnson muttered in bewilderment running his hand through his thinning, baby-fine, strawberry-blonde hair.

"Forward it slowly, frame by frame." I ordered ignoring their astonishment.

Johnson worked the system again and we slowly watched the humanoid figure carry the girl's body in what looked like leaps from the ledge to the dumpster.It knelt down briefly over her body before leaping back to and over the ledge.

Salsa and Johnson were silent in shock. My stomach clenched in fear.

"Sit on this. I don't want anyone to know about this until we verify with IT that this tape is authentic."I ordered.

"Don't worry about me," Salsa told me with a look, "I am not stupid enough to go to the Captain over this. He'll think we are fucking crazy."

"Me either." Johnson looked to me.

"I got to call back a lead." I said walking back to my desk feeling totally fucked.

There is Something About a Woman With a Gun

❧◦◦◦◦◦

I walked out of the suite and headed for the front desk. There was a hole inside of my body, a hollow pit in my guts and an unfamiliar need, an ache for something that couldn't be named. As I stood in front of the desk in the hotel lobby, a sensation like a thousand ants marching up and down my skin nearly overwhelmed me. The human woman behind the desk looked up saying pleasantly, "Hello, Lady Tsoukalous, how may I help you this morning." As she spoke I found myself focused on the throbbing artery in her throat in fascination, swallowing the sudden rush of saliva in my mouth.

Mentally shaking myself, I breathed deeply to control my urges, and with supreme effort replied quietly, "I would like to speak with Nelson please."

"One moment." She told me picking up the phone. As she spoke into the receiver, I found myself wholly entranced by the way the muscles of her neck moved while she spoke. "Sir, Lady Tsoukalous is here she would like to have a word with you. Yes, sir." She smiled at me as she hung up the phone. "He will be out in just a moment, my lady."

I nodded my thanks, not trusting myself to speak to her, as I walked over to the fireplace quickly putting distance between us and found myself gazing into the flames deep in thought. I sensed Nelson approaching me and turned

106

to look at him. He stopped briefly, staring into my eyes. I am sure that he was just as shocked by their red color as I had been this morning as I gazed at myself in the bathroom mirror.

"Lady Tsoukalous, I am so happy to see you well!" He quickly recovered telling me with pleasure.

"Thank you." I replied. "Nelson, I would like you to have a maid pack my things and move me out of the suite."

He stared at me in shock as his mouth opened and closed several times. "But, milady, where would you like to go?" He finally asked quietly.

I thought to the conversation I had just had with Nichola where he had unceremoniously refused to take me to the airport so I could take the jet back home to San Antonio.

"No, Leila! I will not take you back! You can be angry with me all you want, but you are staying here in Peru with me!" He had yelled at me cutting me off, then proceeded to stomp up the stairs to his office.

"I would like you to move me into one of the bungalows." I answered Nelson's question.

"Milady, wouldn't you be happier in the main hotel? It is easier to access the amenities from this building." He coaxed me.

"No. I do not want to be in this building. Are the bungalows not ready for guests?" I asked.

"Well, of course, they are…"

"Then have my things moved into one of the bungalows." I said sternly.

"Of course, Lady Tsoukalous." He then ventured, "Have you discussed this with…" he stopped when I glared into his eyes. "Of course. Right away." He walked over to the front desk said a few words to the human and she handed him a key. He returned, telling me, "The maids will pack your things immediately. If you would please follow me." He led me through the dining room to a side entrance and outside under a covered walk-way to end at a covered porch of a small stone bungalow that wasn't any larger than 900 square feet. He opened the door and motioned me inside.

I walked into a comfortable open living space with a small fireplace, which had a small kitchenette to one side. The living room had French doors that opened onto a small private back patio area with a heated, sunken stone wading pool that would be barely big enough for four people. There were double doors to one side of the living room that opened up into a large bedroom with a fireplace and a gorgeous marble and stone ensuite bathroom with a large soaking tub and separate walk-in shower and dual vanity.

"Will this do, milady?" Nelson inquired softly.

"Yes, thank you, Nelson. It is lovely." I answered.Then turned to see the maids coming in with my clothing and personal items.

"Are you sure about this?" Nelson asked in a nervous whisper suddenly standing next to my shoulder as the maids went about putting my things away.

"I am." I told him steadily.

* * * * *

A short while later, I found myself lonely and bored, so I texted Devin:*Bring my gun to the range. I want to do some target practice. Don't let anyone know where you are going.*

He replied: *Give me 15 minutes and I will meet you there.*

I walked into the dining room entrance of the hotel and made my way through to the lobby. Nelson was just hanging up the phone. "Oh, Lady Tsoukalous, I was just calling you. The master is looking for you." He looked at me helplessly and I felt bad for putting him in the middle of all of this.

"Call him back and let him know that I am using the salon facilities."

"Yes, milady, I will." Nelson said gratefully.

I proceeded to walk out of the building toward the shooting range. If Nichola was stupid enough to try to track me down by heading to the lower level, he would be shit-out-of-luck.

Devin arrived at the range about five minutes after I did.

"Mom! Nick is furious! He came downstairs a little while ago to find your things gone. He called the front desk and they assured him that you did not leave the hotel. Where the hell did you go?"

"I have moved into a bungalow outside of the main hotel." I looked at him.

"Mom, did you know your eyes are totally red?" Devin asked me gently putting the gun bag down next to me.

"Yes. I have totally transitioned." I said quietly. Opening the bag, I pulled my gun case out of it and started to load my gun.

"How are you feeling? You know you almost died. When I woke up this morning and you were not in your bedroom I thought that you and Nick had went to breakfast. After Dene and I went to have breakfast and realized that you weren't in the dining room, we figured that you must have went for a walk, or a drive. We were surprised when Nick came downstairs looking for you. After he found that your clothes were gone, he lost it. Mom, he totally freaked out. It really scared me when I realized that you had left." He told me and I felt terrible, I should have told him that I was leaving.

"I am sorry, Devin. I didn't think about it when I left this morning. I just had to get out of there and away from him." I told him bluntly.

"If you can't be there anymore, Mom, I'm okay with that. I want to come stay with you."

"My bungalow only has one bedroom, besides, you are still transitioning, and you need to stay with Dene and Mansuetus." I put on my ear and eye protection, picked up my gun and shot off six rounds quickly into a man-shaped target 20 yards away. I pushed the button to bring the target back to me as William Burke and Cross-Eyed Fred entered the range building.

"Thought those shots might be you two." Burke said coming up to us, removing his sunglasses. "How are you feeling, Ms. Sutton?" I looked at him with my red eyes. "Ah, I see."

"Well, I am glad that you do, Mr. Burke. So maybe you would care to enlighten me on why my eyes are still red? I am not getting a straight answer out of anyone else." I said sharply as the target halted in front of me.

Burke looked at my target where I had shot a smiley face on the head of the man-shaped target, shook his head, saying softly, "That's some damn fine shootin'!"He then looked down at me and said simply. "You're hungry. You need to feed."

* * * * *

"Sometimes it is not as simple as we would wish it to be." Burke explained to Devin and me as we stood aside, and he loaded his gun. "Feeding can be a complicated business for young vampires. Blood is not the only energy source. If it were it would be as simple as drinking a glass of cow's blood every day and going about your business." He squeezed off a couple of rounds, hitting the target center mass."Each vampire is different. But usually, young vampires are mostly focused on blood until their powers develop. It is why it is beneficial for new vampires to be with an older vampire to keep the body count down on the human population. Personally, I am surprised that you are roaming the hotel unattended, Ms. Sutton."

"So, you think that I am going to just start offing the humans here, Mr. Burke?" I asked offended.

"Obviously, not. Unless you have left a body or two somewhere and just don't want to own up to it." He replied with a side look.

"Of course, I haven't. Don't be ridiculous!" I said, stepping up to the line of my booth and quickly shooting off another half dozen rounds into my target, then pushed the button to bring the target back to the station.

This time I had shot a heart pattern center mass on the man-shaped target.

Burke looked at it shaking his head. "There is something about a woman with a gun!" He chuckled looking at me with a charming smile.

"Told you." Devin said to Burke, stepping forward and shooting off a couple of rounds, hitting his target center mass.

"My advice is to not ignore the signs, Ms. Sutton. Your eyes are red, you are hungry. You need to feed. Come on.Let's pack this up and get you someone to drink." Burke said motioning to Fred.

"I am not going to feed from a human, Mr. Burke!" I protested remembering my experience with that young man from last night. "I am not going to do it! I know that I don't have to."

"Fine. Let's see what they have in the kitchens then. You need to get some blood into you right now. But remember, you are new. Your options for energy consumption are limited. You will need to feed regularly and in a manner that satisfies you; whatever that may entail for you. If you don't, you will eventually lose control! I am here to tell you that is not a pretty sight and more often than not people end up dying. I know what I am talking about here!" Burke exclaimed his voice hard.

* * * * *

110

They had entered the kitchen of the hotel and Burke was greeted pleasantly by the human head chef, who didn't seem surprised at all to see him in his kitchen. He was surprised, on the other hand, to see Leila and Devin there.

He bowed low and murmured, "Lady Tsoukalous! It is a pleasure to see you here. I am Chef Joseph. How may I be of service?"

"Joe, is there any way we can get you to set up a couple of shots of pig's blood and cow's blood? The lady here is hungry, and we are looking for a good combination for her that is palatable." Burke looked at him in inquiry.

"The last time I had cow's blood it made me, for lack of a better term, high.I felt really dizzy and just out of it.I hated the feeling." Leila explained to him.

"Might I make some suggestions? Combining the blood within a beverage is usually helpful." Joseph said as he moved around the kitchen grabbing several green bottles."This is bovine blood, or cow's blood."He said holding a bottle. "It is readily available in most areas of the world.If you are having a reaction to cow's blood that is unpleasant you can try drinking it in a 60-40 mixture with red wine. This seems to provide nourishment with less negative side effects. You can also eat very rare beef, such as roast beef or steak.But, when I say very rare, I mean bloody and barely warmed." Leila nodded as she listened to him intently.

"Now, I would like to suggest if you haven't yet tried it, porcine blood, or pig's blood. In my opinion, it is the one animal that is most similar to human blood." He held out another bottle to her.

Leila looked at it curiously. "I have not tried it. Are the side-effects similar to cow's blood?"

"They don't seem to be. Though it is different for everyone. You see the size of the red blood cells are very similar; as well as the red blood cell life span, the hemoglobin content and overall structure of the blood, to human blood." He explained.

"I see that neither of these bottles are refrigerated." Leila observed.

"A tiny amount of anticoagulant is added to the blood when bottling. If you keep the bottles at a temperature of 50 to 90 degrees Fahrenheit you can preserve the blood without refrigeration from three to fifteen days. Of course, the warmer it is the quicker the blood will deteriorate or go bad." He pointed at the bottle as he spoke to her."Would you like to try some?"

"Okay." Her voice was hesitant. "You seem to know a lot about this." She ventured as she watched him pour her a small glass of pig's blood.

He chuckled good-naturedly. "I have been working for and preparing food for vampires for more than half my life.I am quite an expert in the field."He smiled as he handed her the glass.

She looked at it with a jaundiced eye, then looked over at Devin and Burke. Burke nodded his head in encouragement and Devin gave her a look that said "Gross!".

Taking a deep breath, Leila tipped the glass back and drank it down.The flavor was both rich and delicate, with a slightly sweet, smoky aftertaste that wasn't at all gamey. She closed her eyes and waited for the aftereffects that she had experienced with cow's blood years ago. She felt a warmth in her belly that slowly spread throughout her extremities. But no flipping of her stomach or dizziness. She opened her eyes to find Burke's face close to her own staring at her intently.

"Well?" He asked her softly, his brows arched in inquiry over his beautiful, expressive, chocolate brown eyes.

"I think it is okay." She replied quietly.

"Ewww! Mom!"Devin exclaimed in disgust, directly behind Burke.

"Stop that!" Burke threw over his shoulder at him, then turned back to face Leila intently watching her. "I am sure that she is finding this experience difficult enough as it is. Be supportive."

"How do my eyes look?" Leila asked them both.

"Better. I think the color is slowly changing back to normal." Devin said looking at her intently over Burke's shoulder.

"They look beautiful, Ms. Sutton." Burke said softly looking deeply into her eyes. "Don't you worry! Why don't you have another drink." He continued looking at Chef Joseph who poured her another glass.

"How much do you think I will have to drink?" Leila asked Burke.

"As much as you need to." Burke told her. "It's different for everyone, but Klaus will help you monitor yourself. Remember, you are lucky! You're not alone."

She met Devin's eyes over his shoulder briefly and drank down the second glass.

* * * * *

Feeling satiated after drinking several more glasses of pig's blood, I waved to Devin, Burke, and Cross-eyed Fred as they left the dining room. They were heading back to the cave at Templo de la Luna to finish their investigation of a safe way to break into the antechambers of the cave. They had asked me to accompany them, but I felt exhausted and decided it would be best if I got some rest; besides the cave held some frightening memories for me that I wasn't ready yet to face; I didn't admit this to Devin as I didn't want to worry him anymore than I already had today. Though I don't think that I fooled Burke one bit as his eyes met mine in silent sympathy.

Shaking my head to clear my thoughts of those horrific moments in the cave, I made my way out of the dining room and tiredly headed toward my bungalow looking forward to laying down.

* * * * *

I watched as Leila entered the bungalow and then turned to lock the door after her. I smirked at her ridiculous actions and silently remained still, sitting in the oversized chair in the tiny living area. I watched her as she placed the large, old-fashioned door key on the counter next to the door and proceeded to walk toward the bedroom. She came to a sudden halt with a small shriek, clutching her chest as she finally noticed me sitting in the chair.

"How did you get in here?!" She loudly asked.

"You really didn't think that a tiny thing such as a lock would keep me away from you, did you?" I asked standing. "Besides, I own this hotel. I will come and go from any room that I please." I stalked toward her, and she angrily held her ground. I could tell that she intended to battle me. Fine, if that was the way she wanted it. "My darling," I said, sarcasm dripping from my words as I grabbed her by the upper arms pulling her close, "If I had known that you wanted a private honeymoon, I would have had Nelson move us here myself."

113

"Fuck you, Nichola!" She yelled, glaring at me, attempting to pull away.

"I see that your vocabulary when you are angry has not improved over the last quarter of a century." I told her furiously as I fought to keep her from pulling away. She had the strength of a new vampire, and it wasn't as easy as it used to be.

"You let that boy fuck me, you prick!" She sobbed out as she fought my embrace, pushing and pounding on my chest, and I could feel my heart breaking under her anger and outrage. Pulling her close, I held her tightly.

"I allowed you to feed from him in the most efficient way possible that would keep you from dying." I growled out as I gritted my teeth against her struggling body. "If hanging him by his heels from the ceiling and draining his blood into buckets to feed you, would have guaranteed that you would survive, I would have done that instead. You needed both of us, i psychí mou, both of us. My life force and his, as well as his blood to cure you. The largest amount of life energy consumed in the shortest amount of time is through the sexual act.

I couldn't give you enough by myself and nothing else would have worked.If there had been any other way, I would have done it before I let another man taste of you." I held her tightly against me, enduring her fight, enduring her striking fists as she fought my embrace. "I will do whatever it takes to keep you alive, i psychí mou, including allowing another man to fuck you. I will always do whatever it takes to keep you in this world, no matter how those decisions pain me." I whispered against her hair. "No matter what you believe, that decision, having you feed from him in that manner, pained me.It pains me still. I would apologize if I could, but it would be a lie.I am not sorry, because I had no choice, and you are very much alive! I could not allow you to die. I wouldn't allow you to die."

I opened myself to her, to let her feel my pain, to show her the truth of my words.

She pulled back to look up at me, "You are crying." She whispered.

I moved my hand to touch my face feeling the moisture there in surprise."I suppose I am." I looked into her eyes. "No matter how distressed I am over the manner of your transition, Leila, I just thank God that you did not kill

114

him. That would have been much harder for you to endure." I sighed tiredly.

"What is wrong with you?" She asked softly.

"I am weakened still from your transition. I need to feed." I told her simply, honestly looking into her beautiful, teal-colored eyes. "I see you have fed. Should I ask?"

She looked at me in irritation. "I would never harm anyone!"

"That is what all young vampires would like to believe, Glykó." I told her and the doubt rang through my voice.

"Devin, Burke and I visited the kitchens." She confessed.

"Ah, William took you to see Chef Joseph." I stepped away from her now that she was calm and unlikely to injure herself or me in her anger. "I am surprised that he didn't invite you to feed with him." I kept my voice neutral.

"He did. I told him that I don't intend to feed from humans. The chef had me drink pig's blood."

Though I had paid for all of the furnishings and construction of the bungalow suites, I had never actually been inside one of them, leaving those duties to Nelson. I was overall pleased with the small space. She watched me as I paced the living area of the bungalow keeping my attention on the space as I thought on what she was telling me. "How do you feel?" I inquired.

"Better, but I am tired."

"That is because this method of feeding, while nourishing, is not fulfilling.In addition to blood, you will need to take life essence. The way that I feed." I looked at her.

"How do you know? I am not having sex with a stranger again!" Her voice was harsh and adamant.

"I know because you have always taken essence from me, since the beginning of our physical relationship, and no, I do not want you to do that either, Leila."

"Well, I am not sleeping with you either!" She exclaimed moving to sit on the sofa.

"I am not asking you to," she looked at me in surprise, and I clarified, "not right now in any case." I smiled at her, and she turned her head away from me closing me off, her irritation growing.I sat next to her on the couch taking her hand, stroking it to sooth her. "These intense emotions, this feeling on edge, will pass over time, my love.I promise." I placed my arm gently around her. "I would supply life essence for you, but I am not in any shape to do so at this moment. I too need to feed myself."

"Then what do we do?" She asked turning slightly back to me. "Burke says if I am not satisfied, if I am hungry, I could lose control, and maybe harm someone."

"Did he?" I decided to be direct with her. "You will need to be careful around William; for a while at least."

"What do you mean?"

"When you were injured and in his attempt to save you, he drank some of your blood, he also gave you some of his. I am sure that you both are feeling a fascination for each other because of it."I kept my voice intentionally calm.

"Don't be ridiculous!" She told me in return facing me directly. "I am not feeling a 'fascination' for Mr. Burke!"

"Maybe not." I told her keeping my voice soft, I wasn't trying to fight with her, but was trying to educate her. Regardless of my love for her, she was still a new vampire, and I was her elder. "But *he,* may be fascinated with *you.*A blood exchange creates a bond.Not like ours, but a bond, nonetheless.It is not permanent and will pass soon."I stroked the skin of her arm gently."As to feeding both of us, we will attend a celebration in the employee's village tonight. There I will help you and teach you how to feed from the essence of those around us."

I stood up and looked down on her, reaching out to cup her chin gently, as I gazed into her eyes intently, I realized that my small changeling had become quite strikingly beautiful since her full transformation to full vampire and was growing more beautiful by the hour.

"What are you doing?" She asked, pushing my hand away in irritation.

"I will give you some time to rest." I told her as I turned to leave. "I will be back later this evening to collect you for the celebration."

* * * * *

After Nichola left, Leila went in and lay on top of the bed. She tossed and turned, thinking about what he had told her. She wanted to be angry, she wanted to hate him; but she had to admit that she didn't.She had always known that when it came to her that he was absolutely ruthless, and he would do whatever it took to keep her in his life, to keep her by his side, or to keep her safe, regardless of her feelings and occasionally his own. He had proven it repeatedly.

She also had to admit to herself that she was happy to be alive.

Closing her eyes, sleep finally overtook her.

The Phantom Butcher

The phone on my desk rang startling me out of my thoughts. I was studying the still photographs that we were able to develop from the security video of our killer, with a magnifier. The images of him, either with our victim in his arms or of him retreating after dumping her, were still too blurry to make out any specific details. The killer was obviously male and looked either Caucasian or Latino but could have also been Asian. The video was grainy, and black and white, so hair color was a nondescript 'dark'. The collar of his overcoat looked like it was pulled up, so hair length was unable to be determined. The IT technician that we were working with was adamant still that the video was untainted and whole. The fucked-up part of this scenario was that even in the still photos, the image of the victim in his arms was sharp, distinct, and easily viewable, while the perpetrator's image was blurry and unfocused.

"Sutton here." I picked up the receiver speaking quickly, my attention still on the photographs spread over my desk.

"I want you, Garcia, and Johnson to get your asses in my office right now!" The barking voice of our Division Captain came belting through the earpiece of the receiver causing me to jerk my head back.

"I'll track them down and be right in…sir." I answered keeping my voice calm, then replaced the receiver. *What the fuck does he want?*

Homicide Captain Keith Miles was the most politically-driven, suck-ass human being that I had ever met in my entire life; and sickeningly overtly so.The prick really should consider running for Mayor, because he was absolutely fucking useless leading or supporting the homicide division in San Antonio! God knows that he would do less damage in that position! He could give a shit less about the victims of this city, or the officers he commanded, he just cared about his own personal image and how much positive press that he could garner to push himself up the ladder.

I saw Salsa over at the coffee pot and waved him over to me. "Track down Johnson." I told him. "His fucking highness wants us in his office pronto!"

"What the fuck did you do now?" Salsa asked heading out to find Johnson.

"Wasn't me! I figured it was you!" I smirked gathering up the photos and putting them in my desk drawer. It wouldn't do to have curious eyes on them until we could figure out what the hell was up with the video tape.

* * * * *

I walked in the darkness of my home. My servants, Him and Her, quietly went about their duties, not meeting my eyes as was my want. As long as they performed their duties to my requirements they would live.

My newest acquisition was now secured in the hidden cellar of the house; a chamber carved into the high concrete foundation, with no windows, and accessible only through the hidden trap door in the closet of my master bedroom. She was a truly lovely, and pure, specimen of budding womanhood. Him had outdone himself in acquiring her from the coyote and fully deserved the reward I planned to allow him. I will enjoy defiling her body and soul, in my own special way.

I sat down in my chair, as Her brought me a teacup, I looked at it knowing that this was the last of my previous acquisition. I had every intention of savoring this last bit of her essence over today's newspaper, which Her laid next to the cup. I closed my eyes in remembrance. She had been a delicious acquisition. Though not pure, I still had enjoyed the taste of her as my fangs and cock had pierced her flesh. Experienced from her time on the streets, she had actually tried to use her nubile body in several pleasing ways before she accepted her ultimate fate. I could feel myself grow hard with the memory of how her mouth sucked my cock and how it felt to fuck the deep ragged

119

grooves that my claws had made in the flesh of her body.

I flipped through the San Antonio Express-News as I sipped the thick red deliciousness of her blood from the teacup, pausing on page eight. I could feel my surprise as recognition widened my eyes and I gazed at the still images of my blurred form printed below an article entitled: *The Phantom Butcher*. My surprise gave way to mirth, as laughter bubbled from my lips.

* * * * *

Salsa, Johnson, and I sat around the small conference table in the Captain's office. He slammed the newspaper down in the middle of the table and said scathingly, "One of you guys want to tell me how this fantasy bullshit ended up in the paper?"

I reached over and grabbed the paper that was folded open to page eight with the headline *The Phantom Butcher* in big bold letters above what looked to be copies of the still photographs that I had just placed in the top of my desk drawer. What the fuck? I looked at Salsa and Johnson who both shook their heads.

"It wasn't us, Captain." I told him intentionally keeping my voice calm and direct, as I tossed the newspaper back onto the table in disgust.

"Well, you guys had access to the security footage!" Miles started on a rant.

"Not just us, Captain." Salsa interrupted. "At least a dozen other people in the department had access to that footage also.Besides there is still some debate on whether the footage has been tainted or hacked. It took them a couple of days to comply with the warrant.These pics could be an attempt to cover-up evidence and point us in the wrong direction."

"Obviously, Garcia! There is no such thing as ghosts! You guys need to recanvas the garage, reinterview all of the personnel that had any access to the security area and find out who altered these tapes! Go back over the calls from the tip hotline!It's time to stop fucking around with this thing and get it fucking closed. The city doesn't need to be reading about this fantasy bullshit in the paper! It makes the department look like we are fucking idiots! This is not fucking Ghostbusters you know!"

I gritted my teeth and started to speak when Johnson reached over and kicked me in the shin under the table. I flashed him a quick, sharp look, then closed my mouth, shook my head affirmatively, stood up with Garcia and Johnson, and exited the office.

"Don't kick me again, Johnson!" I growled out to him lowly as we walked back to our desks.

"Buddy, I could tell you were going to blast him. Just doing my part to keep you from getting suspended man." He said as he took a seat next to my desk as Barnes, the skinny, pasty, geeky, department's IT Technician who was working with us on the security video, walked over to flop in the chair on the other side of my desk.

"I just got my ass handed to me!" He bitched to us, straightening his black glasses, and running his hands through his spiky black hair.

"So, it wasn't you?" Salsa asked.

"Fuck no it wasn't me!" Barnes replied. "Officially, the video is now considered to be corrupted."

"Unofficially?" I inquired keeping my voice low.

Barnes leaned in, replying quietly, "Unofficially? There is not a goddamn thing wrong with that video!"

I reached over picked up the desk phone and proceeded to dial a number that had been replaying itself through my mind. "Mrs. Murphy? Hello, it's Detective Zachary Sutton. Yes, it's nice to hear your voice too ma'am. Would you mind if my partners and I came to your home? If you have the time I would really appreciate it if you would accompany us to the scene of the crime and walk us through exactly what you saw." I paused, looking at Salsa, Johnson, and Barnes as they listened intently. "Yes, ma'am, now if you are available. Thank you ma'am, I will see you in a few minutes." I hung up the receiver, stood and grabbed my jacket off the back of my chair.

"Where are you guys going?" Barnes said as Johnson and Salsa grabbed their jackets also.

"We have a lead." I told him as I led the way out of the office.

One Step Too Far

⌒⌒⌒

I was watching Him take his reward for bringing me such a pure acquisition.He had Her bent over the arm of the sofa and was gleefully driving his cock into Her. Her grimaced in disgust unable to hide her feelings towards Him, and I am sure towards myself. Neither Him nor I cared. Afterall, Her was just another female.

After two centuries together, Him's soul was almost as black as mine and that was the way I liked it. Him was loyal and knew his place. Her on the other hand was a fairly recent addition to my household. She had been sixteen when my overzealous bite had made her into my companion almost a century ago. Her was smart, much smarter than Him, and useful in her own way. She tended to the acquisitions and kept them calm and pliable. She hated every minute of her existence, but as my companion, I had trained her harshly and well; so, she endeavored not to show it, though I still knew. Her loathed me and what I was, but as her master she had no choice but to endure and obey. Though, who she really hated with a murderous passion that I had yet to beat out of her, was Him.

Her had tried to kill Him fifty years ago, and damn near succeeded.Luckily for her, she had failed as I would have had to torture then murder her slowly. Him, though ultimately replaceable, was valuable to my household, and I wouldn't like to have to acquire and train another. Upon my direct order Her's assassination attempts stopped, but the hatred increased.

Him was the ultimate companion, but totally boring and needed constant direction. Her on the other hand operated almost autonomously, needing very little direction; and her occasional rebelliousness was not boring, which in my small world made her interesting, for a female at least.

At one time, Her had been quite fetching, with silky brown hair, blue eyes, and smooth pale skin. An innocent young woman on the cusp of adulthood. The last century had turned Her inwardly into a sour, hard, rendition of her former self. Her rarely showed her disgust outwardly towards me and she served me though did so only because I willed it. Him served me with glee and as such was my favorite.

Him was definitely serving me now as he joyfully pounded away into her pussy, holding her hips in a bruising hold. I stroked my cock as I watched them. Her raised her head to cast her look of hatred at me, causing my heart to beat louder, my lips to pull over my fangs in a harsh, cruel, smile, and my hand to stroke my cock faster as I drank in her hatred of us both.

Both Him and I was close to coming, when the doorbell suddenly rang interrupting me and I could feel my anger spike as I released my cock and stood.Him had paused abruptly in his strokes looking toward the front door. I looked at his naked body and tucked my hard cock back into my pants.

"Stay just like that. I will answer it. Do not finish until I return." I ordered.

It was late for any type of visitor. Darkness had fallen an hour ago, and the small rural neighborhood with its large lots and no streetlights, was normally quiet and peaceful, with little activity after dark. Just like I liked it.

I turned on the small porch light in the front of my home, though I had little need for it. I opened the door to three giggling nubile teen beauties, who had the audacity to point their cell phones in my direction.

Smiling at them widely, I used my *voice*, "Come in!"

They immediately stiffened under my compulsion and as I stepped back from the entrance they entered my home single file. As they passed me I took their cell phones from them, stopping their recordings. I closed and locked the front door, then turned off the porch light, leaving the foyer way of my home in relative darkness.

Facing them as they stood stiffly next to each other, I asked softly in my *voice.* "Why were you videotaping me?"

"We were just making a Tik Tok." The one with reddish brown hair and freckles stiffly replied.

"We didn't mean anything by it, we thought it would be funny." Came the monotone response from the cute, plump, dark-haired girl.

"It's just a joke, sir. We are sorry." Came the frightened response from a true beauty. Her sandy blonde hair, sky-blue eyes, delicate jaw line and plump lips intrigued me as did the emotion in her voice. There is always that one that has the will to fight my compulsion; it was a rare occurrence, but it sometimes happened.

"Does anyone know that you are here? Is there someone outside waiting for you?" I asked and I could feel my own special need rising, causing my fangs to descend, my blood to race, and my stiff cock to throb.

"No." The freckled one stated.

"Excellent. Come with me." The two who were in my thrall followed me like lambs to the slaughter. The third was obviously struggling to stop her body from moving. I could remember a time when I too fought the prison of my body against a stronger will.I motioned the two who followed to stop and returned to that rarity of nature even more intrigued than before.Looking deeply into her sky-blue eyes, I pushed my will on her mind forcing her into compliance, then told her, "Now." She struggled still, but her body moved stiffly and robotically to follow her friends.

Leading them through to the master bedroom like the Pied Piper, past a surprised Him and Her, I opened the hidden door in the closet that led to the dark space below. "Go."I said and deleted the videos on their cell phones as they passed me to enter the darkness. My willful beauty immediately balked at the entrance to the darkness. I leaned forward whispering in her ear. "Go or stay here with me."

She turned to look into my red eyes and focused on my smile as I showed her my sharp white fangs. Her body shivered in response as she fought both it and my will. I knew immediately when she had broken my hold.Interesting, interesting, beauty.I grabbed her by the arms harshly and lowered her into the hole to the arms of her friends. She immediately started screaming which set her friends and my other acquisition to screaming also. I closed and bolted the trapdoor silencing the sounds and moved the steamer trunks back over the trapdoor.

I walked back to the living room, where Him still had Her bent over and pinned down with his cock though she was struggling against him."Stop." I commanded her and she went still. "Stay where you are until I return. Him, you are not to finish until I return." I started to walk out the back door with my newest acquisition's cell phones in hand.

"But Master, if I stay this way I will go limp." Him whined at me.

"I did not say do not move; I just said do not finish."

Him smiled at me with evil glee as he gripped Her shoulders and proceeded to thrust his cock in and out of her unwilling pussy again. As I closed the door behind me, I heard Her whisper, "I hate you, you monster!" I smiled as I wasn't sure which one of us she was speaking to but, frankly it didn't matter.

* * * * *

Familiar with today's technology, I had deleted the videos from the phones and the cloud back up, reviewed their social media accounts for auto-uploads, then I took my newest acquisition's cell phones to the mall and distributed them into the back seat of cars that were foolish enough to have their windows cracked to release the Texas heat. I was aware that capturing my new beauties would cause an interest in the media. These beauties were not nameless, nor unwanted; and though this might be a reckless action on my part, I could not seem to help myself. As for the police, they were imbeciles! Besides, who would believe the truth? As far as anyone would know, the last place the girls would have been together was the mall, before they split up.

Females frequently went missing in this century; especially compared to when I was a young man three centuries ago. At least we had the decency to guard and protect our females of the upper classes.Today's society let them roam free and unattended; then lamented when predator's such as myself took them. If they were truly concerned with the safety of their daughters they would watch over them and educate them better on their behavior. As far as I was concerned, it was destiny that they had put themselves in my path.

I walked into the back door of my home to see that Her had some developing bruises on her face and Him was holding her roughly by the back of the neck as he slowly and somewhat painfully, moved his cock in and out of her.I looked at Him, "What has occurred here?" I questioned calmly.

"Her reached around and tried to tear my balls off, Master!" Him replied angrily, and I could tell that he was holding back his orgasm; the obvious pain that she inflicted on him was helping.

I bent to look at her swelling face and my voice was gentle and quiet as she looked at me with hatred. "I thought that I had ordered you not to kill him?"

"I wasn't trying to kill him, just castrate him...Master." Her ground out in pain as Him loosened his grip on her neck so that she could reply to me.

I smirked thoroughly enjoying her rebelliousness. "Finish." I instructed Him as I walked into my master bedroom. I heard several slaps of flesh on flesh and then a strangled cry of delight as he emptied himself into her.

* * * * *

I fastened my new beauty's wrists in the manacles that were secured in the concrete foundation. She shivered in terror and revulsion as I ran my hands over the softness of her arms, then looked up at me with loathing in her sky-blue eyes. Brave, foolish beauty.

I moved to secure her freckled friend in the same manner and as I did so the plump, dark-haired girl jumped on my back and started to hit me in the face, raking her nails down my cheekbone, slicing deeply through my skin. I turned and threw her against the stone steps descending into the cell knocking her unconscious. I turned back to the freckled girl facing her as she watched in horror as the shredded skin of my face started to knit.

"No, no, no..." She shook her head denying her own sight as I grabbed her arms harshly and secured the manacles around her wrists. She reached out to my beauty and held her hand starting to sob hysterically.

Keeping my eyes locked on my beauty's, I allowed my talons to burst forth from my fingertips, then turned in the small space and grabbed the dark-haired girl by the leg dragging her over the concrete floor to pull her close

126

and proceeded to slice her clothing from her body.

"Please don't hurt her." My beauty begged me causing my cock to harden and throb at the sound of her pleading voice."Please don't. We will be good. You don't have to hurt her."

"You need to learn what resistance will get you." I tell her using my *voice* to cause the coldness of the arctic to flow over her skin, making the hairs on her body stand at attention and the nipples of her ripe breasts to harden like pebbles and push against her t-shirt in reaction. I very much appreciated the sight. "Besides, I want to. I want to hurt her." I moaned slightly in need as my fangs grew from my jaw. "And I want you to watch me while I do so."

My original acquisition prayed loudly in Spanish, as if that would deter me, and my beauty and her freckled friend cried and begged me to stop as I pulled my clothes from my body, which only caused my cock to throb with anticipation.All three of them cried out as they saw the whip marks that I had received while I was still human marring my skin.

Keeping my eyes locked with my willful beauty, I pulled her now naked, plump, dark-haired friend close to them, but just out of reach. I wanted them all to be able to see exactly what I was doing to her.

I reached out and gently tapped her cheek, trying to rouse her as I positioned myself in between her legs. "Wake up!"I commanded in my *voice*. "Wake up, girl! All women should be awake during their own depucelage."

She started to rouse slowly, as I held her legs wide and rubbed my cock against her almost hairless slit, spreading my pre-cum there. Her eyes fluttered as I stroked her clit, awakening her body with my strokes and compulsion. Awareness will bring terror and then I can begin.

I worked my cock against her as she became damp, watching her face as she slowly opened her eyes to meet mine in confusion, then in panic. As she brought her arms up to push against my chest I rammed my cock into her pussy, harshly tearing her hymen and she screamed in shock and anguish. The other three's screams joined hers as I buried myself to my balls, reveling in the feel of her tight, now bloody, virgin flesh.

I worked my cock in and out of her harshly, breathing in the scent of her hymenal blood as it ran out of the lips of her pussy to stain the concrete floor of their cell.

I ran my lethal talons over her skin slicing bloody grooves into her flesh as her continuous screams of terror and agony fueled me on. I smiled into my beauty's horrified and disbelieving eyes as I sank my fangs into her friend's carotid artery, spraying my beauty and her freckled friend in blood.

The girl's blood was rich and thick, reflecting her upper-class lifestyle and was as pure and sweet as I had imagined it would be! I groaned in delicious ecstasy as I gulped it down and continued to thrust my cock deeply into her bloody and ruined pussy.

As her gurgling screams rang in my ears, I buried myself one last time inside of her, relishing the blood flowing down my throat and over my skin.As I found my release, it felt euphoric.

* * * * *

I watched Him tie a rope around the little girl's ankles and hoist her plump body up to secure her to the hook set into the low ceiling of the cement dungeon with despair in my heart. With her still warm, dead body suspended upside down like a hog to slaughter, Him removed the large hunting knife from his belt to slice the child's throat, draining the remaining blood in her body into a large bucket. The master would expect me to bottle the remaining blood for his meals after Him brought the bucket upstairs to the kitchen.

In the meantime, I set to cleaning the blood from the cement floor of the dungeon. Tears silently flowed from my eyes, and over the swollen and bruised side of my face from where Him had punched me repeatedly when I had tried to rip his balls from his body while he was raping me. I kept my eyes from going to the frightened, traumatized little girls who huddled together in their chains. They also made no sounds as their tears flowed silently.

I remembered my first experience with the master, and all you hoped for was that no one would notice that you were still present; that you were still alive because you knew if they did, you could be next.

"I can't believe that you still cry for these blood-bags, Her! They are nothing but food for the Master!" Him's voice was derisive.

God I hated him! Him thought that he was as powerful as the master; on the same level of being. He was wrong and if not for the master's orders I would give my last drop of life to kill him. Without Him the master would be hard pressed in this age to secure these children for his sick and lustful appetites.

If I could just find a way to end Him, maybe I could save some of them, maybe I could save at least one of them.

I glanced furtively to the girls still silently huddling together watching me as I sponged the blood from the cement. Dipping the sponge into the bucket of water, to wash and ring the blood from it, I continued to sweep it over the floor; cleaning the floor, but never cleansing the sense of guilt I felt at my own helplessness.

As Him wrapped the body in a tarp and then removed the body from the cell, I let my grief shine in my eyes as I glanced at the three girls. Though outwardly we looked to be of the same age, I knew that their hell would be short-lived and mine would be eternal. I felt both despair and envy at their plight.At least their hell would end soon.My own never would.

The blonde looked at me and mouthed silently, "Help us."

"I wish I could, child." I gently whispered in return, as I picked up the bucket of bloody water to walk up the stairs and out of the small dungeon. The misery at my own impotency, my helplessness, my inability to stop this evil crushed whatever was left of my soul. I could not stop my tears as they continued to flow.

Feeding and Fascination

Nichola woke me up tossing a long sleeved, long gown made of red patterned fabric, and a long red and white patterned shawl on the end of the bed. I sat up as he walked into my closet retrieving some flat-heeled ankle boots.

"What are you doing?" I asked sleepily running my fingers through my wild hair.

"Getting you dressed to attend the celebration in the village." He told me and I could tell from his abrupt tone, flaring nostrils and tight eyes that he was impatient. "Come on, we need to get going."

"I don't want to. I am tired!"I protested with a groan, flopping back down on the bed. "I want to go back to sleep."

"Leila, the villagers are throwing this celebration in your honor!Courtesy dictates that you must go!Besides, we both need to feed, and I need to teach you how to do that. Now get up! I don't want to fight about it."

I looked at him in irritation.

"Leila, if you do not get up right now, I am going to assume it is because you want to stay here and fuck me." He looked at me harshly, surprising me with his language and I met his eyes, noticing that his usually amber eyes were now red.

"Fine!" I snapped."But you go into the living room while I get dressed!"

He humphed in irritation but left the bedroom.

* * * * *

I went to stare out the French doors to the back patio and wading pool, looking up into the dark skies. I knew that Leila still blamed me for the method of her transition, and I was unreasonably, and foolishly, being abrupt with her but couldn't seem to help myself. It had been a very long time since I had felt the ant-like crawling feeling under my skin that indicated that deep need for me to feed. I was centuries away from true bloodlust being a problem but knew that if presented with an open vein I probably wouldn't turn it down. Providing the amount of energy necessary to heal Leila had certainly drained me of both energy and control.

If I would have been honest with myself about my condition, I could have had Nelson provide me with a donor and I wouldn't be on the edge of losing control right now. But I couldn't imagine being with either a human or even another vampire on that one-to-one level that I would have needed to fully recover; nor did I fool myself into thinking that Leila would be okay with it if she found out about it.Needing to feed or not, I just didn't want to be intimate with anyone else. It had been too many years since I had wanted anyone sexually other than Leila and regardless of my level of hunger, I still didn't want anyone other than her.

Having so recently experienced the pain of my mate responding sexually to someone other than myself, even out of a necessity to heal her, I would never want her to experience it. The feeling was even worse because every time I thought about it, I experienced the actual sight, taste, and feel of the act itself. I shook my head trying to erase the sensations, even knowing that I probably would never be able to.

The one redeeming feature, for me at least, was that we both knew that she bore no desire for it. It was an act of necessity and nothing more.

I turned at the sound of her footsteps as she walked out of the bedroom. Her beautiful, teal-colored irises were ringed in a soft pale pink, belying her continued hunger. She was so striking and flawless since her full transformation that she made both my cock and my heart ache with desire. Her hair had mostly returned to its darker auburn color of her youth, with the exception of her long bangs being threaded with white-silver strands. I could see that she had lost weight, but it wasn't unpleasant, and her breasts were still larger than they had been when I had first met her, and her ass was plump and round below a trim waist and flat belly. My hands ached to touch her firm breasts, and I clenched them briefly knowing if I did so right now that she would fight me, and it would ruin our evening.

"Well?" She asked and her voice was annoyed. "Are you ready or are you just going to stare at me?"

I held my tongue as I opened the French doors to the back and held my hand out to her to exit the doors. Glaring at me she walked through the doors onto the patio. I swiftly pulled her into my arms and picked up her slight form as she gasped in outrage. I held her tight against me looking down into her angry eyes then I took flight.

* * * * *

She clutched at his shoulders in sudden fear and buried her face against the side of his neck breathing in his cinnamon, ginger, and sandalwood scent.His scent unfortunately did little to decrease her fear of heights. Feeling her fear course through him, he was slow and careful with her, and though only a short distance, the flight took approximately five minutes for them to reach the village; still a much shorter time than either walking or running.

She felt him land softly and pulled her face away from his throat to look around the village, she slid against his body, as he slowly lowered her to the ground. They were in the village center where a large bonfire burned. There were several people in attendance, both human and vampire, and their attention centered on them. Leila recognized several of the hotel's workers from the shops and spa of the hotel. Followed by Nelson, two humans, Peruvian natives by their looks and clothing, approached them, one was a very old, wizened man, and the other was very young and beautiful, with long dark hair. Leila's eyes widened in surprised recognition, and she looked over at Nichola who stood tall and straight with a haughty demeanor.

The young man knelt before her speaking softly, "Ñusta". Then he bowed his head.

Give him your blessing, i psychí mou, after all he saved your life. She heard Nichola's voice in her mind.

What did he say to me? She thought in return.

He refers to you as Princess. Nichola replied in a somber tone.

Soberly, her heart squeezing in gratitude, Leila stepped forward and reached out with both hands to touch the top of the young man's dark head gently and tentatively. This was the same silky texture that she had touched the night that she had finally transformed. She bent forward slightly and placed a soft kiss on the top of his head. The young man lifted his head to look at her reverently, holding her gaze with his beautiful dark eyes.

"Sulpayki." Nichola said to the old man with a slight nod of his head.

"It is our honor, my Prince." The old man replied in slightly accented English, reverently nodding his head in return.

"I am in your debt, and from this day forward, you and yours are part of my family." Nichola embraced the old man, placing a soft kiss on each of his cheeks.

Nelson stepped forward, motioning to them, as the young man stood to stare down into Leila's eyes in a worshipful manner, "This way, sir, my lady.We have a place for you here.There is both food and drink. Let us serve you."

Nichola took Leila's hand and gently pulled her forward to follow Nelson as the humans followed behind.

As Leila sat down in a tall-backed, short seat, upon stone stairs leading up into a home, though while not large, was larger than the other villagers dwellings. Nichola sat on a lower stair between her legs, leaning back against her and taking her hand to drape over his shoulder, where he softly caressed her fingers.

Leila looked around and saw Devin, Dene, Mansuetus, Burke and Fred seated on one side of the dais; Devin waved at her as he laughed at something that Fred was telling him and was eating what looked to be a chicken and rice dish with his fingers. He seemed to be taking this celebration all-in stride and was fitting in with this mixed community of humans, vampires, and companions well. *Better than I am.* Leila thought to herself.

"Hmmm?" Nichola brought her hand to his lips, kissing her on the palm as music started to play, and dancers, dressed in traditional Andean and Incan outfits, assumed places around the bonfire.

Nothing. She thought at him watching the dancers and listening to the music as they twirled around the bonfire. She looked up to see Chef Joseph by her side. He handed her a goblet and as she took it, she looked at him quizzically.

"It's the same vintage as before, Lady Tsoukalous, except it is mixed in with the local drink, pisco." He bent down to murmur in her ear.

"Thank you, Chef." He smiled at her and took a seat next to Nelson to enjoy the dancing.

The old man and young man from before were now outfitted with headdresses and were twirling around amongst the dancers. *Who are they, Nichola?* She thought at him.

The older man is the tribal leader here. Their chief for lack of a better term. I have been dealing with his family here for more than a century. They are very honorable and claim to be able to trace their lineage back to the Wari, the people that came before the Incans. The young man is his grandson. The old man sent him to us to help heal you. The grandson will take over his rule here upon his death. I employ them all, their family and extended families. My original dealings with the tribe began with the elder's great-grandfather. He thought in return as Nelson passed him a goblet, keeping his eyes on the dancers.

Why do you employ them? Who do they think we are? Why do they refer to us as Prince and Princess?

I employ them because they need the work, one. Two, they are some of the most loyal and hardworking people I have ever encountered. They think that we are the physical embodiment of their gods. You and I know that to be untrue, but they are convinced of it.

She took a sip of the drink in her hand, closing her eyes as both the blood and the alcohol flowed down her throat to spread warmth throughout her body. She hadn't realized how weak she had been feeling until she felt the strength returning to her limbs. *Aren't you afraid of their knowledge? Aren't you afraid that one day they will be a danger to you and the other vampires?* She thought at him.

You mean US, don't you? He questioned briefly then continued kissing the wrist of her hand that he still held. *I don't fear it because I keep an eye on them as well as I do all people who are in my employ. Almost, as well as, I do you.* She could feel him smile against her wrist, watching as pitchers of pisco started to flow and be consumed. She had a feeling that it was going to end up being a wild celebration!

* * * * *

Burke watched Nichola toying with Leila's hand with envy in his heart. He knew that he was becoming increasingly drawn to her and needed to take care of that fascination before he screwed up the fragile truce that he and Klaus had started to develop the night of her transition. He was not a man that usually lusted after another man's woman, but he knew what he was feeling, and knew that he should do something to stop it.

"Billy, what's up? You are awfully quiet tonight." Devin asked and noted.

Burke smiled at him replying, "Just feeling a little peckish, boy."

"Peckish?" Devin asked.

"Hungry for something other than this pig's blood-laced pisco." He told him with a mischievous smile and stood up to join the dancers twirling around the bonfire, grabbing a pretty dancer, and swinging her around. Devin stood up laughing and joined him to do the same.

Oh, no! It looks like Devin is getting drunk. Leila thought making a move to stand up.

Leave him be. Nichola thought in return preventing her from standing. *He is a man, let him enjoy himself. Do not embarrass him.*

You think I would embarrass him? Her thought was laced with irritation.

You may not intend to, but you are his mother. He is pursuing that girl he has in his arms. Do not be a 'cock-block', Leila. He looked up at her as she made an outraged noise behind him.

Since when did you start using that term? She demanded, unsure that she liked the way he was using vulgar language. He had always complained about her using coarse language, so this was definitely something new for him.

I have been learning vulgarity and using it regularly so that I could be prepared to communicate with you more effectively whenever you 'decided' to join me. His thought was acidic, and his look was mocking.

You are being a smartass right now?!

He gave her a small smirk and ran his fangs gently along her wrist, and a hand up her bare calf above her half boot, startling her and causing her heartbeat to race in her chest. Trying to control her reaction to Nichola's bold and public actions, she gulped down her pig's blood-laced pisco, and Chef Joe poured her another goblet.

* * * * *

You seem to be feeling better. Nichola's voice came into her head.

As the evening progressed, the heavily alcoholic pisco (both blood-laced and not) flowed ever more freely and the dancing around the bonfire, got wilder and more suggestive, the more Leila's tension had decreased. Now she was thoroughly relaxed.

Surprised that this was the case, she looked down on him still half reclining between her legs, *I guess I do,* she thought in return.

You are feeding from the life force of the crowd.

How do you know that it is the life force and not the blood-laced pisco? She asked him, feeling a little tipsy as she was now on her fourth goblet of the stuff.

As your mate, I can also feel the life essence flow into you. For vampires, especially those of us who can feed in this manner, this celebration came at the perfect time. But, you need to know how to take this energy intentionally. It is natural for us to do so involuntarily, it is like keeping a battery fully charged all the time. Most of the time, I don't even realize that I am doing it. But, though feeding in this manner is a gift, your control over it is very important; you need to know how to do this purposefully. He thought to her sipping his drink.

I don't understand what you mean.

I mean that it is easy to siphon off the excess emotions in places where there are many people who are boisterous, such as this celebration, nightclub, concert, or other large venue. But there may come a time where you are on your own needing to feed but there are only a few quiet, unemotional humans nearby. You need to be able to concentrate and control the siphoning of their life essence, either combined or individually. For instance, I once fed on the midnight route of a Toronto city bus that traversed the whole city, where most of the passengers were dozing or outright sleeping.

So, you concentrated your efforts on just a few people?

Yes. His thought was direct.

Did you have to touch them to do it? Since they were sleeping I mean? She felt her curiosity peak.

No. This ability that you and I have is advanced, and we do so psychically. Touch is not necessary, but proximity is. It will be helpful for you to hone this skill; especially if you are still going to try to live your life as a 'vegan vampire'. She could hear the humor in his thoughts.

You act like I don't have a chance to accomplish that, Nichola. She returned in irritation.

That is absolutely untrue, mikró! I am a large believer in your willpower and know that you can do anything that you put your mind to. But your success is going to depend on your learning to identify, control, and properly wield those abilities. She felt him stroke up her calf again.

Ignoring his wandering hand, she thought about it. *So, am I able to feed from other vampires also in this manner?Other than you, I mean?*

He turned giving her an intense look. *Yes. Though I wouldn't suggest that you do so.*

Why not?

What we do with humans, could be considered involuntary because they aren't aware of us doing it. So, if you attempted to do so with a vampire on an involuntary basis, One, it would be very rude. Two, many would take it as an assault on their person. Three, you wouldn't get away with it for very long as most of them would feel what you are doing fairly quickly. The sharing of essence on a voluntary basis between vampires is usually done through a sexual encounter.

She pondered that information for a while, then asked, *So, how do I do it? Siphon life essence from an individual?*

Yes. Without having sex with them, of course.

He looked around at the humans at the celebration seeing several of them congregating on the other side of the bonfire chatting amongst themselves. *See the pretty female there, with the low-cut blouse? The one touching the chest of the man she is speaking with.*

Yes.

Concentrate gently on her... He started explaining.

Should I point at her to focus my thoughts? Leila interrupted.

Only if you want to look silly. He chuckled, ducking, as she swatted him in the back of the head. *Seriously, these are all mental skills, i psychí mou...*

* * * * *

Burke leaned back against a wall in one of the village cottages looking out the window, watching as Leila swatted at Nichola and how he laughed and smiled at her. He knew enough about vampire soul mates to realize that they must be having a private conversation between the two of them. He looked down at the pretty native girl on her knees in front of him as she undid his pants, pulling them down over his hips, and caressed his half erect prick.

She gazed up with a hunger in her dark eyes as she slid her moist lips over him softly, using the suction of her mouth to pull him erect. His voice escaped his lips in a soft moan, and he placed a gentle hand on her dark head as her head started to bob up and down on his now hard shaft. He closed his eyes as she cupped his balls and ran a finger gently over his puckered asshole.

His balls started to tighten as he grew close to coming when he suddenly saw beautiful, teal-colored eyes in his mind causing him to suddenly pull her head away from his cock.

He opened his eyes as he pulled the girl to her feet, lifting her skirts to rip her panties from her body. He slid his arms between her legs lifting her body up and placing her against the wall next to the window, one leg over each of his arms holding her wide open to his gaze as he slid his rock-hard prick into her wet channel. She cried out in both pleasure and pain as he rammed himself into her. He drilled her body with his cock, his hips and muscular ass grinding himself against her clit and felt her wrap her arms tightly around his shoulders holding him close.

He turned his head intently watching Leila and Nichola out the window as he fucked the girl in his arms. Jealousy nestled itself in his chest as he watched Nichola's hand caress up Leila's bare leg to wrap his hand around her shapely knee.

As the girl he held convulsed around his thrusting cock in orgasm cried out softly, he closed his eyes, driving his fangs into her throat drinking of her deeply. As he came, he imagined Leila's face in his mind, her streaked auburn hair haloing her as her head was thrown back in ecstasy, her voice calling out his name, as her pussy pulsated around him.

* * * * *

Leila and Nichola walked slowly through the trees surrounding the village on their way back to her bungalow at the main hotel. Leila was feeling relaxed and a little drunk, which wasn't surprising with how much pig's blood and pisco she had consumed.

"I psychí mou…" Nichola began softly.

"Don't Nichola." Leila told him quietly in return. "I am still really fucking angry with you. I understand that you thought I was dying. But you knew how I felt about drinking blood from a human being. I now feel like I am some kind of cannibal!Not to mention the fact that you lay next to me while you let him fuck me! I can't even wrap my head around that. I know vampires are an oversexed, kinky kind of species; Es and I talked about it, and I've felt my own off-the-wall desire levels before you pumped me full of venom years ago, but that shit you did was really fucked up!"

He let her get a few steps ahead of him before he said. "Leila, I cannot be without you. I know that you are angry. But since I have found you we have been apart more than we have been together, and now that you are vampire, I can no longer be without you."

"Nichola," she said over her shoulder as she walked on, her voice sharp and hurt. "You don't even care about how bad and upset I feel about this. You can't even acknowledge how fucked up it is! Just go to hell and leave me alone!"

"The only hell I know is being without you. So, I have already been there!" His voice was angry and bitter.

She rolled her eyes at his dramatic response and walked on. Turning around to berate him for whining about past decisions, she saw that he was gone. *Good! At least he listened to me this time.* Turning back towards the hotel, she took several steps before she heard what sounded like several branches snapping behind her.

Turning, she looked hard into the darkness of the trees, when a large dark shape stepped from them and moved toward her. She froze in fright thinking it might be a puma that Burke had warned her about. Looking steadily, she realized with frustration that her vampire sight wasn't fully developed yet and not knowing what the shape was, as it slowly approached, terrified her to the point of bolting.

When the shape was about six feet away, she realized that it was an enormous dog. Exhaling suddenly in relief she patted her leg saying, "Oh, thank God! Come here. Are you a nice doggie?" She made a smooching sound with her mouth. "Come here, baby. It's okay, don't be afraid. What are you doing out here?"

The dog yawned loudly exposing its large sharp teeth and suddenly its tongue lolled out of its mouth like it was smiling at her and with a wag of its tail it came to sidle up to her body. Its massive head came up to the middle of her chest and it laid its head upon her breasts almost pushing her down as she tentatively pet its huge frame."Woah, buddy." She said as she steadied herself. "God you are huge! Are you lost?" She baby-talked to the gigantic beast and it raised its huge muzzle to quickly slobber her face with its long tongue. "Yuck!"She giggled. "None of your doggie kisses!" She looked at its mottled coat, unable to make out a color in the dark."What am I going to do with you?"It roughly nosed her hand when she stopped petting it and she continued to stroke it as she spoke to it. "I suppose I will have to take you home with me tonight. If a puma got you I would feel terrible! I will talk to Nelson tomorrow morning, I am sure that he knows who you belong to.You are too large not to be pretty well-known."

She continued towards the hotel and the large animal kept pace with her.

* * * * *

As she approached her bungalow, the beast stopped and let out a low growl.She stopped also feeling a spark of fear, and out of the darkness of the bungalow's porch across from hers' came Burke's soft drawl, "Evening, Ms. Sutton! What have you got there?" He stepped out to the porch doorway and smoke from a cheroot swirled around his head.

"Oh, Mr. Burke! You frightened me. I found him in the woods. You don't happen to know who he belongs to, do you?"

Burke glared at the beast, which leaned its body against Leila's protectively."Can't say I have ever laid eyes on him before." Burke smirked around his cheroot as he took a draw. "A mangy looking cur isn't he? Have you asked Klaus?"

"Oh, no! He's beautiful." Leila pet the animal's large head, and it wagged its tail at her and looked up at her in adoration, then bared its teeth in Burke's direction again with its low growl."Hush. He's okay, he's a friend." She told it, then said to Burke who still had the smirk on his lips as he looked at the dog, "Nichola got back before I did. I will check with him in the morning." She headed over to the door of her bungalow followed closely by the dog.

"I didn't know that you were staying in the bungalows, Ms. Sutton."Burke's voice was curious as he walked a few steps toward her but halted suddenly at the warning growl and bark of the enormous beast who was guarding her back as she was opening the door.

She turned in the doorway, to say repressively, "It's a recent development."She looked at the dog facing off with the wary vampire. "He doesn't seem to like you very much, Mr. Burke. My aunt told me a long time ago that one predator senses another."

"He's obviously aggressive." Burke told her, his glaring eyes never leaving the dog. "But neutering would take care of that.Hopefully, he's not rabid. We'd have to shoot him then." He said harshly as if it understood him, and it obviously understood the sentiment because it barked and snarled harshly in warning once more at him before hiking it's leg and peeing on the bush in front of Leila's porch, glaring and growling at Burke the whole time. Then it turned to Leila and walked through the doorway of her bungalow.

"Good night, Mr. Burke." Leila said to him softly, and he nodded to her as if put out, as she closed the door.As she locked the door, she glanced at the dog who was sitting still on its haunches watching her actions intently."That wasn't very nice." She told it, and it let its tongue loll out of its mouth again as if smiling and wagged its tail briefly at her.

141

She walked past it into her bedroom, and it followed her to leap up on the bed to watch raptly as she took off her clothes and put on a short nightgown."Now, you better not potty in this bungalow. Nelson would be furious with both of us if you messed this place up." She told him as she went into the bathroom to brush her teeth and her hair.

In a few minutes, the dog was next to her, his head well above the counter sniffing the top and looking at her in the mirror. He nosed the elbow of the arm that she was brushing her hair with."Do you want me to brush you too?"She looked in the drawers of the bathroom knowing that they always supplied a set of personal grooming items in each of the rooms. Finding the spare hairbrush, she told him, "Okay, come on." She headed back into the bedroom and climbed onto the bed to sit cross-legged on the bed and the dog leaped up to lay in front of her. She looked at his shaggy multi-colored coat as she started brushing him.

"You seem to be well-taken care of," she spoke to him as she brushed his soft fur. "You have obviously been eating well!" He huffed at her as she brushed. "I am sure that your owner is missing you terribly." She pet him as she brushed, and he gave her a groan of pleasure.When she was finished, she sat the brush on the nightstand. "Well, at least you don't seem to be a shedder. Now, look at you! You are so handsome!" He stood up on the bed to tower over her and proceeded to lick her enthusiastically.Pushing her with his body down on the bed and laying across her, effectively pinning her to the bed with his greater weight. "Oh, my gosh!You are such a monster!" She giggled as she struggled and wiggled out from under him and got up turning off the lights.

She climbed underneath the covers and the dog snuggled against her side, his long muzzle tucked against the side of her neck and shoulder as she wrapped an arm around his large head. "I miss my dog," she told him softly with a little hitch in her voice, as she stroked his soft fur. He breathed deeply against her, giving her a little groan. "She's so tiny compared to you. I hope Zachary is taking good care of her." She felt him softly lick her throat as she relaxed and fell asleep.

* * * * *

She woke to the sound of the shower running. *What the hell?* She thought as she got out of bed and headed for the bathroom. Nichola turned off the shower, stepped out and wrapped a towel around his waist.

"What are you doing here?" She demanded.

He gave her a look with an arched brow, grabbing her hairbrush and brushing his hair. "What's it look like?" He asked snarkily.

"Where's the dog?"

"It disappeared when I got here." He replied.

"Do you know who it belongs to? I was hoping to find its owner."

"No." He told her."Zachary called and left a message on Mansuetus's phone last night. He wants us to call him back after breakfasting this morning. Why don't you get in the shower and let's have breakfast." He headed into the walk-in and Leila saw that there were several sets of clothes hung up and in the drawers of the closet..

"Nichola, you can't just move in here with me!" She protested.

"Why not?" He asked simply, pulling on a pair of jeans.

"I am in here because I am pissed at you and don't want to be around you!"She said heatedly.

"Well, I am not going to accept your torture of me this time, Leila, and I refuse to fight about it! You can be angry with me if you like. But you are not getting rid of me! I am taking time off from my business responsibilities and we are going to spend more time together. After all of these years apart, it is something that we need to do in any case.Staying here in the bungalow, sleeping, and living separate from everyone is a good start. Now get in the shower and let's go to breakfast so that we can call Zachary back." He turned his back on her and headed into the living room.

She stood there and gritted her teeth in frustration for a moment then headed into the bathroom.

* * * * *

Leila sat in silence next to Nichola and sipped pig's blood out of a juice glass as she waited for the waiter to bring her breakfast. Nichola was reading the newspaper off of the tablet that he always seemed to have with him.

He gave her a sideways glance and spoke softly, "You can decide to not speak to me if that is what you want, Leila. But you and I both know that eventually, you will see that I had no choice in what I did. You can't stay angry with me forever, you are just being stubborn."

She drained the juice glass and poured herself a cup of coffee ignoring him.

Burke, Devin, Cross-Eyed Fred, Mansuetus and Dene joined them.

"Good morning, Klaus, Ms. Sutton." Burke said with a nod.

"Good morning, Mr. Burke." Leila murmured. Nichola nodded in his direction and returned to reading his tablet.

"Have you heard anything more from Zachary, Mansuetus?" Leila asked. "Did he say in his voice mail what he wanted to speak about?"

"No, Kyría." Mansuetus replied proceeding to order his breakfast.

"Did you find that mongrel's owner?" Burke sipped his coffee.

"What mongrel?" Devin asked with interest.

"Your mother took in a stray last night. Huge, ugly, aggressive beast! Probably is in early stage of rabies; I am sure he was frothing at the mouth last night." Burke told him.

"That is not true!" Leila exclaimed. "He was a really sweet dog! And, no, he took off this morning when Nichola let him out."

"Did he try to bite you?" Burke asked Nichola.

"No." Nichola replied still reading his tablet.

"Well, he sure was thinking about biting me last night!" Burke exclaimed to the table in general.

"I am sure that isn't a first for you, Burke." Mansuetus smirked.

"Besides, you are a vampire, are you trying to say that you were scared of a little dog?" Dene chuckled.

"I didn't say that! Besides, he was huge!" Burke said indignantly.

"He was protecting me!" Leila defended her furry friend. "I told you, one predator recognizes another. Besides, he didn't try to bite you. He just barked and snarled."

"So now you are afraid of barking dogs?" Mansuetus grinned.

"He had huge teeth!" Burke yelled.

"So, now you are a vampire who is afraid of teeth?" Dene asked

144

incredulously; he tried to keep his voice even, but you could hear the laughter in it.

"Oh, never mind!" Burke said in a huff. "If you run across him and he bites one of you, remember I warned you!"

The Hunt Begins

Devin, Burke, and Fred were making plans to head out to the cave after breakfast when Mansuetus's tablet rang. He glanced down at his screen with a surprised look. "It's Zachary video calling."

"Well, answer it Uncle Man!" Devin demanded.

"Hi Zach!" Mansuetus said.

Leila came to look over Mansuetus's shoulder and wave at the screen."Hi Honey!"

"Hi Mom! Wow, you look different!" Zachary exclaimed in bewildered shock. "How are you doing?"

"I am good, Honey! Mansuetus said that you called him last night and left a voice message. We haven't finished breakfast yet or we would have called you back."

"I'm sorry, Mom. I just couldn't wait anymore. There is a lot of shit going down right now that I need to talk to you about."

"What is going on?" Leila asked concerned.

"You know that case I have been working on? The one with the murdered girls? It has been really frustrating because we haven't been able to identify any of the victims, all of them were Hispanic and because no one has claimed them or reported them missing, the media have assumed that they were all illegal aliens, so it hasn't gotten a lot of media attention despite the number of victims.Do you remember me telling you about that case?" He asked.

146

"Yes, I remember. It sounds like a gruesome and heartbreaking case."

"It is. Well, it has suddenly become front page news! But, what's worse is that I think the killer is a vampire." Zachary told them calmly.

Nichola reached over, took the tablet from Mansuetus, and looked at the screen.

"Hey, Nick." Zachary said.

"Do you remember me?" Nichola asked quietly, surprised.

"I remember everything I have ever seen." Zachary answered. "It's a gift... and a curse." His voice was soft.

"Why do you think this murderer is a vampire?" Nichola asked him gently.

"The victims are killed elsewhere and then their bodies are discarded in ever increasing public locations. Like he is playing with us. All of the bodies, in addition to some pretty horrific wounds that has been determined to have been made by some sort of claw instead of knives, have all been totally drained of blood. But the strongest evidence to date is a video that we obtained from last week's site where he abandoned a victim's body. I have uploaded the security video to Mansuetus's email. You tell me what you think it could be." Zachary's voice was calm and professional.

Mansuetus reached over and pushed a few icons on the tablet. By this time, they all, including Burke and Fred, were gathered around Nichola, who was holding the tablet and he pressed the play button to watch the slow-motion video that Zachary had sent.

"Oh, no." Leila murmured quietly as they all watched the video.

"Meet San Antonio's Phantom Butcher." For the first time since describing the killings Zachary's voice showed emotion and it was harsh. "From what my mother has told me of vampires and how their images are affected by photographic equipment, I believe that this is a made vampire." Zachary stated as Nichola looked at him on the screen.

"I concur." Nichola's voice was dangerously quiet.

"That video was more than a week ago, but now it gets more complicated because three teenage white females were reported missing two days ago, and all indications are that they were taken together. The news is now all over this case and are having a field day with it.It is only going to get worse because we found one of them last night, meaning we now have a name for a victim, and she meets all of the physical characteristics for a media frenzy: she's pretty, white, was a good student, and comes from an upscale family. Reporting on this case will become big business for the news outlets.

She was killed in the exact same manner as our Jane Does, so there is no doubt that this is The Phantom Butcher. But he's changing, something has definitely set him off because his usual action has been to dump one body per month, and the victim was usually killed at least two days prior to him dumping her. Well, he's escalated his timeframe, he has given us two bodies in the span of slightly more than a week and the newest little girl's death probably occurred within hours of her going missing.

Frankly, the police department, nor the FBI who is now taking up space in my office, are equipped to handle this type of assailant." Zachary's voice was bitter. "According to my mother, you lead a group that manages these issues when they become public. I need your help to stop this monster, Nick."

"You will have it." Nichola vowed dangerously.

* * * * *

"You are not going!" Nichola ordered, looking at Leila and Devin as they started talking about packing after Zachary hung up.

"I am not staying here!" Leila glared at him as he sat at the table holding the tablet in his hands looking at her and Devin with concern and no small amount of frustration.

"Neither am I!" Devin stated.

"I am going!" Burke said surprising the three of them before they could start arguing.

"Why would you go, William?" Nichola asked him incredulously.

"Because there is a rogue operating out of my territory. Do you dispute that I am the oldest vampire residing in that area of Texas?" Burke looked at Nichola hard.

"No, as far as I know you are the oldest vampire in the area."

"My territory then. I am going to be involved in any hunt for any monster killing little girls in my territory!Besides, where are you all going to stay if not at my ranch?"

"The windows of my home are UV protected." Leila told him. Then she looked at Nichola hard, "and I am going!"

Nichola started to answer her when Burke cut in. "My ranch house will sleep everyone here and then some. I have a cook and housekeeper as well as ranch hands for security. Plus, the location is rural. You can't have a bunch of vehicles and vampires at your house in a neighborhood without drawing undue attention. Besides if any of your neighbors know you, they will see right away how different you look." Upon Leila's glare on him, Burke continued. "Not that you aren't beautiful, you very much are, but you have definitely changed since your transformation and any human who knows you is going to notice it straight away."

Nichola looked at Burke in speculation then said, "Fine." He looked at all of them, handing Mansuetus the tablet, and immediately took control. "Vampires need to spend time in the spray booth. That includes you, Devin. Mansuetus please make our travel arrangements and get a hold of the Dragonfly's crew. Dene, we may need a doctor on hand, so you are coming also. We will leave tomorrow if at all possible, so everyone needs to get their packing done."He stood and took Leila by the elbow to lead her back to the bungalow.

* * * * *

"I don't like this Leila, it's dangerous…" Nichola spoke, trying to keep his voice reasonable, as he walked her into the bungalow.

"Don't start with me, Nichola!" Leila exclaimed. "I am not your slave nor a weakling! My whole existence I have spent doing someone else's bidding, always doing what I am told; to get by or to get along. I am going.My son needs me! Could you imagine what would happen if Zachary cornered this rogue vampire without vampire backup? He could easily get himself killed. I am not going to let that happen."

He pulled her close, wrapping his arms around her, enveloping her in his scent. He felt her relax against him as she placed her head against his chest to listen to his strong and steady heartbeat.

"I know his profession is dangerous, Nichola." Leila whispered against him, wrapping her arms around him."But I never really worried too much.He's so smart, and physically, he's strong and fast. Preternaturally so. Against a human those worries were small, something I could live with. But against a vampire? Basically, Zachary is still just a human."

"Leila, you are a new vampire. You are not fully in control of yourself…"

"Garbage! Just stop!I am not going to go off the deep end and start attacking humans and if you were really concerned about that you wouldn't even suggest that you leave me here unsupervised! I could kill your whole staff at the hotel after all!" She pulled back to look up into his amber eyes."I will make sure that I am drinking plenty of blood. I will do what I am supposed to do. I will take care of myself so that I can help my son." She attempted to pull away from him and he held her tight.

"And you will feed from me, Leila." His voice a low order against her hair.

"I should have known this was about sex!" Her voice was disgusted as she tried to push away from him and was unsuccessful.

"This is about you! You've only been a vampire for less than a handful of days. I am your mate and your elder and as a new vampire you shouldn't even be in the general public for at least a year. You are dangerous, whether you want to believe it or not. It is one of the reasons why I am taking time from my businesses: to be with you, to teach you." Nichola whispered against her temple.

"Whatever! But you will be teaching me in Texas!" She grumbled and felt his lips curve in a smile against her face.

"You are stubborn, yet I still spoil you, agapitós, do not make me regret it."He murmured.

"I won't Nichola. I will do everything that I have to in order to remain in control and be strong so that I can keep my son safe. I promise."

"We will keep him safe, agápi mou, and we will stop these murders and protect both the human community and our own." He tilted her head up and kissed her lips softly, reluctantly pulling back when she started to deepen the kiss to look down into her eyes. "I need to call Rom and have him meet us in San Antonio."

"Rom? Why?"She asked surprised.

"Because Rom is the best tracker I know and if Zachary is right, we need to stop this bastard as soon as possible before this becomes a worldwide story."

* * * * *

Nichola entered the darkened bungalow just after midnight. Her scent of licorice, jasmine and peppermint permeated the space claiming it as her own, and he breathed deep of it relaxing his tired mind. He made his way into the bedroom to see her curled up in the bed slumbering like a child.

His lips twisted at the sight in a small smile.

We never seem to have any peace do we Glykó? He thought to himself. The years that they spent apart had been boring and tedious for him and he had absorbed himself in his businesses and in the doctor's experiments. As soon as she entered his life again and he had finally made arrangements to take a much-needed hiatus to spend time with her, all hell breaks loose. He shook his head at the irony as he stripped himself of his clothes.

Just as Mansuetus had predicted years ago, his life with her was never tedious or boring; but just once he had hoped for some peace and quiet.

Sliding beneath the blankets with her, he pulled her body across his to straddle him as he softly kissed her tender lips when she woke against him.

"Nichola?" Her voice asked sleepily in the dark.

"Who else would it be, i psychí mou?" He murmured against her mouth, then ran his tongue over her lips as his hand stroked over her back toward her ass, pulling her close against his erection.

Ignoring his question, she asked, "Where have you been all day?"

"Taking care of business." He said softly as he ran his lips down her jaw to kiss along her throat.

"You know I basically know very little about you or what you do. I am tired of you not including me in your life.I am tired of not really knowing you."She was fully awake now.

"Our souls already know each other, don't they?" He asked sliding his erection against the silken panties that covered her pussy causing her to groan slightly.

"Nichola! Just because we are soul mates doesn't mean we have a relationship! If that were the case, you wouldn't have spied on me over the last 25 years! You know almost everything about me. Yet you share very little about yourself."

"What would you like to know, Leila?" He asked softly against her ear as his hands continued to stroke up and down her body feeling her tremble in response to him.

"Let's start with something easy." She placed her forearms against his chest and looked down at him; somewhat surprised that she could see him so clearly in the dark. "What did you do all day? You left here to call Rom and I didn't see you for the rest of the day, including dinner."

"I made calls to the other small council members to discuss the murders in San Antonio with them. Peake as you may remember holds much sway over information networks, which includes news agencies throughout the world. He is having his people look for any similar crimes in other locations in an attempt to identify this killer. He will also take steps to discredit any news agency who reports on any supernatural aspect of these cases. We are walking in darkness without knowing who in our community is committing these crimes. The more information, the more 'knowns' that we have, the better our plans will be and the safer our hunt is. Unfortunately, at this moment we are going in blind. This situation is extremely dangerous."

"Why? Are you afraid of the murderer?"

"No." He smirked. "But our mission on these hunts is always two-fold. We must apprehend and dispose of a highly dangerous killer, without getting ourselves killed, and we must make sure that we do so with little to no indication that supernatural forces are in play to the outside world. We must stop the killings and keep our community secret at the same time."

"Did you get everything done that you needed to do?" At his inquiring look, she clarified, "Are you packed? Did you go through the spray booth? Are you ready to leave tomorrow?"

He smiled at her with just a hint of fang. "I am ready." He stroked his erection against her. "In many ways. And you are hungry."

"I am not!" She protested trying to pull away from him, but he held her hips tightly and rolled himself against her causing her breath to catch in her throat.

152

"Yes, you are. I can feel it." His voice was a sexy growl in the dark room. She shook her head negatively biting the inside of her lip to keep from moaning aloud as he rolled against her once more and she could feel her panties become soaked with her juices. "Yes, i psychí mou, I feel your hunger and it makes me hungry too." He pulled her face down to him to claim her lips roughly, thrusting his tongue against her own, nicking his tongue against her sharp fangs; fangs that she hadn't even realized had descended. She drew on his tongue for a brief moment before pulling away abruptly.

"Nichola, stop." She murmured weakly as desire and bloodlust flowed in her veins. "I am afraid. I don't wish to hurt you."

"You can't hurt me, Leila. I am the one person in the world that you can't hurt with your feeding. You need me and I need you." He moved his hands up her sides stripping her nightgown from her body as he sat up, still holding her straddling his hips, then fastened his lips against one of her nipples with a soft groan; he loved to suckle her and cause her nipples to grow pebble hard.

Her head fell back with a groan and her hands made their way over the sculpted muscles of his arms and shoulders, and through the softness of his thick hair. His skin felt like satin and his hair felt like silk against the sensitive vampire skin of her hands. His scent enveloped her; that heady scent of cinnamon, ginger, and sandalwood which she had always been drawn to, now set off fireworks in her nerve endings almost overwhelming her. She ran her fingers deeply through his silken hair pulling his head back hard to fasten her lips to his, suckling and nibbling against the tender skin that she found there, eliciting a moan from him. The taste of him, his mouth, his skin, was heavenly, making her want to submerse herself in him. She tried to fight the desire for him that was quickly overwhelming her. She tried to pull her anger forward, her anger against the part that he played in her transformation. She failed as her need for him grew, causing her pussy to weep her desire and her mouth to water in her need to taste him.

"Oh, my angel," Nichola whispered in longing to her, following her body down as he easily picked her up to gently lay her against the sheets. "I have waited so long for you to become vampire. So, so, long." He kissed and licked his way down her body as she squirmed against him, quivering as the skin of her body pebbled in desire and he pulled her soaked panties from her hips and down her legs then settled himself between her legs keeping them wide with his shoulders.

Her control shattered. "Please.I need...I need..." She moaned, her eyes fluttering, as she felt his breath against her drenched pussy as a fire spread in her veins and over her skin.

"Yes, love. I know what you need." He whispered as his finger encircled her clit causing her hips to buck involuntarily.He gave one long lick to the slit of her pussy, and she gave a little cry of shock as electricity flowed throughout her body. "Yes, it feels so much *more* now doesn't it?" He whispered against her and pierced her vaginal vein with his fangs drawing her into his mouth to feed, causing her to cry out and lurch against him, holding his head to her.

Leila could feel her life force flow into him with her blood and was powerless to stop the waves of pleasure that were coursing throughout her body.The pleasure that she was receiving was a meal in and of itself. She could feel the power of his life force flow into her as he pulled from her in a loop of desire that sated the hunger, but not the desire in her body.

She felt him lick her to heal the bite. "Please, Nichola..."

"Yes, my love?" He placed small gentle kisses directly against her clit, and she groaned loudly.

"Nichola, I need you to make me come!" She cried out straining against the small kisses of his lips, seeking completion.

"How would you like me to do that?" He glanced up teasingly from between her legs and his eyes glowed with amber light as he gently stroked her with one of his long fingers causing her to further squirm.

"Just do it!" She growled in frustration as he continued to stroke her clit gently, steadily.

He kissed and nibbled his way up her body to her breasts, his hand never stopping it's gentle, steady stroking between her legs. He licked her nipple, which had turned into a hardened pebble.He scraped his fang gently over the sensitive surface and she pushed herself against him. "Tell your lover what you want, Leila." He instructed against her skin then gave her a small nip causing her to gasp.

"Oh, please! I…"

"Yes?" He murmured as he lapped at her nipple, moving his hand up to stroke against her belly.

"I want you, Nichola!" She shrieked out as the pleasure decreased when he removed his hand from between her legs and her frustration grew.

"Hmm?" He took her nipple between his teeth to roll it gently.

"Ah! I want you to fuck me, Nichola!" She gasped out on the verge of losing all control and weeping.

"Yes?" His collected voice was cool, and he patiently circled her belly button with just the tip of his finger.

"I want your cock! I want your cock buried deep inside of me!" Her voice was desperate in her desire. "God, what is happening to me?!" She felt like her skin was on fire as her need grew to a fevered pitch and a painful desire ripped through her veins.

"It is the ache from the mate bond. You've just never felt it this intensely before because you weren't a full vampire. It is the need to mate with me. Only me.It is the same ache that I have felt since I first laid eyes on you." He explained his voice still cool, but then she felt him tremble as he continued huskily, "Beg me, Leila. Beg me and I will stop this ache inside of our bodies." He shivered against her, moving to gently nibble her lips and she realized that his need was almost as great as hers. "Beg me, Leila. I want to hear it from your lips, just once, just once how much you love and need me…and I will make this ache inside of you burst like rockets in the sky. Just once, Leila."

Her pride fought hard against it, this total submission. She knew that is what he wanted from her. As the craving spiked through her veins once again, she whispered, "I need you, Nichola. I need you to drive your cock into me, I need you to claim me as yours.I love you." As the words left her mouth she realized how very true they were.

Upon her declaration he pushed his cock into her wet channel deeply causing both of them to cry out in pleasure as he did so. He thrust deep and hard, in abandon, as she wrapped her legs and arms around him, pulling him into her. As he plunged into her she ground herself against him time and again crying out in frenzy as she reached for completion.

The feelings that were overwhelming her were so alien to what they had ever been as a human, and the rough way that he handled her as he drove himself into her was thrilling. It was as if he was unafraid of harming her and he could finally take her the way that he had always wanted. It was more than sex, it was more than love, it was a bonding of bodies and souls.

He sank his fangs deeply into her throat, drinking of the ambrosia of her blood, his hips ever rolling his cock into her as she screamed out her first orgasm; the energy of it feeding them both. Her pussy milked him as he drove her second orgasm crashing over her, and she bit into him to pull his blood into her mouth to taste of his spice and power, groaning as electricity flowed in her veins.

He felt her claws against his back, leaving grooves that healed almost instantly as he drank of her power. As she reached the crescendo of her third orgasm, she did see stars and he let go of his own control, to drive his cock deeply over and over until his own climax ripped through him like an earthquake and his cum erupted from him like a volcano to drench her womb.

They held each other tightly, reluctant to part, until both fell into a deep satiated slumber, their bodies two halves of a whole, still connected, wrapped in each other's arms.

A Song Only Our Souls Understand

꧁ꪆꫀꪆ꧂

To say I was experiencing some frustration and irritation would be to say the least. Since I woke up this morning after experiencing the most mind-blowing sex of my entire existence last night, every time I glanced at Nichola he was giving me a little knowing smile and his eyes positively glowed with what I can describe only as arrogant, male delight. It was really getting on my nerves!

Yes, the sex was great, transcendental in fact, but I hated that I had totally surrendered to him. I always thought that when I became a full vampire that I would be in control of my own life; not tied or enslaved to someone else's desires, thoughts or wishes.

I had accepted the fact that we were soulmates years ago, but the more I settled into my vampire self, I realized that I truly had no idea what it really meant. As a vampire it was as if I knew him on a cellular level. He was still basically a stranger in his actions and life, I knew so little about him, just superficial things, but I didn't know what made him tick as a person. Yet I wholly recognized him as mine. When I looked at him I discovered myself. He was there to strengthen me and only me, as I was here to do the same for him.He was a mirror opposite to me, but I knew he was the only person who had the keys to the locks of my heart.

This bond was eternal, and ancient, older than the universe. It frightened me because I also realized that he wouldn't always be the one to make me the happiest or even the most contented, but that he would eternally be the one that made me feel the most: the burning, the anger, the worry, the yearning, the sweet mad desire and need that threatened to take my sanity. There would be no escaping him ever and he had the absolute power to take me either to heaven or to hell!

I had never wanted to feel this way about another person because I was always afraid of losing myself to grief if it didn't last. Fear ripped through me as I realized that in all the universe there would be no one for me like him. He wasn't a choice, he was my other half – and he scared the hell out of me!

Last night I had given him power over me, and I hated it, but at the same time I craved to do it again. I was such a mess!

* * * * *

Leila and I sat across from Burke on the plane while we were getting ready for takeoff at around noon. Mansuetus, Dene, Fred and Devin were sitting across the aisle at the table and Fred was shuffling a deck of playing cards. Burke looked at us irritably and his face was set into a sour expression.

"Did you rest well last night, William?" I inquired solicitously.

"Not really." He stated with a glare. "I kept hearing these strange screeches and screams in the night that were distracting and kept me up."

"I am sure that Nelson would accommodate you upon our return with a room inside of the main hotel, Burke. It is much quieter there." Mansuetus stated picking up the cards that Fred had dealt him.

Leila flushed intently flipping through a magazine that I knew she wasn't reading, and I felt her embarrassment. Reaching over to rest my hand possessively on her thigh that was clad in a calf length black skirt, I gave a small smile and looked out of the plane's window as I thought back to the conversation that Mansuetus and I had this morning in my office.

"Nikolaos, I feel the need to warn you…" He had started hesitantly.

"Mansuetus if you are concerned about Leila and Devin, there is no need I assure you. It will be easy enough to keep them grounded to Burke's ranch and with its rural location they will be out of any danger from this killer." I had stated packing my laptop and tablet in their cases.

"Nikolaos, that is not what I am speaking about! I am not sure if you are aware, but Burke is interested in Leila.Between what Devin has revealed and my own observations, I believe that he is captivated by her. Physically." His voice held a hint of outrage.

"He is fascinated with her. He has tasted her blood after all, but this will eventually wear off…"

"Nikolaos, please listen to me. You have been busy, with reason, and not in attendance for most of their interactions.I have been attentive. He is pursuing her, and it is not because he has tasted her blood." Mansuetus was blunt. "He watches, complements, and ingratiates himself. His looks are contemplative and intent. He is physical with her when there is no need for it. The pursuit is light touched, but he is pursuing her nonetheless."

"What do you mean by physical? Inappropriately so?" I felt myself grow cold at his words.

"He touches her at every availability. Not inappropriate by human standards, at least not while I was present, but vampire standards are another matter. In fact, he acts very humanlike around her. Like he is besotted."

"He is young, and she is exquisitely beautiful." I replied neutrally but inside I was seething.

"If you believe that, he shouldn't be the only one to tell her so."

I could see that Mansuetus was serious.

"My friend, you forget the preference of the lady, and the lady herself.Leila is not interested in William, nor has she had time to grow bored. She has enough to keep her interested at the moment." I gave him a small smile.

"Kýrios, she sparks emotions from him. I don't believe that he presents a danger to her, but she is a young, volatile vampire, who is still very human-like in her thoughts, and he is handsome, charming, and attentive."

Knowing that she fought against and was fearful of our soul bond, I met his eyes in consideration for a moment. "I will take care, Mansuetus."

* * * * *

"Will we be able to stop by my home before we head to the ranch?" Leila asked Nichola.

"Yes, Mansuetus has made arrangements to rent a Yukon at the airport."

"My ranch manager is meeting Fred and I at the airport. I want to get to the ranch to make sure that your accommodations are ready, Ms. Sutton." Burke stated giving her a soft look.

Nichola noticed the look with a scowl, "Rom is also meeting us at the airport.If you would like I can text him your address and he could meet us at your home instead?"

Leila nodded to Nichola, then spoke to Burke. "Mr. Burke, may I bring my dog to your ranch?"

Burke answered her in surprise, "What kind of dog is it?"

"She is a terrier, Mr. Burke. She is a small, indoor dog."

"A ratter? She doesn't bite does she?"

Leila smiled, "No. She is very friendly and playful. She is just a little over a year old, but she is totally housebroken and not destructive."

"I don't see why not then. I like dogs after all."

Mansuetus and Dene snorted with laughter and Burke glared at them.

* * * * *

About halfway through the flight Leila headed into the lavatory. She was checking her makeup in the mirror above the small vanity when the door opened and Nichola slipped in behind.

"I am sure that I locked that door!" She snapped at him. She was stressed out from the situation and tired from having gotten little actual rest the night before.

"You did." Nichola said looking at her in the mirror over her shoulder with a cheeky smile as he closed the door behind him.

"Well, you are going to have to show me your trick."

"Telekinesis will come to you when you are older." Nichola rubbed his hands up and down the long sleeves of her red silk blouse. She heard an audible click as he turned the lock with his mind, locking them in the lavatory.

"Exactly what do you think you are up too?" She tried to make her voice strong, but he was nuzzling the nape of her neck and she could feel his fingers on the outside of her thighs inching her skirt up her legs, so she was failing miserably.

"Initiating you into the mile-high club, mikró." He murmured against her skin, letting his scent envelop her. "I can't wait to feel my cock thrusting into you several thousand feet in the air."

"Stop." She gasped out as she breathed in his scent, growing wet, which caused her fangs to descend, as he slid her panties to the floor. "They will hear us."

"Let them." He told her bending her over the vanity and thrusting deep within her wet channel.

She tried to stifle her moan by biting her lip as he moved roughly within her, gripping her hips hard. Her pussy trembled around him, and she gripped the vanity for support. She looked up into the mirror meeting his glowing amber gaze and with a knowing smile, he reached his hand around to stroke her clit with his fingers. She cried out softly, never taking her gaze from his in the mirror and responded by thrusting back against him meeting his pounding cock which caused him to groan.

Come for me, ómorfi adelfí psychí mou! Nichola commanded in her mind as his hips drove his cock deeper and faster into her pussy. She could feel his cock grow harder and knew he was close; causing her own orgasm to crash over her. She gave out a soft cry of release which she tried to stifle with her own hand across her mouth.

He quickly followed her, and his cock expanded then burst within her sending his seed deep, causing him to cry out. She quickly reached back to place her hand over his mouth to muffle him. He nibbled against her skin and flicked her palm with his tongue groaning loudly against her hand.

Stop it, you loud-ass vampire! They will hear! She thought at him.

"I don't care." He told her as he withdrew moving to stand beside her and clean himself up. He smiled broadly at her as he zipped up, then pulled her against him to kiss her deeply. "Welcome to the club." He whispered against her lips with a small laugh.

"Out!" She ordered him whispering back.

He chuckled in response, patting her ass through the skirt which was now back in place properly falling straight, and left the lavatory.

She looked at herself in the mirror, shaking her head, then smiled broadly at his behavior, as she put herself to rights.

✳ ✳ ✳ ✳

As she walked back to her seat, she passed the table where Devin, Mansuetus, Fred, and Dene were playing poker. As she was passing Devin murmured with a cheeky smirk "A little bit of a walk of shame thing you got going on there, Mom."

Leila punched him in the arm at the same time as Mansuetus, who sat next to him, hit him in the other arm causing him to yell, "Ow!" and throw his arms up over his head in expectation of more blows. Leila then ignored him as she took her seat, curled up next to Nichola, pillowed her head against his shoulder, and promptly went to sleep.

✳ ✳ ✳ ✳

About an hour out of San Antonio, Burke who had been reading through several magazines that had been provided by Jared, the Dragonfly's steward, looked at Nichola across from him who was engrossed with his tablet. He looked at Leila who still slept deeply and peacefully against his shoulder.

Nichola felt his perusal and looked up in inquiry.

"She seems happy." Burke murmured to him.

"She is for the most part." Nichola told him with a smile, then glanced down at the top of Leila's head. "She is just headstrong, volatile, and unsure of herself, like all young vampires. But, eventually, she will come into her own."

"What's it like?" Burke asked suddenly and Nichola looked at him in surprise.

"Being a soulmate? Or being *her* soulmate?" Nichola was direct.

Burke smiled briefly in chagrin, "Both." He too had decided to be direct.

"Terrifying." Nichola chuckled softly, also with a bit of embarrassment.

162

Brother Mine

As Mansuetus pulled the Yukon into the long drive of Leila's home, the exterior security lights came on. I was impressed with the stucco and stone exterior and was thankful that her husband had provided her with a charming home, since I know that she would never have allowed me to. Knowing her stubbornness I hoped that now that we were together, she would allow me to take care of her.

As she unlocked the double front doors, I followed her into the tiled entryway automatically sending out my senses for any possible hidden danger in the house.

"Princess! Mommy's home!" Leila called out and I could hear small, clawed feet clicking against the ceramic tile of the floor.

A high-pitched yipping bark accompanied a small fawn gray brindle dustmop barreling around the corner of the dining room off of the entrance. The yapping ten-pound ragamuffin who was now leaping around our shins, its tail wagging uncontrollably, was followed sedately by a man with intense blue eyes, short reddish caramel colored hair and a trimmed, darker reddish-brown beard. He was dressed in a long-sleeve dress shirt, pressed jeans, and western style boots.

"Hi Mom!" Zachary said as he gave Leila a quick hug. "Hi Nick." He said and held his hand out to me. I smiled clasping it in greeting.

"Come here, rat dog!" Devin said scooping up the animal. "Let's take you outside for a minute. Hey, Brother!" Devin greeted Zachary as he walked past him into the house. "How's it going? You must be Rom." I heard Devin say from the other room.

Leila rushed up the hallway and into a wide-open living space."Rom! How are you? Is Es here also?"

"Leila!" I heard a deep voice exclaim as I followed her to watch her give Romulus a hug."You are as pretty as a jewel! Es is still at home with our daughter, but they will be heading to Peru in a few weeks."

"Your daughter?!" Leila exclaimed.

"Yes. It's a long story! We have a beautiful daughter that we adopted about ten years ago. She just graduated college, summa cum laude. We are very proud of her!"

"I am sure you are!" Leila said with a wide smile.

"We wouldn't have done it, if not for you, Leila. You showed us what life could be like with children. How so very important that they are. She's been such a blessing to us." He told her with a sincerity that caused her eyes to fill with unshed tears and she hugged him tightly to her once more.

"Hands off my woman!" I chuckled reaching out to grip Romulus by the forearm. "I am glad to see you, my friend. This is a nasty business that we find ourselves in."

"Zachary was filling me in on the case file." Rom indicated photos and reports scattered over the table in the breakfast nook. "This one is a truly evil bastard. Any idea who it is yet?"

"None. I have Peake on it. If he has repeated these murders elsewhere we will know about it, hopefully soon. Let's gather up the files; we will read them when we get to Burke's ranch."

"That's something I thought I would never hear. I always thought you expected to get a knife in your back from the American!"

Leila looked at me quizzically. "It was a misunderstanding on my part." I answered Rom with a small shake of my head.

"It is a misunderstanding that we are going there at all, seeing as he is trying to seduce Leila into his bed!" Mansuetus said as he came into the living room.

"Mansuetus!" Leila whirled, admonishing him for his words.

"It's true." Mansuetus grumbled heading out the back to join Devin in the backyard with the dog.

Leila gave me a glare, to which I held up my hands helplessly. "I can't control him! The older he gets the grouchier and outspoken he is!"

"Do you believe that's true?" She demanded with her fists on her hips.

"True or not, I trust you, i psyhí mou." I said as I wrapped my arms around her. "Besides, who could blame him? You are a ravishing creature."

She gave me a quick kiss; her lips softly brushing my own, then pulled away with a smile to head into what I guessed was her bedroom. "Don't be a suck-up, Nichola."

* * * * *

When Leila returned to the living room her arms full, carrying a medium-sized dog crate, bed, bowls, food, a bag of dog toys, and a small blanket, she noticed the dog sitting on Nichola's lap staring at him intently. They looked to be having a stare down.

He glanced to her, "What is all of that?"

"This is Princess's things; well, some of them anyway." She stated simply and Mansuetus took them from her to load in the car.

Nichola looked back at the dog doubtfully, "Why Princess?" He questioned and the dog speedily wagged its tail at him.

"Because…she's…a…princess." Devin said snarkily as if he was speaking to someone that was slow.

The dog barked once at Nichola, tail never stopping. He squinted at her and murmured low, "You know dog, there was a time I would have eaten you just for amusement." To which the small dog stood to place her tiny paws on his chest and proceeded to lick him in the face, much to his amazement.

"Don't bother trying to put her in her place." Zachary told him laughing from the couch. "She doesn't have any fear and is not impressed by us. We were going to call her Cujo, but it didn't seem to fit with her size."

"We were never going to call her Cujo!" Leila chided opening up the refrigerator and looking inside. "Zachary, are we out of bottled water? I am thirsty." She closed the refrigerator door to find Nichola standing next to her gazing down at her.

"You are hungry." He told her softly.

"What I need is some ice-cold water." She told him firmly.

He backed her up against the kitchen island and she gazed up at him with wide-eyes. He reached behind her and unzipped a small soft-sided cooler, pulling out a bottle of pig's blood. He uncorked it and handed it to her. "Mansuetus brought it from the plane." He answered her unspoken question. As she glanced into the living room to see both Devin and Zachary watching her with fascinated disgust, Nichola pulled her face to him and looked deeply into her eyes. "You gave me your word that you would do what was necessary so that you could be here for your son. Now drink."

Facing him and not facing her children, she tipped the bottle back and drank deeply. She sighed. Nichola whispered in her ear. "Extreme thirst, is a sign of our hunger."

"Everything seems to be a sign of hunger." She mumbled in a whisper taking another long drink.

Nichola looked at her then spoke in her mind, *You might not be wrong. At least when you are young.*

Mansuetus walked into the living room, "Are we ready to go?"

"Yes." Nichola answered, placing a kiss on Leila's forehead, pressing the bottle into her hands, and zipping up the cooler to hand to Mansuetus. "I am going to ride with Rom so that we can discuss the case."

"Uncle Man, would you drive my truck please?" Devin threw a set of keys to Mansuetus. "I am going to ride with my brother."

"But who will drive your mother?" He asked bewildered catching the keys.

"Me!" Dene said gleefully and snatched the Yukon keys out of his hand heading for the front door.

"But you never drive!" Mansuetus exclaimed following after him.

"Only because you never let me." Dene replied.

Nichola kissed Leila briefly, before taking her hand and pulling her to the front door.

* * * * *

"So, you leave because Mom thinks that you are transforming into a vampire, then you come back the same and Mom is a vampire? What the hell, Dev?" Zachary said as soon as he pulled onto the interstate following the directions of his GPS, heading to Kerrville.

"She damn near died, Zach! She got bit by a giant centipede and there was a cave-in! Nick didn't really have a choice, it was push her change or let her die.Would you have wanted that?"Devin started.

"What the hell were you doing in a cave?"

"Searching for Incan treasure!"

"What?"

"You heard me. Some of the people that I have met are really interesting."

"You mean vampires, don't you?" Zachary said dryly.

"Yeah, vampires. But that doesn't mean they aren't people! This guy's ranch that we are going to, his name is Billy Burke, he was a spy for the union army during the Confederate War. He is really cool, Zach! He knew Doc Holliday and Wyatt Earp! He has a gold mine in California. He found all kinds of Incan treasure in Peru. He's also an old-time gunslinger."

"You know, not all vampires are 'cool', Dev! You know what this evil fuck has been doing to these little girls, right?" Zachary growled.

"Zach you are the least judgmental person I know. Don't let this case sour you. They are just like humans. There are good and bad. Would you judge the whole human race if this had turned out to be just a plain-old human serial killer?" Devin asked reasonably.

Zachary was quiet for several minutes. "I suppose not." He finally replied. "So, this Burke dude; he likes Mom? Does Mom like him?"

"I think he does. No, Mom doesn't like him that way. If she did, I think Nick would try to kill him." Devin snickered.

"I don't know. Nick seems pretty even-keeled. It's hard for me to imagine him being violent."

"Well, he's nothing like Dad, that's for sure. But you didn't see him the day Mom got hurt. He was set on hurting Billy. He blamed Billy for Mom getting hurt."

"Was he to blame?" Zach asked quickly.

"Hell no! But he and Nick had some long-standing bullshit between them.

Nick was convinced that Billy had done something intentional to her. I think they have put it past them now though. Which is good, cause I kind of like them both, though Nick can be kind of bossy." Devin said quietly.

"Even though Nick is Mom's 'boyfriend'?" Zachary laughed knowing that Devin had issues with their mother ever being with another guy besides their father.

"Well, I had some issues with him at first, and still kind of do. But I really think he loves her. He seems to make her happy. When she isn't pissed at him anyway. She doesn't stay pissed at him for long. He doesn't let her." Devin smiled.

"Does she love him?" Zachary asked in surprise.

"I don't know, to tell you the truth. I think she tries really hard not to. I'm pretty sure she thinks that he would try to control her if she was in love with him."

"Does he? I can't see that working out so great!" Zachary observed, after having experienced his parents mostly volatile relationship his whole life.

"Actually, no, he doesn't. He pretty much let's her have her way. But he doesn't let her bully him either. She tried to leave him after she first transformed. She moved into one of the separate bungalows at the hotel. He just decided that he wasn't going to let her do that, and now he is living with her in the bungalow. Their relationship is weird and hard to describe. Still, she seems to be happier with him than she is without him."

"It would be nice to really see her happy for once." Zachary's voice was quiet.

"Yeah, it would be." Devin agreed, then changed the subject. "I am glad that Mom told us about our family history."

"Me too. If I didn't know I would never have understood what I was looking at when I first watched that video tape. Maybe now we stand a chance at stopping this murderer." Zachary's voice was firm.

"The way I see it, Brother. This sick fuck was bound to screw up."

"How do you figure?" Zachary asked.

"Because I have learned that there is one enormous difference between the attitudes of vampires and humans. Vampires, because they have lived for so long, have a tendency to think that they are infallible. It's arrogance. That arrogance causes them to make mistakes. We are going to catch this motherfucker. He just thinks that a bunch of unaware human police are searching for a regular serial killer. He never counted on you or anyone like you seeing that video tape. He never considered that he would be recognized for what he is.That's arrogance. Now he can deal with our badass vampire partners." Devin chuckled.

"You know there is no arresting this asshole, right? There is no way we get out of this unbloodied." Zachary's voice was thoughtful.

"I know, Brother, I know." Devin replied soberly in return as they turned off the interstate heading for the ranch.

My Special Beauty

I watched Her approach me in a calm unhurried stride with my dinner goblet; her face now completely healed from Him's fists. Since Him had harvested the dark-haired girl's remaining blood, there were more than enough blood stores in the house to last a few weeks.As Her set my goblet next to me, she refused to meet my gaze, which angered me greatly, though I didn't outwardly show it. Usually, Her would cast a small look of disgust in my direction when she presented me with my food, which entertained and amused me. Ever since I had collected my newest acquisitions, and my loss of control when I took the dark-haired girl, she had been studiously avoiding my gaze.That did not amuse me.

"Her, is there something that you would speak to me about?" I inquired failing to keep the anger from my tone.

"No, Master." Her said meekly, eyes downcast.

"Are you feeling neglected by myself?"

Her looked at me with shocked amazement. "Absolutely not, Master!" She said quickly.

I had forgotten how beautiful Her's pale blue eyes could be, and it had been many years since I had taken Her to my bed or played any of my games with her.My cock stirred at the remembrance.

"If you are feeling neglected, I could make time for you." I murmured looking for her reaction.

A look of loathing flashed through her eyes, before quickly being replaced by a passivity I knew that she did not feel. I smiled at her reaction, there is my amusing beauty. "No, Master. I do not feel neglected." Her's voice was calm and quiet.

"Know this Her, you will always hold a special place in my heart. If you ever feel neglected, you would only have to say so. I would neglect you no more. Do you understand?" I gave her my most charming smile.

She flinched in reaction, entertaining me thoroughly, then nodded once quickly.

"You may go." I waved my hand in dismissal, picking up my goblet to sniff and then sip the fragrant ambrosia that she had brought me.

My chuckle followed Her as she rapidly left my study.

* * * * *

"Good evening, my beauties!" I greeted as I walked naked down the short steep flight of stairs into my dungeon. Sharp screams of dismay greeted me in return. "How are you beauties tonight?" I asked pleasantly.

"What do you want with us?" My special, brave, beauty addressed me. Obviously, her bravery made her the spokesperson of the trio, much to my satisfaction.

"What does any man want of the ladies in his life? Love and affection of course." I smiled at their looks of terror and drank in their emotions.

"You raped and killed our friend, you sick fuck!" She burst out angrily.

"Language child, language." I walked over and slapped her sharply, careful to keep her unmarked. "Ladies do not use such foul language. I apologize about your friend, I had not intended to dispose of her so quickly. But she did attack me, and sometimes these things happen." I said conversationally, smiling pleasantly and showing my fangs.

Tears flowed over her cheeks as she asked in a shuddering voice, "What are you?"

"Why I am God, of course. Your god. That makes me the only god that matters." I knelt before her, wiping her tears from her beautiful face as she froze in place from my touch. "But I need not be a harsh god." I told her as I stood and uncuffed my Latin beauty who whimpered piteously in terror.

171

"Why? Why are you doing this to us?" The little freckled beauty ask trembling in voice and body as she gripped my special beauty's hand.

"Because I can." I answered her simply with a small smile, as I pulled the Latin beauty's resisting body to a fairly clean mattress on the other side of the small dungeon, but well within the view of my other two beauties. "You will find as we get to know each other better that I can be a merciful and kind god. I can even give you pleasure. All you have to do is worship and obey."

"What the hell does that mean?" My brave beauty burst out.

I pulled sharply on the Latin beauty's black silky hair, baring her throat to me, causing her to cry out. "Language!" My special beauty looked at me in horror. "Be warned. Your sharp words to me will cause harm." She placed her hand over her mouth, nodding to me as tears ran from her eyes.

I extended my long tongue and ran it over my dark beauty's throat causing the other two beauties to gasp in panic and the dark little beauty to mewl in terror like a frightened kitten. "As with any god, I can give pleasure or pain." I ripped the clothes from her body as she screamed.

"Oh Dios, por favor, sálvame de este demonio!" She begged squeezing her eyes shut tightly.

"No más oraciones, mi belleza oscura. Eres mía." I returned softly gently cupping her small breast. "Mírame. Mirame ahora."I ordered and she opened her eyes to gaze up at me starkly.

I captured her gaze with my own, willing her to relax. Willing her to want me; to give herself to me. Willing her to love me.

I felt her body tremble first in panic as she tried to fight my will, then in desire as she succumbed. I felt her heartbeat quicken against my palm on her breast and the bouquet of her arousal met my nose as I brushed my lips gently against her skin.

"Yes, my sweet." I breathed as I laid my dark beauty tenderly down on the mattress with me and her arms rose of their own accord over my scarred back with a small moan. Glancing toward my other two beauties. "You see, I can be gentle. The choice is yours." I whispered beaming at them.

I looked down into the pleasant, fresh face of my dark beauty and took her full lips in a deep kiss, nicking her plush bottom lip with my fangs. I sipped at the sweet spicy blood drawn there as I ran my hands down her slender but budding body causing her to gasp out in passion.I then looked over at the horror upon the faces of the other two beauties.

"When you learn that you are all just glorious sluts to be taken and used as the whores that you all are, you will be fulfilling your purpose and you will enjoy your life so much better; and, so will I." I murmured to them as I kissed my way down the dark-haired beauty's almost hairless body.

* * * * *

Her knelt in the corner of the bathroom upstairs trying to hold in her sobs of horror with her hands over her mouth, knowing what that monster was doing to one of the young girls in the dungeon, remembering her own experience at his hands years ago. She looked up in supplication to silently pray, *Please God, please do something to make it stop.*

Homo Sapiens Lupus

＿✦✦✦＿

Well, Mr. Burke was right about one thing, his ranch was definitely rural. Dene, Princess, and I had been slowly driving for five minutes since turning off onto the rutted dirt road of his ranch. Still there were no lights for a ranch house in sight; nothing but wide-open land.

"Dene, I really haven't had a chance to talk too much to you, privately, since Devin and I arrived in Peru. How are you really doing?" I started hesitantly.

He gave me a quick smile, before turning his attention back to the dark rugged road. "I am doing really well, Leila."

"Really?" I questioned.

"Yeah, really! I am not going to pretend that I don't know what you are talking about. But, to tell you the truth, it's been more than ten years since Iris moved-in with Aleksei. At first I was crushed, sure. I really loved her, Leila. But she didn't love me; not in the same way that I did her. Not like that. Frankly, a lot of our time together was hell for me. She was only faithful for a short amount of time. She tried to hide it at first, and then she was just right out in the open about it. If I hadn't been tied to her through the companion bond, I would have left her years before she left me."

"So, you no longer have a companion bond?" I asked surprised.

"I do. Nick replaced Iris's bond with his own. His bond keeps me sane.

When she left, I was beside myself with anguish. I hurt so bad I couldn't even bury myself in my work. It was actually crippling; I have never felt so much mental and physical pain in my entire life. Nick helped me big time, Leila. I wasn't sure I was going to make it. Nick helped me get past her. He is a better guy than I ever gave him credit for. He could have just ended me, a lot of vampires would have. But he always treated me with respect while Iris and I lived with him, and after she left me with him, he still believed in me.I owe him everything, Leila."

I was quiet for a minute considering everything that he had told me.I felt bad for him. Until he had gotten involved with my family he had so much promise as a doctor.

"Leila, I know what you are thinking." Dene said softly.

"Do you?" I asked.

"Yes, I know you. Listen to me.You can't change the past. I have learned so much about so many things that I never would have had the opportunity to even know about if I had remained in the 'regular' world." He smiled his sexy boyish smile as he emphasized the word 'regular'. "Having Nick as a sponsor, I still have my research. He supports me in all of my projects, and he is not stingy with funding! Look at everything I have done with my sun block product. Look at what I have done with my DNA testing and database. I am changing the way vampires think and the way that they behave; and it's been really positive for their community. Hell, I am indirectly responsible for Rom and Es having a daughter!"

"What do you mean?" I asked shocked.

"Well, I heard Rom tell you about his daughter. They adopted her because her parents were killed by what vampires are now referring to as a rogue. It happened about eleven years ago. Some made vampire went crazy and started killing what we originally thought was random people. Well, it wasn't so random. His victims were all humans and their families who carried the same type of vampire gene."

"What?!" I exclaimed shocked.

"Yes. He had been trying to take out his maker's human line." Dene looked at me for a moment and I was speechless. "Yeah, hard to wrap your head around, right?

You know, Nick really threw himself into his businesses and his duties for the small council when you chose to remain human. I think that giving himself something important to do kept him sane." He faced forward again, sliding me a glance out of the corner of his eye, making me feel guilty.

"Well, anyway, during the investigation, Rom and Nick personally took him out. They ended up saving the little girl, though they weren't able to save her parents. I ran some cursory tests on her blood. She does carry the vampire gene but had no one in the vampire community still living who was related to her, so was bound for a life in a human foster home. Well, once Esmerelda found out, she insisted on adopting her. They have actually been really good parents to her, and they love each other very much."

I smiled glad that Es had been happy all of these years.

"So, Leila, I answered your questions. Now answer one of mine. What's it like?" Dene glanced at me briefly.

I uncorked the bottle of pig's blood that Nichola had insisted I take with me and took a long drink. "Being a vampire? It's different and then again it's not. It's intense."

"Thanks, Leila. That's a little vague." Dene smirked at me.

"I always feel like something is missing inside." I whispered facing forward to look at the high beams on the rutted road. "Nichola says that is the hunger. Basically, he says that everything I feel is hunger. But to be honest, after Nichola gave me his venom to stop my transformation all of those years ago, I have been feeling empty inside anyway. That's what I mean when I say that it's different, but then again it's not." I took another sip from the bottle. "I feel more anchored today, than I did the very first day. The first day, I just felt adrift. On the edge of losing control."

"Well, you are definitely changing daily. I can see it, and not just physically either but in the way you move, in your attitude. You seem pretty calm, overall. You seem calmer than most young vampires that I have seen. They all usually seem to be, I don't know how to explain it, a little jumpy maybe, sort of uncertain in their own skin. You definitely are much calmer than when you were transitioning all of those years ago." He grinned. "That probably has a lot to do with Nick. He really helped Iris when we first moved-in with him. Just being around him helped. She was able to pull herself together and to regain control of herself. I don't know if you realize how bad it was, but she was really on the edge for quite a while."

"Yes, she was kind of a mess." I agreed. "So, in your medical opinion, how's Devin doing?" I asked changing the subject.

"In my medical opinion? Dev's doing okay. He's moody, but that is par for the course. He's hardheaded like his Mom, so he's difficult to pinpoint exactly." He gave me a cheeky, playful grin, and I shoved him gently on the shoulder. "But he seems to be transitioning normally. There hasn't been any sign of fang growth yet."

"That didn't happen to me until after I was with Nichola a few times." I didn't want to go into any details.

Dene smiled. "Well, he was okay the other night. Mansuetus, Fred and I kept an eye on him."

"Excuse me?"

"You know how it gets sometimes when vampires have sex. We didn't want him to get wild and hurt her since she was just a human, so we just all stayed in the same room..."

"Stop!" I said suddenly realizing what he was telling me. "I don't want to know any of the details!"

"Okay...Mom." He chuckled.

"Exactly, Mom does not want to know!" I put my fingers to my temple. I could feel a headache coming on.

✴ ✴ ✴ ✴ ✴

When Leila and Dene finally arrived at Burke's ranch house, there seemed to be something going on in the circular-drive in front of the large stone home. Devin, Zachary, and Mansuetus were leaning against Zachary's car, Devin looked disgruntled and irritated with his arms crossed, watching. On the other side of the drive, there were several people, men who looked to be ranch hands, a few women, and even a couple of children to one side watching Nichola and Burke having an intense discussion. Leila knew it was intense as they parked the car because she could see Nichola gesturing

177

to the people animatedly as he spoke to Burke, and she could tell that Rom was standing behind him ready in case something broke out.

"Now what?" Leila murmured to Dene as they got out of the car and approached them.

"You didn't think to mention that your people were wolf-shifters before I brought my family out here to your ranch, William? Do you care so little for my family's safety?" Nichola ground out between clenched teeth.

"Don't be ridiculous! This pack has sworn their loyalty to me for the last three generations! My guests no matter what their stripe, are always safe here!" Leila noticed that Burke was standing with his arms crossed in much the same manner that Devin was.

"C'mon Nick!" Devin interrupted, causing several sets of eyes to fall on him in surprise. "You are just being prejudiced! If Billy says his people are fine, then they are fine."

"You are too young to know what you are speaking about, boy!" Nichola used his *voice*, pushing his power at him.

To which Devin came off of the car defiantly, standing straight with his hands fisted, to snap, "And you are just too goddamned old to keep up with the times! None of us here are human! What good does it do to hold old grudges? We are better off learning to cooperate with each other..." to which Mansuetus wrapped an arm around his chest to hold him in place.

Leila knew that it was for his own protection as Nichola's eyes flared red and he took a step towards him. She quickly stepped up to Nichola and pushed Princess into his arms, who proceeded to nuzzle against him happily. He looked down at the dog bewildered by how she had gotten there.

"Mr. Burke, do you personally guarantee our safety while we are here?"Leila asked him calmly.

Burke placed his hand on his chest looking around Leila to look at Nichola sincerely, "I do, Klaus." Nichola once again glared at him. "I give you my word that your family is safe here. You are my guests, and my people hold no danger to you or yours. They will give their lives to protect you as well as they do me. Isn't that correct, Mitch?" He looked at a large man with arctic blue eyes, who looked to be in his early forties, and was almost as tall and muscular as Mansuetus. He stepped forward to stand next to Burke.

"That's right, Boss! You have my word also, Mr. Tsoukalous, that neither my pack or I are a threat to you or your family." His voice was a deep gravelly bass. "We keep all those who reside here safe from harm. It is our job, and we take it very seriously. We are looking forward to being a part of your hunt for this sick killer."

Leila could feel his sincerity. She looked at Nichola who looked at Rom, who in turn shrugged.

"How are your noses?" Rom asked the big man with a twinkle in his dark eyes.

Mitch grinned a toothy smile in return, "The best."

* * * * *

I was unpacking and putting away our clothes in the room that Mr. Burke's housekeeper had shone me to, and Princess was lounging on the king size bed making sure that I didn't leave her sight, when I heard from the doorway, "Kyría, would you like some help?"

I turned to see Mansuetus standing in the door, and Princess's tail started to make a speedy staccato beat against the bedspread. She rolled over onto her back as the big man walked over to rub her belly.

"No, thank you, Mansuetus. I am almost done."

"You have put Kýrios's things away also?" He asked softly.

"Yes." I looked over my shoulder to him realizing that he was the one to always take care of Nichola. "Is that okay?" I asked gently.

"Absolutely, Kyría. I have more than enough to keep me busy." He gave me a grin.

"You mean with Devin, don't you?" I softly returned his smile.

He gave a laugh. "Yes, life with the young master is not going to be boring."

"Where is he?" I asked.

"He is in Burke's office gathered around the conference table with the others. Zachary is briefing them on the details of the case file for this killer."

"I am surprised that you aren't there."

"Fred is taking care of some ranch business, Dene is unpacking, and I am here visiting with you." He smiled at me as if in explanation.

"You are here to protect me?" I asked raising my eyebrow in his direction knowing how he was. "Are you worried about the wolf-shifters?"

"No, I am not worried. The man who spoke outside, Mitch; he is their alpha. Wolf-shifters are very honorable for the most part and his tone was sincere.Besides, he is also being briefed.I read the case file earlier on the plane. Zachary sent it to me." He smiled at me widely.

"So, you are a head of the game?" I smiled at his nod. "If Mitch is there who is guarding Nichola and the boys?" I was suddenly concerned.

"Not worried about the wolf-shifters, remember? Besides, Kýrios would kill him before he could even see it coming." He grinned at me.

"Then why was he so upset about them?" I asked sitting down on the bed on the opposite side of Princess to join in petting her; she was in heaven at all of the attention she was receiving.

"Burke is too young to know, but at the end of the thirteenth century, vampires and the shifter world in general were at war with each other. It was a bloody, dangerous time and there were massive casualties on all fronts. That's when the vampire race made a decision to band together under a governing body instead of going solo or in isolated communities like they had for millennia."

"So Nichola is worried about old resentments?" I asked.

"Not for himself, but he is always concerned about you and your children.The fact that Burke has aligned himself with wolf-shifters would be nothing if you and the boys weren't involved on this trip, or if he had been upfront about it in the beginning. It was just a shock to see.

I know that Kýrios agrees with Devin's sentiment of collaborating with non-human factions; especially since overall, the vampires were the victors in the war.It is one thing to agree with that sentiment, and quite another to leave the security of his mate and son to what was at one time an enemy. He is also smart enough to know that he cannot control the actions of other species as well as he can other vampires and you will be here on your own much of this trip."

"Oh, that's not happening!" I told him with a laugh. "I am not sticking around this ranch bored. I live in this area. I know my way around and I don't have the sun keeping me from going anywhere."

"Kyría…" Mansuetus began.

"No, Mansuetus. I will agree that I probably wouldn't be great on the investigation, and I would feel better knowing that you are with Nichola and Zachary. Besides, I will have Devin and Dene with me."

"And me, Ms. Sutton!" Fred said smiling from the doorway. "The Boss has told me that he wants me to keep an eye on you and Master Devin." Princess jumped down from the bed with a sharp bark and ran to Fred to jump up against his knees. He bent down and picked her up and she gave him little kisses as her tail wagged enthusiastically against him. "What a sweet little dog! She looks like that dog on *The Wizard of Oz*!" Fred exclaimed with a smile holding her close.

"Have you seen *The Wizard of Oz*, Mr. Fred?" I asked smiling at the man's obvious affection for my dog.

"Oh, yes, ma'am! Several times. I loved the moving pictures when they came out! I loved Judy Garland. Better than dance hall girls any day! This dog is not the right color, but she sure looks like the same dog!" Fred said scratching Princess under the chin, much to her delight.

"Well, she is the same breed as Toto. She's a little on the small side though. Her name is Princess." I told him.

"Well, Princess!" Fred exclaimed to the dog, holding her up to smile up into her small face. "I'll bet you that there is some leftover beefsteak in the fridge, let's see what we can dig up for you to eat and fatten you up a bit."With that statement, Fred headed off down the hall with my dog.

I looked at Mansuetus, who shrugged. "It's strange how you all don't seem to get the whole pet thing. You all seem to like them very much." I told him.

"It takes a special animal to bond with a vampire, Kyría. Though you showed us the way when we first met you and your children. Even Rom and Es obtained a cat for their daughter." He smiled standing. "We had better see that Fred doesn't overfeed Princess."

I laughed and followed him out the door.

* * * * *

Devin, Zachary and Nichola walked into the kitchen where Princess was

181

eating the steak pieces that Fred had prepared for her. Mansuetus and Leila were sitting at the kitchen table watching her and Fred had disappeared to make sure that the rest of the guest rooms were ready.

"I would speak to you privately, Devin." Nichola addressed him quietly.

"What do you want?" Devin's voice was belligerent as he sat down at the kitchen table with his mother and Mansuetus.

"Devin, you do not know the history between wolf-shifters and vampires…" Nichola began in a reasonable tone.

"Oh, give me a break!" Devin spat out argumentatively. "You are just overly sensitive and prejudicial!"

"Devin." Nichola was obviously struggling to maintain his composure. "You need to listen to me on this…"

"You're not my father!" Devin snarled at Nichola.

Immediately, Nichola's whole demeanor became hostile, the threat of violence flowed from him as his eyes flashed red at Devin. "No. I am not!"He said harshly in his *voice.*"I am your elder, I am your mother's mate, I lead this family and you are a member of my family, my bloodline!Until you understand the dangers that wolf-shifters are to vampires you will follow my guidance and take care! Also, I will not expect you to interfere again when I am having a conversation about the safety of this family. If you have concerns or comments to make, you may bring them up to me privately. In public, this family shows a united front!"

"You don't tell me what to do…" Devin returned, though his voice was much quieter in awe of Nichola's fury and power that was washing over him.

"I do tell you what to do!" Nichola pushed harder with his power. "I am your elder and you will obey me!"

Devin stood with difficulty, struggling to push Nichola's power from him which had become almost a physical force, and walked out onto the back porch slamming the door behind him.

Zachary, Mansuetus and Leila looked at Nichola who glared after him.Nichola walked over to Leila bent down and kissed her hard on the lips, then began, "Your son…"

"I know, he's very stubborn. It's not easy being a parent is it? But you are being very patient, and I am so proud of your control. At least he didn't cuss at you. You know how much you hate that." Leila said with a small teasing smile.

Nichola closed his eyes, breathed deeply, then kissed her softly.

* * * * *

Devin stood on the back porch crossing his arms in anger after slamming the door. Zachary quickly followed behind in concern.

Burke stepped out of the shadows, blowing smoke from his cheroot. "What's up, young bucks?" He asked with a smile.

"Devin and Nick had an argument." Zachary told him with a smirk walking over to Burke.

"He's a dick!" Devin threw a thumb over his shoulder towards the door and walked over to where Burke was leaning against a stone column holding up the back porch.

Burke gave a sharp laugh, "Yep, he can be, when he gets his back up over something."

"Well, he doesn't get to tell me what to do! I'm not a kid! Just because he's putting the wood to my mother doesn't make him my father!" Devin ground out furiously.

Zachary looked shocked and opened his mouth to say, "Hey!"

"Whoa! Don't talk about your mama like that boy! She don't have anything to do with this! You show her some damn respect!" Burke's drawl was sharp as he pointed the butt end of his cheroot at him.

"Sorry, Billy. I shouldn't have said that about mom." Devin said ducking his head and flushing in shame at Burke's rebuke. "That damn Nick pisses me off is all."

"Well, he is old as dirt, but he is your family. Gotta respect your elders. Gotta respect your family. I've known him for a long time and he's okay. Even if he wasn't involved with your mother, he woulda' still taken you in during your transition, 'cause you're his family. Gotta respect someone who loves their family and wants what's best for them. No matter what the disagreement. I envy you young men." Burke's Texas drawl was heavy, and he suddenly clapped a hand on Devin's shoulder to address him. "You are lucky, boy. You are a young transitioning vampire, and you continue to stand toe-to-toe with that long-toothed old dog in there and he lets you get by with it. But don't push too hard because he's not as soft as you think.Come on boys, I got a bottle of whiskey in my office." Burke smiled as he led them along the expansive back porch to a door that led into his brightly lit office.

* * * * *

I was stepping out of the shower when Leila and her dog came into the bedroom.The small dog walked into the bathroom to stare up at me and when I looked down into its eyes, it wagged its tail wildly, making me smile.

Walking out of the bathroom with a towel wrapped around my waist I was drying my hair with another towel when I looked up to see Leila staring at my body hungrily.Her voracious eyes stirred more than my own appetite and I could feel myself grow hard under her gaze.

"I psychí mou, if you continue to look at me like that…" I began then found myself pushed against the wall.

Surprised that she had used her vampiric speed, I met her red eyes briefly, slightly shocked at her aggressiveness, then her lips covered mine in a rough deep kiss. I could feel her sharp fangs against my lips. *This is different.* I thought enjoying my aggressive mate's soft lips as I felt her remove the towel from my body to wrap her hand around my now raging stiff cock. I groaned into her mouth as she pumped me. I tried to pull away to take control and she was having none of it.

With one strong hand on my chest, she held me against the wall as she knelt before me. Briefly looking up, her red eyes shone devilishly into my own, as she first blew on the head of my cock, compelling me to arch toward her, then took me deeply into her mouth, running her strong tongue over me. A deep moan involuntarily escaped my lips. *O Theé mou, I love when she does this!*

I wrapped my hand into her silken strands and fucked her mouth deeply pushing myself into her throat, half expecting that she would pull back and release me, instead she ran her hands around my hips to grab my ass clutching me to her, sucking my cock ever harder. I could feel the muscles in my legs tremble as she fellated me, and extreme pleasure ran up my spine. I didn't even try to stop the moans that escaped my lips. I could smell her heady arousal in the air, and it made me wild as I gripped her tightly to me and thrust myself over and over into her mouth.

I rode the edge of release as I quickly stroked and with a shout I came, then felt her fangs pierce me and she drank deeply of my seed and my blood. I moaned as she drew on me making small mewling sounds deep in her throat. I felt her tongue run over the base of my cock, sealing the puncture marks made by her fangs, then she pulled back to look up at me wickedly.

"God, I love you." I whispered sincerely gazing down in her now teal-colored eyes.

"Well, I should hope so." She laughed, pulling me over to the bed, forcing me to lay down. I laid their feeling weak, in a haze of pleasure, and after a minute she climbed up my body, naked, to straddle my face, making me moan and I buried my tongue in her wet channel, greedily drinking in her succulent juices.

I adored this dominant sexual side of her that was emerging with her vampire nature, her vampire hunger, and was more than content to worship at the temple of her body. I quickly and repeatedly flicked my tongue over her clit and then held her tightly to me as she came on my face with a shocked cry.

I flipped her onto her side, moving behind her to grip her leg and pull it up to her chest and swiftly thrust up and into her body, enjoying the way her tight muscles gripped my cock and fluttered around me in the aftershocks of her orgasm. She cried out in ecstasy as I thrust deeply, moving my hand to stroke her clit.

"Oh, Nichola!" She gasped out thrilling me. I loved to hear my name on her lips.

"Yes, moró. Come on my cock." I whispered into her ear, feeling her heart beating rapidly through her back against my chest, as I thrust even deeper until I was buried in her tightness to my balls.

I continued thrusting and stroking her, as she moaned out her desire, pacing my passion with hers. She yelled out as I felt her clamp down on me with the muscles of her pussy as she came again, and I thrust deeply, coming also, softly groaning out in pleasure, feeding her my orgasmic energy. She was my sweetest desire and I loved to give her every part of me.

Holding her shivering, spasming body tightly against my chest, I then gently bit down on the side of her throat to sip her fragrant, delicious, blood.

* * * * *

Nichola slowly roused to feel Princess move from where she had been sleeping in the middle of his chest to go over and stand on Leila's shoulder. He smiled contentedly as he heard her whisper to the small dog, "Okay, Mommie will take you."

Feeling his vampiric internal clock, he knew that though it was very dark outside that dawn wasn't too far away. Through half-opened eyes, he watched as Leila put on a short, white silky nightgown, then covered it with a peignoir, then led the small dancing dog out the bedroom door.

* * * * *

I gazed up at the dark cloudless sky, watching the stars twinkling brightly, as Princess roamed the yard. There is something about a Texas Hill Country night sky, so clear, and bright with stars that was always soothing to my soul.

"Couldn't sleep, Ms. Sutton?"

I heard Burke behind me and looked over my shoulder at him. His dark silky hair was sleep-tousled, his feet were bare, and he wore dark pants and an open white shirt, exposing his beautiful muscular chest.

I smiled at him briefly, "I was sleeping fine until Princess woke me up to take her out. Too much beefsteak from Mr. Fred, I think." I turned to look back up into the sky.

"Yes, he seems to be enamored of your dog." Burke's quiet chuckle was near, just over the back of my shoulder. "It's pretty out here tonight." His voice was soothing.

I turned to find him behind me, too close, looking down at me with a gentleness in his eyes. "Mr. Burke, Mansuetus made a comment earlier that disturbed me." I turned to look back up into the sky.

"Really what was that?" He whispered in my ear, and I knew that he was breathing in my scent.

"He says that you are trying to seduce me."

There was a brief silence behind me, and then I felt his warm breath against my ear, "And if I am? Are you tempted?" His voice was deep, soft, tantalizing, and hungry.

"I wish that you wouldn't, Mr. Burke." I told him sincerely, not looking at him. "For many reasons, my relationship with Nichola notwithstanding, but mostly because you seem to be a good man and my sons like you. This blood bond that we have because of our accident, this fascination, will go away, eventually. If we act on that fascination, it will only leave ashes in its wake."

"My fascination for you began before I ever tasted your blood, Leila." His words were soft, and his breath caressed my hair. I could feel the heat from his body in the cool Texas night.

Suddenly, Princess started barking frantically. I looked into the darkness for her, not seeing her as her barking became high-pitched and fearful, I moved into the darkness yelling, "Princess, where are you?"

* * * * *

A massive shape from the direction of the house leaped past Leila and Burke into the night. Suddenly, there were high-pitched snarls and then terrorized, pained barks and yips, and smaller dog-like shapes rounded the side of the house to join in the melee that was occurring just out of sight on the edge of Burke's expansive yard. Leila moved to run to the sounds, screaming, "Princess!"

Burke grabbed her quickly and held her back. "No, Ms. Sutton! Don't get into that, you might get hurt, the wolf shifters are killing something."

"Princess!" Leila shrieked, yanking away, and moving with vampiric speed ended up in the middle of a battle where wolves were tearing a pack of coyotes to bloody shreds. A few stragglers ran away into the night and as Burke arrived behind her, the bloodied wolves turned to look at the massive creature standing over a small animal facing off with the wolves.

Leila recognized the dog that she found in Peru but looking between it and the wolves she realized that it was a different type of wolf, at least a foot taller and much heavier. Compared to the wolves facing it, it was huge.

The larger multi-colored wolf showed no fear and faced off with the pack.The wolves facing it slowly crouched submissively, one by one. The large wolf bent down and took the small animal in its mouth gently turning to bring it to Leila who knelt and reached out for it crying out, "Oh, no!Princess!"

She is unharmed, agapitós. She is just frightened. Leila heard in her mind.

As she took Princess from the wolf's mouth pulling her into her arms against her chest, Leila felt Princess move against her and softly nuzzle and kiss her throat, as her small body trembled in fear.

"Nichola?" Leila questioned reaching out a hand toward the large wolf, who moved into her embrace as she sobbed in relief, holding both Princess and the wolf tightly against her.

The wolf looked up at Burke and gave a snarl.

"I knew it was you all along!" Burke pointed to the wolf and the wolf gave a sharp warning bark and snapped at him, causing Burke to leap back.

* * * * *

Mansuetus, the boys, Romulus and Dene came bounding out of the house in various stages of undress to stare at them. "What's going on?" Mansuetus asked in concern.

Rom looked at the wolf that was walking towards the back of the house with Leila and Burke following behind. "Nikolaos? Were you on a run?"

"Princess was almost attacked by coyotes!" Leila exclaimed.

"Is she alright?" Zachary said worriedly walking to his mother.

"Yes, Nichola and the wolf shifters saved her." Leila told him as he pet the shaking dog in her arms.

"Did you know that he could shift?" Burke asked Rom.

"You are still relatively young, Burke. Most born vampires develop this ability as they age." Rom replied to a shocked looking Burke.

"Can you do this also?" Burke asked him.

Rom answered with a smirk, crossing his arms. "We rarely discuss abilities, Burke. If you and I were to battle, why should you know my strengths or weaknesses?"

"Okay, that's a yes." Devin said snarkily.

To which Rom gave him a good-natured, but enigmatic smile.

Nichola made a huffing noise and Mansuetus opened the back door for him.

Come back to bed, i psychí mou. Leila heard in her mind.

She responded out loud, "Okay, I am coming," and the others looked at her.She ignored them and followed Nichola into the house, as she heard Mansuetus urging everyone to go back to bed since they all needed to be up in a few hours.

Leila sat down on the bed and placed Princess next to her. Princess immediately jumped down and ran to Nichola, who had sat down next to the bed after Leila had closed the bedroom door, to dance around his large wolf form, jumping up to try to lick him in the face.

"Do you think she knows it's you?" Leila asked him.

Somewhere in her animal mind she probably does. My vampire scent is intertwined with the scent of the wolf.She is most assuredly not afraid of me in this form. Wolf Nichola placed a paw gently on the top of Princess's head, and she nipped playfully at his paw dancing out of the way.

"We are soulmates, you are not supposed to be able to lie to me!" Leila suddenly exclaimed.

When did I lie to you?

"You made me think that I had found a dog in Peru! You didn't tell me it was you! You even slept in my bed! You made me look like a fool! You tricked me!" Leila said getting angrier as she thought about it.

I have been very straightforward with you about my not being separated from you anymore. I will not be banned from your bed because you are angry with me. You will always be angry with me over something, Leila. We are a couple, disagreements will occur. So, I refuse to be kicked out of your bed because you decide you are angry about something, and I will never live separate from you again. Did I trick you? Yes.But I didn't lie to you; I just let you believe what you were inclined to believe in order to be near you.Since you have become a full vampire, the need to be near you is overwhelming. Besides, if I weren't in your bed that night I am sure that William would have worked his way into your bungalow and into your bed. Jealousy poured from his thoughts.

Leila gasped in outrage glaring at him. "That is not true!"

189

Well, we will never know now because I was there in this form and made sure that it didn't occur. After overhearing the conversation between the two of you before the dog was attacked, I wouldn't have been surprised! He obviously has been interested in you from the beginning and you weren't very strident in deterring him. Wolf Nichola paced back and forth in irritation, and Princess jumped up on the bed next to Leila to watch him.

"If you heard our conversation then you know what I told him!" Leila said hotly.

Please Mr. Burke do not attempt to seduce me, you are such a good man, and my children really like you. Great deterrence, Leila. Nichola's thoughts were mocking.

"I am unused to men pursuing me! I didn't even know that he was, until Mansuetus said something about it!I was trying to be kind and polite!"She snarled in reply. "Are you going to change back? Or does this shit wear off?" Leila demanded angrily with a wave of her hands.

Since he is terrified of me in this form, I am trying to decide whether I am going to track him down and frighten him until he pisses himself! Nichola thought at her then met Leila's shocked eyes for a heartbeat.

Suddenly, she burst out laughing and she could hear Nichola's answering chuckle in her mind. She then said, "He certainly is afraid of you like this."

He would be afraid of Princess if she were larger. It's amazing that he allows wolf-shifters to manage his ranch.

"Well, they aren't animals. Are they?"Leila asked curious.

It is different from when I shift. They are more controlled by their animal instincts than I am. Most types of shifters take the actual size of their shift animal regardless of how large or small they are in their human form. This is why my wolf form is so much larger than a normal wolf, because I am as a man larger than a wolf. The wolves contend that their animal form has a separate soul.But still others when they shift, take a form that is a cross between their animal and a human. Such as the Naga; a truly cold, uncaring, and dangerous species. They shift into a snake-man and have a tendency to steal human women indiscriminately for breeding. Though their kind may be extinct. We did our best to ensure that, during the vampire-shifter war, in cooperation with many other mammalian shifters such as the wolves, tigers, and bears, I should add.

"There are a lot of things that I still have no clue about, isn't there?"Leila interrupted his thought looking at him and feeling lost.

He leaped up on the bed, causing her to gasp in surprise and wrestled her down to lay across her body. *You are so young, i psychí mou.* He nuzzled against her throat, and she thought that he was trying to comfort her. *There are so many things for me to teach you. But you have centuries to learn them. You could learn something new today by having sex with me in this form...*

Sleuthing for a Killer

―――

As they followed Zachary through the police station to his captain's office, Nichola thought back to parting with Leila after breakfast. He intentionally gave Leila a disgruntled look as she quickly leaned up to give him a small kiss goodbye against the side of his mouth. *Don't look at me like that Nichola. You didn't really expect me to have sex with you in your wolf form. You look very nice by the way.* Leila thought soothingly as she smoothed her hands over his navy, light-weight pin-striped suit and solid, gold tie.

You disappoint me, i psychi mou. You always tell me 'no' and do not accept me as I am. I feel as if you do not love me for my whole self. He had pouted at her.

That is not true! She was appalled that he would think such a thing and then realized what he was up to. *You are so kinky!* She thought shocked, squinting her eyes in irritation at his attempted manipulation of her future capitulation.

You have yet to experience the half of it.But you will eventually. He thought in return smiling wickedly at her in promise.

Nichola focused his attention on the task at hand as Zachary knocked on his captain's door once, then followed him as he entered upon hearing the captain's voice.

Captain Keith Miles looked up in surprise. He had been sitting in his office pissed off because he was feeling sidelined by the Feds who seemed to be

192

taking over the outer spaces and the investigation. He wasn't the center of attention on this case, and as far as he was concerned their interference made it seem like the San Antonio Police Department couldn't toe the line. A fault he firmly placed on Sutton and his team.

"Sir, I would like to introduce you to the specialist teams that Washington and Austin have sent down to assist with the abduction and murders of these girls."Zachary began as Mile's look turned sourer. "This is Dr. Nick Tsoukalous, his assistant's Dr. Richard Romulus and Mr. John Mann.Dr. Tsoukalous's team works with both the FBI and Interpol in the profiling, tracking and apprehension of serial killers. This is Professor William Miles and his assistant Mitch Matheson, they are consultants for the Texas Rangers and the division of Intelligence and Counterterrorism Division of DPS."

Miles ignored what he considered to be outsiders to focus on the two obvious Texans. William was wearing a black lightweight blazer, white button shirt, and boot cut black jeans, black western boots, and a black Telescope hat. Mitch was wearing a brown blazer, white button shirt, pressed dark blue jeans, deep brown western boots, and a camel-colored Cattleman hat.Both wore bolo ties.

"Professor Miles." Captain Miles held out his hand.

William stepped forward to grasp it firmly returning, "Captain."

"Where's your family from, Professor?" Captain Miles asked.

"Kerrville, sir."

"My family is from El Paso." Keith Miles smiled warmly, much to Zachary's surprise.

"I am sure we have a distant relation between us then." William Miles a.k.a. Burke used his folksy Texas drawl and gave him a charming smile like he had just met his brother from another mother.

"What can I do for you and your teams?" Keith Miles sat down and motioned them to sit. Nichola and William sat in the two chairs in front of the desk, while the others assumed the chairs around the conference table and Zachary stood against the wall.

"Captain," Nichola began using his *voice*. "We have been discussing the case in detail with Detective Sutton, who has been very helpful by the way. We find ourselves in a quandary, sir. You see, neither myself nor the professor, travel with or have the inclination to hire a public relations assistant. I believe I am speaking correctly when I say that the last people that we like to interact with is the press." Here he looked to William.

"You are correct, Doc," William acknowledged with a nod.

"Detective Sutton has told us that of all the people he has seen deal with the press, you are the most skilled." Nichola told the captain who glanced at Zachary in surprise and then sat up proudly at the praise. "We were wondering, if you would lead the efforts in interacting with the press?Run interference so that they don't pollute this investigation any more than they already have. The professor and myself have found that they have a tendency to alert the quarry, of pursuit, despite it not being in the best interests or safety of the public. Would you be willing to take point on that front, Captain?" Nichola's *voice* persuaded.

"Well, I don't know..." Captain Keith Miles started in surprise.

"Captain, we," William motioned to Nichola, "need a man of your skill.Besides, it won't be without a mutual benefit. We will directly supply you all of our investigative findings, before we report them back to our respective agencies." Here Keith Miles eyebrows rose as William's *voice* flowed over him."We desire no contact with the press whatsoever. In fact, we find it better for the investigation if they don't even know that we exist. Full credit for any of our findings would go straight to you and to the Homicide Division.We are only interested in stopping this bastard. But we need a skilled man like yourself to keep those sidewinders in the press at bay."His Texas charm rolled off of him to wash over the captain.

Captain Keith Miles found himself mildly surprised when his own words were sincere, "I would be honored to assist you in this way gentlemen.Anything that we can do to catch this killer. Myself, Detective Sutton and his team are at your disposal."

* * * * *

"I am so going to get fired if they find out that you guys aren't who you say you are." Zachary mumbles as they walk down the hall, away from the captain's office.

"You must have faith in me and Mansuetus, son." Nichola claps him on the shoulder in reassurance. "Your mother refers to me as a stalker. But I prefer to think of myself as prepared for all possibilities, wherever she lives. Out of necessity in the last several decades, my contacts and influence in law enforcement run broad and deep. Mansuetus and I have made our phone calls to secure our cover stories.Besides this is exactly what Rom and I end up doing more often than we would like to see." Nichola's voice was poignant as he told Zachary.

William sidled up to him on the other side, "This ain't his first rodeo, boy."

"Detective Sutton, I would like to get a look at the last two victims.Get a scent that the perpetrator is the same in both deaths." Mitch said behind Zachary.

"Okay, let's go to the morgue." Zachary said quietly surrounded by his supernatural team.

* * * * *

On the fifteen-minute drive to the morgue, Burke and Nichola good-naturedly sniped and bickered with each other.

"I was impressed by your handling of the captain, William. After Zachary's less than stellar description of his personality, I am sure that it was pleasant for you to meet a human so similar to your own character." Nichola praised, then alternately, insulted him subtly, as he and Rom sat in the back seat of the Yukon behind Zachary, who was driving, and Mansuetus who occupied the front passenger seat.

"It was your decision to establish a commonality for him to focus on."Burke, who sat with Mitch in the third row of seats in the Yukon, responded referring to the cover last name that Mansuetus had assigned to him and planted in the Intelligence and Counterterrorism Division of DPS data system as a civilian consultant.

"Humans respond well to commonality and bond quickly. Making suggestion easier. It was less likely that a man of his temperament would welcome either Rom or myself as he immediately saw us as foreign entities."Nichola replied in a lecturing tone.

"I agree. Commonality works well in all relationships. Which is why Leila

195

and I get along so well." Burke's soft Texas drawl was brazenly dangerous.

That statement caused the others to stiffen in surprise. Even Nichola was quiet for a few seconds before responding.

"How are you and Leila anything alike?" Nichola questioned dangerously in return.

"Well, to begin with, we are both Americans and Texans. She and I also seek knowledge and adventure. Then there is the fact that we are both vampires.She is very young, but as you know I am fairly young myself. You could say, on a vampire age scale, that relatively, we are of an age; unlike yourselves. And I am sure you would agree, scientifically speaking, that commonality breeds affection."Burke's voice was smooth.

"Scientifically speaking." Nichola agreed. "But when it comes to my Leila her affections are firmly, immovably engaged elsewhere."He stressed the words.

"You sure about that?" Burke questioned with a smirk.

"Positive." Nichola drawled as if bored.

"Would you care to place a wager?" Burke asked snarkily.

"Okay! That's enough!" Zachary's voice was loud and pissed off. "That's my mother you are speaking about!"

"Sorry, boy, we're just two bulls poking each other back here."Burke said good-naturedly throwing a smirk at Nichola. "No harm or insult meant."

"I respect your mother too much to ever wager in a game of chance with her affections, son." Nichola responded sincerely. "And I will do whatever is necessary to keep them secure." He fairly growled over his shoulder at Burke who gave him a large grin in return.

* * * * *

Zachary and Nichola sat and waited in the sterile hallway outside of the doorway to the morgue, where the others were speaking with the coroner and viewing the bodies of the last two victims.

"You know he seems to really like you one minute and then pushes the edge of getting his ass-kicked the next." Zachary, who was leaning his elbows on his knees and letting his hands dangle tiredly between them, murmured softly to Nichola as they waited patiently for the others.

"He and I have known each other for a long time, relative to your frame of thinking as well as his own. I was one of the first two vampires that he ever met, almost directly after his transformation." Nichola relaxed back with his legs crossed in the plastic chair next to Zachary. "I like him also." He told Zachary who sat back to look at him in surprise. "Did you think that I didn't? He knows that I do. I am very old, Zachary, and very powerful. I would never tolerate another vampire whom I did not like, to 'poke' at me in the manner that William does." Nichola smiled at him gently. "Your mother is not the first lady that we have competed over. But as her soulmate, I am very aware of how your mother feels. I am a jealous creature, if I had doubts about your mother's veracity I would not tolerate William's pursuit of her."

"Well, he thinks he's got a chance." Zachary smiled at Nichola good-naturedly.

"He doesn't know your mother as well as I do."

"You seem pretty self-confident and self-aware." Zachary stated suddenly, his tone like the methodical detective that he was.

"I am very old, Zachary. I wouldn't have lasted this long if I weren't aware of both my strengths and weaknesses and actively worked to improve myself. Your mother is both a strength and weakness for me. Her existence and expectations of me make me a better person.Wanting to please her also makes me more tolerant, which in our community can be seen as a weakness. I behave less ruthlessly because I know that she doesn't care for it. She is very human in her beliefs, and very trusting in her actions. This naiveté makes me cherish her and frightens me at the same time." Nichola smiled.

"You really will always protect her won't you? Even from herself?" Zachary asked almost surprised.

"Always. With everything that I have and everything that I am. I would give my life for hers. I will do anything to keep her safe." Nichola told him simply and sincerely.

The others walked out of the morgue doors and Zachary and Nichola stood."Well?" Nichola asked.

"It's the same killer, sir. Scent is the same on both bodies." Mitch nodded positively.

"This guy is rabid and needs to be put down." Burke told Nichola in a disturbed voice.

"There is something familiar about those wounds." Rom stated thinking hard as they exited the building.

"What?" Nichola inquired.

"I can't really pinpoint it, but they remind me of Gervais without the cannibal aspect." Rom's voice was also disturbed. "But Gervais's victims were all over the spectrum, male, female, independent of age.Nothing like these. With the exception of the last victim, all of the previous victims could have been copies of each other; unknown, unwanted, teenage Latinas. Our kind have a tendency to have 'types' also in our victims, just like human serial killers.I don't understand this recent change in victim type."

As they all settled in the car, Mitch popped up with "Opportunity."

"What do you mean?" Mansuetus asked from the front seat looking behind him at Mitch.

"Well, take my wolf. It's very favorite food is ground grouse. It just loves it. But if a rabbit easily presents itself, well, its rabbit for dinner. So, opportunity."

Mansuetus nodded his head in agreement thoughtfully.

"Zachary would you please take us to the mall? That was where the last victim was found, and where you believe that the girls were abducted from, is this not correct?" Nichola asked.

"Yes. That is the last place all three of their cell phones pinged from at the same time.Before splitting up, I mean."

"Splitting up?" Rom asked.

"Yes. Location services has them going in three different directions from the mall.Before service stopped for them."Zachary explained.

"What do you mean stopped?" Burke asked.

"The signal stopping. Could be because the phone was disabled in some way, the battery died, or they entered a 'dead zone' for cell service. We're not sure." Zachary told them.

* * * * *

After the others left to head into San Antonio, Leila, Devin, Dene, and

Fred sat around the kitchen table after breakfast reading through the case files while Princess slept on top of Fred's boots. It seemed that with all of the snacks that he was passing to her when no one was looking, that she had found her new best friend.

"I am sure that Uncle Man said that you told him that you would not be investigating these murders!" Devin sounded bored and disgruntled.

Leila looked at her youngest son, whom she had conscripted into assisting her absorb the information in the case file, with irritation. She hated it when he whined. What else was he going to do anyway? He might as well use his time constructively!

"I did not say that. I said that I was sure that I wouldn't be great at helping them with the investigation."She told him giving him a dirty look.As Leila read the most recent victims information and the information on the two girls still missing, something wasn't adding up for her.

"Dene, did you read here that they think that the last three girls were abducted together at the mall?" She pointed out a document to Dene.

"Yes, I saw that." Dene told her with a nod looking at the document.

"Doesn't that seem strange to you?" She asked.

"Well, it is believed that the last victim, who is one of these three girls, was killed within hours of their abduction." He responded looking at the medical report on the latest victim.

"But that doesn't make sense to me. Why would the killer dispose of her body at the same place that he abducted them?Should we assume that he killed her there at the mall? And if that is the case, where the hell would he have kept the other two little girls?Did he have a large vehicle? A van possibly, or a bus? That has to be the police department's assumption. He wouldn't have abducted them in public, at the mall, drove away, killed one, then drove back to the mall to dispose of the body. That is making two trips to the same public location and would be too risky, even for an insane vampire. There is a lot of surveillance at a mall..." Her voice trailed off as she thought about it.

"He couldn't have." Dene stated as he read the coroner's report and going over the pictures in the file."He obviously took his time with her.He raped and tortured her to death." He passed a photo to Leila, and she blanched in disgust. "See here. There is evidence of some clotting on these cuts. These were made before death. Besides, there is no way that he had a vehicle large enough to hang her for exsanguination."

"What do you mean? Didn't he just drink her dry?" Leila asked.

"No. Her body was nearly bloodless. There is no way that one vampire would be able to take in, what I would estimate looking at her weight and height here, would be six to eight pints of blood in one kill." Dene was focused on the medical report. He then took hold of another photo and passed it to Leila, pointing at the photo. "See this. Her throat was cut, but no clotting. This was obviously done postmortem. In order to get that much blood out of her body after her heart stopped beating, he would have had to have hung her.

Let's see." He rifled through the photos in the file, and his eyes lit up in discovery as he grasped another photo which he passed to Leila. He pointed out some faint marks around the girls ankles. "See this? I would bet my medical reputation that these are postmortem ligature marks, made by a rope it looks like. No bruising, just the indentation of the mark where he hung her and drained her corpse of blood by cutting her throat."

"How long would that take?" Leila asked as Devin looked at Dene in disgust at his description.

"Draining of the blood? Forty to sixty minutes, give or take. The rape and torture?" He flipped through all of the photos again focusing on the damage done to the body. "Another hour? Possibly more with the amount of clotting in some of these wounds."

"How do you know so much about this?" Devin asked impressed.

"Doctor of Hematology." Dene said pointing at his chest. "Besides, I work for a vampire and have spent the last couple of decades being part of their community. Even though I am just a companion, I know them pretty well, have seen some of the damage that they can leave behind, and have treated some of that damage as a doctor also."

"What we know for sure is that he disposed of the body at the mall." Leila said looking at the men. "There is no way he killed her there. I would bet money that he didn't make two trips to the mall. One trip to grab them, leave, go someplace else to kill, torture, and drain one of them. Then drive back to the sight of the abduction to dispose of her body? That's too risky and too stupid and we know this guy is not stupid. Obviously, crazy, but not stupid." Leila thought hard.

"Where did they find the girl's car at the mall?" Fred asked and Leila looked at him to find Princess sitting on his lap looking over the files spread out over the table in interest; though most likely to see if there were more snacks to be had.

"They didn't. None of the girls had a license." Devin replied looking at another document.

"Well, who drove them then?" Fred asked him.

"No one knows," Devin answered. "None of their parents knew that they had been going to the mall and no one has come forward to say that they had been with them that evening or had given them a ride to the mall."

"Well then, how do they know that all three of them were at the mall?" Fred questioned looking at him.

"Because their cell phones pinged at the mall and then the report says that they left in three different vehicles before," Devin read directly from a report "location services lost connectivity with the phones."

"Where were they before they went to the mall?" Leila asked in confusion.

Devin looked at a map that had a red line graphic on it. "Looks like the last place that they were at before the mall was the neighborhood of Tanner's Creek. Hey, I know where that's at. It's about halfway between Boerne and the Mall." Devin said excited.

"It's also where two of them live. The third one lives in another neighborhood about a mile away." Dene said looking at his report. "It says here that her mother dropped her off to spend the night with the little girl that was murdered. That was the last time that she had seen her daughter."

"I don't think that they were taken from the mall." Leila stated pointing to the red line cell point location map in the middle of the table. "I think that they were abducted from their own neighborhood."

"Come on, Mom." Devin said looking at her. "That's not what the police think, including Zachary."

"I am telling you as a mother, when your children do not have a license you end up running them all over. We have three sets of parents who did not take those girls to the mall. They had no idea they were at the mall. So how did they get there?"

"Okay." Dene said."Let's say you are right. How do we prove it?"

"We do up fliers with their photos and we canvas the neighborhood."Leila stated seemingly coming to a conclusion.

"Mom! We can't do that. Two of the families live there and one of those families lost their daughter. The police have already interviewed the families.It would be inappropriate to question these families again and it could be considered interfering with the investigation." Devin looked at her like she was crazy.

"Nonsense. Yes, it would be inappropriate to bother their families. That just means that we don't. That doesn't mean that we can't knock on all of the neighbor's doors, show them a flier, and ask them if they have seen the girls and if they have, when was the last time they saw them. As long as we report our information to Zachary, that would not be interfering with his investigation. That would be helping with the investigation." Leila told him.

"Mom! Have you ever been in Tanner's Creek? It's a big neighborhood. It has at least two hundred houses and they sit on at least an acre of land each, it will take us a full day, even if we split up in two teams, to visit all the neighbors. Besides, if their neighbors had any information they would have already passed it to the police." Devin told her, not wanting to spend his day walking from house-to-house ringing doorbells.

"Devin, do you watch the local news?" Leila calmly asked him.

"No." He answered quickly, bewildered.

"Most people don't, and the police are releasing very little information about the case. In fact, they are actively playing it down. I'll bet you that most of the neighbors have no idea that there are two families in the neighborhood who have missing children. Most neighbors don't even know each other in today's society; at least not more than a passing wave as you are in the front yard or driving down the street.We have very little interaction with each other anymore. It's worth looking into."

"Ms. Sutton," Fred, who had been sitting back listening to the exchange petting Princess, began, "let's say you are right. Don't you think it may be a might dangerous?"

"We won't be doing it at night, Mr. Fred. In fact, it is even too late to start today. We will start bright and early tomorrow. Today, we make up the fliers, get them printed, then print out a list of the property addresses of the neighborhood, mark where the families live and prepare to canvas tomorrow. Would you like to be my canvassing partner, Mr. Fred?" Leila asked him smiling at him persuasively.

"Okay?" Fred answered looking at Dene and Devin in question.

"Great!" Leila said happily. "Let's get to work on those fliers and then we can take them to the print shop and have a couple of hundred printed out. We can pick up pizza for everyone on the way home." She smiled at him.

"Pizza?" Devin asked bewildered.

"Sure, why not? Everyone is working, and we shouldn't expect Mr. Burke's housekeeper to feed us all."

"I don't think I have ever had pizza." Fred said suddenly.

"Really?" Devin was amazed as Fred nodded at him.

"The Boss only eats meat and potatoes, mostly steak and sometimes the occasional egg. I eat what he eats." Fred replied.

"I haven't had pizza since I became a companion." Dene said wistfully as Devin looked at him in surprise.

"That settles it then. Flyer creation first, a trip to the print shop, and then we will stop at the Boerne Pizza Factory and bring back pizza for everyone to enjoy!" Leila exclaimed with a smile.

* * * * *

The whole wolf-shifter pack, which including the children numbered slightly over thirty, were milling about the kitchen, formal dining room, and out on the expansive back porch eating, when the guys returned to the ranch just after 6:30 pm.

"What's going on here?" Mitch asked one of the ranch hands.

"The lady brought pizza back from town, Alpha, and invited us all over to eat." He replied smiling, then quickly nodded his head in a submissive gesture.

Mitch looked at Burke in surprise who in turn looked at Nichola.

"Your mate has taken over my ranch." Burke stated in wonder.

"Welcome to my world." Nichola murmured with a broad smile, then said, "But at least you got her title correct.My mate."

Rom walked past them exclaiming, "Pizza!" and headed out to the back porch where Leila and Mrs. McKinney, Burke's wolf shifter housekeeper, had set up two long tables that had about fifty pizza boxes on them and was helping the children put pizza on their paper plates.

Burke and Nichola followed after Rom looking around curiously.

"She doesn't really expect us to eat this and on cardboard plates too?"Burke asked Nichola quietly as the children laughed uproariously at something Rom said as he helped them get pizza.

Nichola looked over to see Devin, Dene and Fred at a smaller table stuffing their faces only to be joined by Rom, Mansuetus and Zachary. "My recommendation? Don't offend her." He said as Mitch walked past taking a bite out of an oversized slice of pepperoni pizza.He approached the long tables trepidatiously with Burke beside him.

Leila smiled broadly at him. "How was your day?"

"Informative and productive." He answered returning her smile hesitantly looking at the pizzas."What do you recommend?"

"For you? Garbage Pizza." She handed him a paper plate with a large slice. "Mr. Burke we specifically got you steak pizza." She told Burke who took his plate from Mrs. McKinney looking at the pizza doubtfully.

Nichola looked at his slice critically. "What's on it? Don't I need silverware?"

Leila walked around the table to him and undid his tie and a couple of buttons; she took his tie, folded it, and put it in his suit pocket, then handed him a large paper napkin. "No silverware, you eat with your hands. This Garbage pizza has Pepperoni, Italian Sausage, Bacon, Black Olives, Artichokes, Eggplant, Mushrooms, Garlic, Goat Cheese, and Red Sauce." She turned him about saying, "Rom has saved you a seat."

"It's Italian, Nikolaos!" Rom said as Nichola sat next to him looking at his pizza; Burke accepted a chair on the other side of the table next to Devin and Fred. Fred reached down to give Princess, who was standing on her hindlegs perched against his leg, a piece of pizza crust.

"It's Greek!" Mansuetus exclaimed as Mr. McKinney started passing around red plastic cups of wine at the table. Burke looked up at him in astonishment.

"The lady and the missus say we are not doing dishes this evening, Boss." He murmured as he handed him a cup.

"It was created in Naples!" Rom argued vehemently.

"Naples was a Greek port!" Mansuetus returned. "Kýrios try it. It is plakuntos it just has more toppings. It's good!"

"Try it, Boss! It is really good!" Fred said to Burke next to him as he chewed loudly.

Nichola took a bite of his pizza, raising his eyebrows in surprise, it was very similar to plakuntos with additional toppings, and was quite good.He looked at Rom quizzically, "Since when do you eat anything other than chocolate?"

"Since I obtained a daughter." He replied with a smile, holding his pizza high. "Pizza is my second favorite food! We have had many a pizza party at my home over the years."He looked around at the children squealing and running around on the back porch. "Children change you my friend. For the better." He said with a shrug of his shoulders.

"You have a daughter? How is that possible?" Devin asked.

"We adopted her about ten years ago, she just graduated from college at the top of her class! Would you like to see pictures of her?" Rom said pulling out his wallet and freeing a very long accordion-style wallet insert of pictures.

After the whole table exclaimed over the beauty of Rom's daughter, Devin looked at Nichola and said quietly, "You need to tell my mother: No."

"About what?" He returned softly. "Telling her 'no' doesn't usually work out well for me I have discovered."

"I heard that, Devin!" Leila said loudly coming over with a slice of pizza herself but finding no open chairs.

"Here Ms. Sutton, take my chair." Fred said starting to stand.

"Oh, no, Mr. Fred. I will be quite comfortable right here." Leila replied sitting down on Nichola's lap; much to his delight, and Burke's chagrin."But thank you!" She told him with a smile.

"C'mon, Zachary! Tell her she can't!" Devin told his brother.

Zachary gave his brother a put-upon glance before looking at his mother, then asked, "What do you want to do, Mom?"

"She wants to knock on all the doors of Tanner's Creek and pass out fliers and ask if they have seen the missing girls. Tell her that you...that you have already done that!" Devin answered for her, his voice desperate.

"We haven't done that." Zachary told him and Leila smiled triumphantly at Devin.

"Why not?" Devin demanded.

"Because, frankly, we don't have the manpower and it crosses jurisdictional lines with the BPD. That doesn't mean it's a good idea. When are you wanting to do this, Mom?" Zachary stressed the word 'Mom'.

"Tomorrow, honey." Leila answered sweetly. "During the day, in the bright sunshine, there is no danger. According to Dene, the only other spray booths in existence are at Rom's home in Utah and Nichola's Toronto home because the formula is still under testing, so it's not like our vampire serial killer is going to be running around in the sunshine."

"Thank God for that!" Rom murmured.

Leila faced Zachary with a reasonable, expectant look on her face.

"You will, of course, text whatever you find out to me." Zachary stated.

"Of course, we will!"

"Well, I guess, I don't see any harm in it." Zachary's voice was disgruntled. "Nick?" He tossed the ball in Nichola's court.

Leila turned to look at Nichola expectantly.

"I suppose it will be fine." He was quiet as she smiled at him widely. "But you three will be with her and you will be armed. Correct?"

"Zach!" Devin moaned out.

"Dev, I couldn't really stop her anyway. Hell, she is free to start up a civilian advocacy group and knock-on doors if she wants to. As long as she shares any information with the authorities, there is not a lot I can tell her."

* * * * *

"I am sure that 'pizza' is not on your menu for control." Nichola murmured holding Leila's hand as they walked Princess along the back of Burke's expansive yard.

"I drank my pig's blood and the interaction with the activities of the pack was an additional source of energy. I am doing what I am supposed to do." Leila assured him. "Didn't you like the pizza? You had three slices!"

"I did enjoy the pizza." Nichola smiled at her. "It was unusual."

"Just because we are different from the majority of society doesn't mean that we can't enjoy the small things in life. I understand now why Mr. Burke has developed a relationship with the wolf-shifters. They are interesting and changing. They have their own society, and he is an integral part of that. They must fill his desire for a family." Leila told him. "Mrs. McKinney told me that before Mitch became Alpha he sent him to school for agriculture and ranch management."

"I am not surprised. Most vampires have a tendency to take care of those who we feel belong to us. It satisfies our natural need for control." He smiled good-naturedly at her and pulled her into his arms.

"Do you feel a need to control me, Nichola?" Leila playfully asked him amazed at how well she could see him in the darkness. She could feel herself changing day-by-day, and her abilities were growing.

"Yes." He murmured, surprising her by answering affirmatively. "But I am making an effort to curb this need. I realize that you are an individual with your own desires and goals that may not always coincide with my own. I only wish to protect you. You are my everything; you are my forever."

Leila's heart swelled to overflowing love for him upon this confession as he lifted her up and lay her on the plush grass of the lawn to kiss her deeply.

"You will ruin your suit." She whispered against his lips wrapping her arms around his neck.

"I don't care." He replied capturing her lips with his own once more.

Princess took the opportunity to leap up on Nichola's back to stare over his shoulder, looking down at Leila, tail wagging, causing her to giggle.

Burke's voice came from the darkness. "You know that the wolves patrol out here in the night. Unless you are wanting to give them a show, of course. I am sure it would be the talk of the pack house."

"Both he and that dog are cock-blocks!" Nichola swore softly running his lips down the side of Leila's throat as she laughed even louder.

"You know I can both hear and see you!" Burke called out once more.

Nichola rolled his eyes in irritation smiling down at Leila before getting up from the lawn, causing Princess to jump down from him and dance around his feet. He reached a hand down to Leila and pulled her up against him, holding her close. "Let's grab that dog and take this to the bedroom."

* * * * *

Nichola returned to the bed to hold Leila's heavily slumbering body against him, spooning around her protectively. He ran his lips over her silken shoulder to place his face in the curve of her neck to breathe deeply of her unique scent. As with most newly transformed vampires, his mate, when she did sleep, slept hard and deep as her body gradually achieved full transformation.

He ran his left hand down over the silky-smooth skin of her left arm to gently hold her left hand in his briefly, before he slid a beautiful, five carat, oval diamond ring over the third finger of her left hand. The heavy gold band was intricately twisted and worked, with small marquis diamonds decorating each side, that looked like leaves decorating a strand of English ivy. It fit perfectly, as he knew it would, since he had it made for her years ago. He gently, reverently, brought her hand to his lips.

The more her body adapted to its new reality, the more bonded he felt to her and the more he felt her bond to him. When this hunt was over, he vowed to take her into Cusco for a small vacation to show her the city before the large council activities began. After that he would take them all to his home in Toronto to drop off the others, and then he would take her to his hotel in Katerini to show her his homeland. He curled around her and closed his eyes to dream of their future.

The Last Ride

ince Zachary and the others left in the Yukon again in the morning
to go into San Antonio, Devin and Dene drove Devin's truck and
Leila drove Zachary's car with Fred as her passenger to Tanner's
Creek to start the day of knocking on the neighbor's doors.

Leila smiled and spread the fingers of her left hand out over the steering
wheel to admire the beautiful diamond ring that she had found on her finger
when she had woken up this morning. Sometimes Nichola just made her
feel like the most loved woman on earth.

"Brake! Brake! Brake!" Fred yelled beside her, stepping on an imaginary
brake pedal, clutching the arm rests in the car.

"Mr. Fred!" Leila admonished him, gently slowing to exit the interstate.
"You are such a horrible rider! You are perfectly safe with me; I have been
driving for forty years!"

"Women shouldn't drive!" He hollered putting a hand on the ceiling of the
car and clutching the armrest in panic, as she turned into the subdivision.

"Mr. Fred, that is an extremely sexist attitude!" She pulled the car over to
park in the first street of the subdivision.

Devin pulled up next to them with a Cattleman's hat and sunglasses on
and Dene rolled down the passenger window and Leila rolled down hers.
"How you doing there, buddy?" Devin asked Fred. "You okay? Dene and I
saw you bouncing around." Devin and Dene were snickering.

"If I could have one, your mother would give me a heart attack!"Fred shouted leaning across Leila to yell up at the other two men in the truck.

"Mr. Fred, you are being ridiculous! You have arrived safe and sound!" Leila yelled at him in return.

Devin chuckled. "We are going to park at the other end of the neighborhood, and we will meet you in the middle. There is a park and pavilion. If you beat us there when you are done, just wait till we get there. You don't have to worry about disturbing the parents, it looks like those addresses are on mine and Dene's list."

"Leila, please make sure that you have your cell phone on. Nick will be really pissed if he knew that we are splitting up to do this." Dene told her.

"If we don't, we will never make it through the neighborhood in a day. Time is short and we still have two little girls still out there who are hopefully alive." Leila replied.

"I understand, just be careful." Dene told her worriedly.

* * * * *

"Your new buddies seem pretty unusual." Sammy 'The Salsa' whispered to Zachary as they were sitting at a workstation viewing the many hours and multiple camera angles of the security video tapes from the mall.

Zachary glanced at the three vampires who sat in front of three workstations and Mitch and Mansuetus who stood over their shoulders looking at the screens. All five of the men had decided to dress down today, wearing jeans, boots, and casual blazers. "State and Feds. What do you expect?" He replied.

"Well, they seem to be working. Are they at least competent? The other morons in the outer office have been on one long coffee break since they have arrived. It's like they are tourists on a boondoggle. I heard them yucking it up about their trip to the Riverwalk this morning.Worthless, just worthless."Johnson muttered in irritation, they had spent all day looking at the footage from the multiple cameras of the large mall and parking lots with nothing to show for it, and he was tired and grouchy.

"These guys aren't like that. They know what they are doing." Zachary replied.

"What's that?" Burke asked pointing to the screen.

"Back it up and slow it down." Nichola told him leaning over to look.

Zachary and his partners got up to stand with Mitch and Mansuetus to look at the screen in front of Burke. "What the fuck is this!" Johnson exclaimed as he saw the same blurry image that they had seen from the surveillance footage in the parking garage, approach a car in the mall parking lot and lean against it.

"This bullshit again?" Salsa asked in disgust.

"Something is not adding up." Rom said to Nichola ignoring the human's outbursts. Nichola looked at him in inquiry and Rom looked at the others."Has anyone seen the girls on any of the surveillance cameras from the mall?" The others shook their heads. "Billy, see if you can zoom in and see what he is doing to that car."

Burke looked lost for a moment and Mansuetus said, "I got it", and motioned for him to give him the seat. Mansuetus made the necessary adjustments then played the image slowly forward once more."Looks like he is putting something in the window. See here,"Mansuetus pointed at the screen."The back window is down an inch or so."

"This is a distraction!" Nichola exclaimed suddenly. "He didn't abduct these girls from the mall! He snatched them from somewhere else. This is just another drop spot for the last victim." He thought for a minute then looked at his watch. "Fuck!" He yelled.

"What?" Zachary asked in alarm, never having seen him lose his cool before even when Devin was pushing his buttons.

"Your mother!" Nichola replied in panic, and they all scrambled for the door as Johnson and Salsa followed bewildered.

* * * * *

Fred and Leila sat in the park pavilion waiting for Devin and Dene as the sun submerged behind the horizon in the distance. She wasn't surprised that most of the neighbors that they had spoken with had no idea that two neighborhood girls were missing. Though something was bothering her about one of the people that they had talked to. She just couldn't put her finger on it.

* * * * *

Zachary's cell phone rang in the Yukon. "Yeah." He said throwing it on speaker.

"Where are we going?" Salsa asked.

Zachary looked in the rearview mirror to see Salsa and Johnson following them. "We are going to Tanner's Creek."

"Buddy, we can't! It's not our jurisdiction!" Johnson said.

"Bullshit! I don't give a fuck! My mother and brother are in that neighborhood knocking on doors and passing out fliers. Think about it! It's why we haven't been able to figure out how they got to the mall! They were *never* at the mall! Only their cell phones. They got snatched from their own neighborhood!" Zachary yelled.

"Your brother nor Dene are answering their cell phones!" Mansuetus told Zachary.

"Neither is your mother!" Zachary heard Nick say from the back, and he heard the fear in the vampire's voice.

"Fred either." Now he heard Burke's panicked voice from behind him.

"It's hill country out there. Cell phone reception can be spotty." Johnson said through the speaker of Zachary's cell phone.

"Fuck!" Zachary hollered leaning on the horn to get a car to move over from the left lane as he watched the setting sun.

"It's okay, buddy. We got you." Salsa's voice came from the phone and then lights, and a siren came on behind them. Zachary moved over and let Salsa take the lead and moved directly in behind him to follow closely.

* * * * *

"Still no bars." Leila said to Fred. "How about you?"

"Nope." Fred said looking at his phone.

"Did you think that something was off about that teenage girl answering the door at," Leila looked at her address sheet, "1519 Converse?"

"Pretty girl, weird eyes though." Fred looked at the sheet, thinking aloud. "Said she didn't know the girls; never have seen them. Strange. Girls of a certain age always seem to know about all the girls of their age if they live close by each other; even if they ain't friendly."

212

"That's true. Don't you think she should have been in school too?" Leila was asking him then looked up to see the subject of their discussion walking towards them hurriedly.

Her approached them and blurted out. "You guys have got to get out of here before the sun fully sets! He knows that you are here walking the neighborhood."

"What are you talking about?" Leila asked her.

"The Master! You're a vampire aren't you?" Her asked desperately trying to get them to understand. "I don't know how you are in the sun, and he doesn't either, but he saw you from the window. He wants to know. You have to leave the neighborhood right now!"

Leila stood up with Fred to ask the girl more questions, then heard faintly, *Leila! We are almost to Tanner's Creek. Where are you?*

I don't know where Devin and Dene are at, but Fred and I are at the park by the pavilion waiting for them. There is a girl here who says that he knows we are here.

He who?

Her Master.

Fuck! Watch your back! Don't let her anywhere near you. She's his companion! She could be under his orders. Tell Fred to get out his gun! We will be there as quickly as possible.

Leila speedily reached out to clutch Fred by the arm as he approached the girl to talk to her, stopping him. "Get your gun out, Fred, and stay away from her." Leila told him as she glared at Her suspiciously.

"It's not me you have to worry about. As soon as he realizes that I am gone, he's going to know that I came to warn you. Then he will kill me for sure and honestly it will be a blessing because I won't have to live like this anymore." Her told Leila and Fred, then turned around to see Him approaching, she edged closer to them, then whispered, "Shoot Him! Shoot Him now! He's just as dangerous as the Master!"

"Her what the hell are you doing out here?" Him yelled as he hit the edge of the sidewalk by the park.

"Your name is Her?" Leila whispered appalled.

"That is the name that the Master gave me." The girl looked at Leila with

213

desperate eyes. "Please shoot Him. He will kill us all."

"Hey, how's it going?" The man approached them smiling in a friendly manner, waving at them with one hand and reaching behind his back with the other as he got closer.

Fred shot him in the shoulder with his 45 caliber and he fell to the ground with a scream. Leila and Fred quickly ran to Him, and Fred leveled his gun at Her saying, "Stay back."

Her stopped with her hands up. "You need to kill him!" She told Fred.

Him again reached behind him as they looked down on him. "Don't do it, partner. I'll blow your head clean off." Fred threatened, his voice low, capable, and dangerous, pointing the gun at his head."Let's see your hands!" Him raised his left hand up, but his other hung by his side useless.

"You broke my shoulder." Him told Fred with a grimace.

Leila kicked him then rolled him over. He had a huge Bowie knife in his back waistband, it was at least eight inches long. Leila took it and put it in her waist behind her belt as the sun sunk below the horizon.

"You need to kill him right now and then run for your car! Now!" Her begged in a whisper urgently to Fred as he kept his gun pointed at Him.

"Her! You slut!What are you doing here? Go back home immediately! Be assured I will punish you harshly for your betrayal." A cruel angry voice came from the wooded greenbelt on the edge of the park.

Her fell to her knees with a surprised cry, cowering in terror.

Leila pulled her hat and sunglasses off to see better in the growing dusk; flinging them to the ground to face the vampire who now stood about ten feet behind them. "Leave her alone!" Her *voice* was a low threat drawing his attention to herself.

"She is mine to do with as I wish. What have you done to my manservant you day-walking slut?" He growled at her, his skin flushing dark with rage, his long straight brown hair flowed around him as he saw Him bleeding and lying on the ground with Fred's gun pointed at his head. Leila was awash in his power.

As far as Leila was concerned, she had been on the receiving end of much more power than this. "Your manservant came to attack us, on your orders I believe." She responded haughtily as if she was speaking to the Devil at a tea party. She gave him a push of her own power in return to which he reacted in surprise."You are lucky he is still alive." She pushed her claws from her hands and felt her teeth lengthen in preparation to defend herself.

"Oh, you magnificent whore! Tell me, how do you walk in the sun?" His *voice* was coaxing as he looked at her with hot desire in his red eyes and she saw his own claws descend from the tips of his fingers.

"Only pureblood vampires have the knowledge to be able to do so," Leila lied with supreme arrogance, stepping to the left to pull his attention and himself farther from Fred, Her, and the prone Him. The vampire did as she wanted stalking her to open ground. "Obviously, from the looks of you, you're a mongrel.So, you have no need to know." She smirked knowing it would infuriate him.

"I can always drink it from your veins!" He snarled flushing even darker as his fury grew to new heights and his teeth descended from his gums.

"You can always try!" She challenged openly hoping Nichola was close.

"Latour, stand down!" Leila heard his voice with relief then felt Nichola's presence about ten feet behind her and to her side, though she didn't dare take her attention off the vampire in front of her to look at him.

I psychí mou, are you unharmed?

Yes. Whatever you do, don't hurt the girl next to Fred, I feel she is a victim in this. The man on the ground is his companion, Fred shot him. He came to capture me and kill Fred. The girl has been trying to get Fred to kill him, she seems to think he is just as dangerous as this asshole. He hasn't moved since Fred shot him though. This psycho here wants to know how I walk in the daylight!

The man whom Nichola called Latour nodded his head looking behind her."Baron! And the Count! It is good to see you again after these centuries! Is the Master with you also?"

"Gervais is dead, Latour!" Rom responded stonily from behind her and to her other side; she could here death in his voice. Pain flashed through the vampire's eyes at this information.

Leila saw Burke and Mitch in his wolf form silently approaching the vampire from behind and started to walk backwards as she felt Nichola, and

215

Rom flank her.

"How did he die?" Latour asked and grief colored his words.

"I removed his head from his shoulders." Nichola responded in a low growl.

"But why?" Latour wailed in pain.

"Because he wanted me to." Nichola told him his voice icy.

Faster than light, Latour snatched Leila to him, pulling her back against his chest like a shield, placing his claws at her throat, piercing her skin causing her blood to flow down her front.

"Is this glorious slut yours, Baron?" He snarled next to her ear.

"No!" Came Burke's roar out of the darkness behind him, startling Latour and Leila brought the heel of her boot down on top of his foot as hard as she could, feeling satisfaction when she heard a bone snap, then she rammed the claws of one hand backwards and into Latour's groin. He screamed in agony dropping his claws from her throat, as Burke grabbed him, and then he turned digging them into the middle of Burke's chest deeply. Burke gave a surprised gasp his chest rattling as he dropped to the ground and Mitch leapt through the air knocking Leila down, and tackling Latour, his teeth snapping around his throat.

Leila crawled to Burke as she heard Devin's voice screaming, "Billy!"

She watched Fred drop to his knees screaming in pain and Him leaped up to tackle him, striking him sharply in the face. Her jumped on Him's back, wrapping her arms around his neck to pull Him from Fred and he tossed her over his shoulder to wrap his hands around her throat shaking her slight body as he worked to choke the life from her.

Her dug her thumbs into his eyes in desperation and though blood flowed down his face and Him screamed in agony, he didn't release her throat.

Watching as Her gasped and struggled against his superior strength, Leila ripped the Bowie knife from her belt and tried to launch it at him as she covered the gruesome wound with her hand, trying to stem the spurts of blood flowing from Burke's chest.

The knife landed short of her target sticking in the ground next to Her who grasped it and gutted Him, pulling the knife through his intestines, and carving up with all of her might until the knife lodged in the middle of his sternum. Him screamed once before going limp and Her shoved his lifeless body to the side gasping for air through her bruised throat.

Fred crawled to Burke wailing as Leila pressed down hard on the gaping wound and she could feel it sucking air around her hands every time he drew a breath.Devin was now beside Burke clutching his hand and Dene came over to Leila's side to look at the wound. He shook his head once at Leila and covered it with his own hands to try to stem the flow of blood that rushed and ebbed with every beat of Burke's heart. Leila could barely see through the tears in her eyes as she lifted his head to cradle him gently against her lap.

"Fred, damn it! Stop that caterwauling!" Burke's voice was weak, and he looked up briefly at Leila with knowledge in his eyes.He reached out and grasp Fred's hand and placed it in Devin's. "You are the best friend a man could ever have. See this boy? You belong to him now, you serve him as well as you did me…better even!" Fred's shoulders shook in pain and grief as he clutched both Devin's hand and Burke's.

Burke coughed then moaned in pain and Leila smoothed the hair back away from his forehead with bloodied hands. He looked up to see Mitch standing naked next to Nichola who gazed down at Burke with grief etched on his face. A short bloody sword was clutched in his hand.

"Mitch," Burke's weak voice continued. "You are a damn good man. The Sutton boys are going to take over the ranch. You pledge your loyalty to them. They will make sure that you and your line have a place on the ranch forever."

"Yes, Boss." Mitch whispered as Burke looked at Devin and then looked up past Leila's shoulder and she turned slightly to see Zachary behind her with tears in his blue eyes.

"Yes sir." Both boys said in unison to him with a nod of their heads and their tears flowed down their faces at what they realized was happening to the charismatic vampire gunslinger.

He leaned back to look at Nichola. "Klaus. You kill that bastard?" Nichola nodded then swallowed. "Give Fred a bond. Give my people your protection.

217

Just until the boy is old enough to do it himself. I am glad that we finally buried the hatchet." His voice was barely a whisper. "I always considered you my friend."

"I am your friend, William, as you are mine. I will take care of them, I give you my word." Nichola's voice trembled with emotion but was sincere.

Burke looked up at Leila's tear-streaked face, breathing deeply with pain; though his body was failing, and his voice was weak, his eyes were tender. "Don't cry. I have never met a vampire woman like you before. You are an above-board, ace-high lady, Leila," Burke's voice weakly caressed her name, "and I am proud to have known you and your boys." He coughed painfully and Leila couldn't stop the tears from flowing down her face as she watched his life drip away, as the blood flowed from his wounds. "Kiss me before I go, I know you always wanted to." He whispered and tried to smile as his beautiful brown eyes fluttered in pain. Leila bent close and pressed her warm lips to his cool ones. "So sweet. Just like I imagined." He murmured, took one more, deep, rattling, breath and then he was gone.

"Billy!" Devin called out in anguish, pulling on his lifeless hand.

"Boss!" Fred screamed throwing his body across Burke's, pulling him tightly to him to rock his lifeless body back and forth wailing in agony.

Leila covered her face with her bloody hands and sobbed; heartbroken in a million pieces at his death, and grateful for his sacrifice for herself.

* * * * *

Leila stood in the shower, bracing her hands upon the tiled wall, and let the piping hot water flow over her skin washing the blood from her body as the activities of the night flowed through her mind.

Latour's companion, Her, who seemed numb with relief, had led them to the girls. To their surprise they found three girls in the dank, dark, dungeon that the monster Latour had built for his sick, sadistic activities.

Mansuetus, Dene and Mitch had drove the Yukon to the ranch with the bodies of Burke and Latour. Nichola was adamant to Zachary that they couldn't leave Latour's body for human's to find. The physical differences between a full vampire and a human was readily evident during autopsy. Zachary was relentless though, he had to have a killer to solve the case and

218

put it to rest.It was settled that Him, the companion, would be left behind to fill that role. Zachary was not happy with this deception, but according to Her, really it was only half a lie as Him had always played a proactive role in obtaining all of Latour's victims with the exception of the last three.

If Latour's evil greed hadn't taken hold of him causing him to abduct the last three girls, his activities may have continued on in perpetuity. It was both a sad action because of the little girl's life who was lost, and a fortunate occurrence for the future lives saved.

Leila had driven Zachary's car carrying Devin and Fred, and Her. Fred clung to Devin in the backseat, sobbing with grief and pain as he tried to cope with the severing of his companion bond and the loss of his friend and master. Her, who was also dealing with the severing of her own companion bond through the death of Latour, had sat in the front seat next to her dry-eyed and silent.

Nichola, Rom and Zachary had stayed behind to deal with the aftermath of everything that had happened. But most especially to deal with Zachary's two partners who seemed to be traumatized with what they had witnessed of the vampire battle. Knowing her son the way she did, she knew that he would balk at having his partner's memories wiped or altered. Knowing Nichola and Rom, she was sure that would be their intention because at a minimum they had to come up with a cover story that would account for Him's injuries and wipe away the girl's memories of the vampire, Latour. She did not envy them; they all had their work cut out for them.

Leila, feeling almost crippling grief and anger over the death of Burke, tiredly got dressed in a pair of jeans and a t-shirt, slipping on a pair of open backed canvas tennis shoes, and headed into the kitchen. Mitch and Mr. and Mrs. McKinney after their initial bouts of grief, had taken Burke's body to prepare him for burial. Fred had been insistent that he wanted to be buried here on the ranch with his family. After they had taken Burke to the pack house, Fred had collapsed and Mansuetus had carried him to his room.

Mansuetus and Dene sat at the table with Her, they had cleaned up as best they could from all of the blood that had covered them, though their clothes still carried the signs of the tragic evening. They were all silent as Leila poured herself a glass of pig's blood and sat at the table. "Where's Devin?" She asked Mansuetus.

"He and the dog are with Fred." He replied sadly.

Leila looked across the table at the girl who must have been no more than sixteen or seventeen when Latour had forever changed her life.

"What is your name?" Leila asked.

"Her." She replied softly, glancing at Leila with eyes that were such a light blue that they were almost ghostly.

"No, what is the name that you were born with?" Leila tried again.

The girl thought hard for a few minutes and Leila had almost given up hope of an answer when she finally mumbled, "Cass...Cassandra." Then flinched in preparation for a blow.

"Cassandra." Leila commanded using her *voice,* causing Cassandra to meet her eyes. "What part did you have in the abduction and killing of these girls?"

Cassandra looked down at the hands in her lap. "I fed them."

"You fed them?" Leila asked surprised.

"Yes and kept them clean. Tried to take care of their wounds when the Master..." her voice faded, then she continued softly. "I wanted to help them. I was never allowed to leave the house alone. Even when I had to go food shopping, Him drove me; had to go with me. The Master insisted. If I tried to disobey, the Master would punish me or give me to Him..."

Here Mansuetus rumbled deep in his chest and Leila looked briefly at him. The big man was sitting with his hands fisted on the table and a glance at Dene told her he was just as furious over the girl's words.

Cassandra continued. "Today was the first day in decades that I left the house on my own. I was only able to because the Master had sent Him to trail you, after you had left and then went down to... So, there was no one to stop me." Cassandra's voice faded into silence as she continued to look down at her hands.

Leila looked at her with pity. "Why didn't you run, Cassandra, to at least try to escape, when you got your opportunity to leave the house this evening? Why warn us?"

"Where would I run to, that he would not find me and kill me anyway? I

220

figured since I was now marked for death for leaving the house when they weren't paying attention, that I should at least try to warn you. Maybe it would repay the universe for not being able to do something more for the master's girls." Cassandra looked up to face Leila telling her, "I do not blame you if you must kill me, lady. The Master always said that we are made to serve and without him, we would die in agony or other vampires would kill us. That this was the way for our kind. I must be broken inside because I do not feel agony over his death. I feel nothing but relief. I only ask one boon, that you will kill me quick." Cassandra's voice was a soft murmur.

Leila looked over her head and realized that Nichola, Rom, and Zachary were in the shadow of the front entrance and must have heard the whole sordid story.

* * * * *

Dene and Mansuetus took Cassandra into the living room and Leila, Zachary, Nichola, and Rom went onto the back porch.

"You really can't be thinking about killing her!" Zachary glared at the three vampires. "She's just as much a victim as the others. Maybe more so as her torture was unending!"

"It is our law!" Rom responded hotly.

"Did you just hear what you said, Zachary?" Nichola asked. "Sometimes death is a reprieve."

"Not to mention the fact that she is now unbonded. She is not held in check by anything. I don't think that you understand exactly what companions are, though you basically grew up calling one Uncle." Rom was adamant.

"Then explain to me exactly what they are, Rom." Zachary's voice was dangerous and Nichola was reminded of his mother, who was choosing in that moment to be unnaturally quiet.

"We create them to help us. They serve us. But they can be dangerous also. They are basically vampire lite. They have almost the same strength and speed as we do and can live almost as long as we do. They'll never be able to shape-shift or fly, but they have few of our weaknesses also. They get their life energy through their bond with their creator, so don't have any bloodlust. Plus, they walk in the sun.

221

Without a bond controlling them, could you possibly imagine what it would be like for us to hunt them if they became homicidal toward humans? A lot worse than it was tonight. They blend better and have the opportunity for more damage. When the bond breaks it cripples them, for a reason. They are not meant to live beyond the master. This one feels nothing about her severed bond; she is definitely broken." Rom told Zachary.

"I want to keep her." Leila said softly.

Rom threw up his hands to pace back and forth, then he looked at Nichola. "Christ! Would you please talk to them?"

"I am going to give Fred a bond." Nichola told him quietly.

"That is different!" Rom exclaimed.

"How so?" Zachary asked.

"Fred's maker was not homicidal. He was not abused his whole existence. He is not broken. The only thing broken inside him is his bond."

"Like what you did for Dene?" Leila asked Nichola.

Nichola looked at her in surprise. "Yes."

"I want to keep her, after everything that she has endured at the hands of vampires...our kind...she deserves a chance. We owe her one chance." Leila said to them, and Zachary smiled at her in agreement.

"Under our law, you are then responsible for her actions. You would pay a price if she went crazy and starts killing people." Rom told her emphatically.

"She won't go crazy if Nichola bonds her." Leila said fixing her gaze on Nichola.

222

Companions Are Our Family

❦

"Wake up, Lady Tsoukalous!" A voice rang out enthusiastically as the door opened to the bedroom.

"Cassie!" Nichola groaned. "I am in here also."

"I know Lord Tsoukalous!" Cassie's cheerful voice rang out as she opened the drapes to let the light in.

He pulled a pillow over his head as Leila got out of bed. Leila had kept him up most of the night. She seemed to be getting more amorous the longer that she was a vampire! Not that he was complaining, but with over one hundred vampire guests and their servants in residence at Temuco de Wila Tatitu gearing up for the special gathering of the Large Council, many people seemed to 'need' him more than usual and he was grouchy as a result. He just wanted to relax with his Glykó and close the outside world away.

Then there was the issue of Cassie. After he had bonded her with his venom, he had expected her to cling to him like most companions, instead she had strongly cleaved to Leila and happily followed her everywhere. Which was good, since she wasn't under his feet as some companions were, and Leila seemed to like her very much, so she had more patience than he did. Still, Cassie had a tendency to walk into their bedroom at some very inopportune times; causing him to tell Leila last week that he had firmly placed Cassie in the cock-block territory; right along with that dog.

He had ended up paying thousands of dollars in bribes to get that dog in country and not submitting it to quarantine regulations, only to have it sleep in their bed usually on top of him. Cassie came over and gathered up the dog who had settled itself against his side. The dog also groaned in protest at being woken up.

"None of that Miss Princess!" Cassie scolded, as Nichola looked out from under the pillow, and proceeded to snuggle the dog closely against her. "Let's go outside, then I will have Mr. Fred fix you your breakfast."

Yes, everyone loved that dog!

Then he had to deal with Fred who when bonded followed William's last order to the letter and cleaved to Devin, which initially Nichola had also taken as a blessing until he realized that it would require him to scold them about proper decorum at least twice a week for drinking, pursuing the village women and of all things gambling. He suspected them of holding a moving gambling den in the hotel and had assigned Mansuetus to keep them out of trouble; and Mansuetus was unhappy about being a babysitter. That is until they broke through one of the cave walls under the Templo de la Luna and found more treasure! Then Mansuetus developed the treasure hunting 'bug' also. Still both he and Aleksei received their typical cut of one-third, so that was a plus.

So, if he wasn't irritated with Cassie, he was irritated with Devin and Fred, or he was irritated with Mansuetus who wanted to spend all of his time in the cave.

Then he had to listen to Leila and Cassie 'chit-chat' about the different 'attributes' of Dene and Fred; both who seemed to be courting favor from Leila's new companion. The constant giggling and laughing nearly drove him over the edge.

Yes, all-in-all, he found himself to be profoundly and crazily happy in his new life with his Glykó.

Leila walked out of the closet just as he was sitting up in bed. "Well, what do you think?" She asked nervously holding up a tailored black suit coat and mini skirt.

Nichola stood and shook his head heading into the closet, "Half of the Large Council for this session will be female vampires."

"You are sure about that?" She asked from the bedroom.

"Positive. They have been doing nothing but complaining for the past ten days." Nichola came out of the closet holding up a champagne-colored, long sleeve, lace covered blouse and long lace covered skirt. The skirt was cut short in the front and would come about mid-thigh on her. "Wear your brown knee-high boots, and your matching brown floor-length duster. The one with the slits up the sides. Walk tall, take names and kick ass!" He leaned into her for a kiss while she giggled against his lips.

"You really are killing me with this new way of communicating with me. Killing me with laughter that is!"

"I love to hear you laugh." He murmured running his lips down her throat, growing hard as he took in her scent.

"I love you." She whispered running her hands up his naked body to encircled his neck.

"I love you more." He returned to softly kiss her lips nibbling gently.

"Oh, my lord!" Cassie screeched out from the patio door.

Since he was standing stark naked, half erect, holding women's clothes in his hands and kissing Leila, he should have expected that to happen. He looked up and Cassie had Princess held in the air in front of her eyes.

"Cassie! If you would stop entering our bedroom without knocking first you would stop walking in on me naked and us in compromising situations that lead to your embarrassment!" He snapped.

"I am so sorry, Lord Tsoukalous!" She fairly squealed, keeping her eyes averted and clutching Princess to her, hurriedly exited the bedroom.

"Shame on you, Nichola!" Leila admonished and headed into the bathroom to take a shower.

He was positive that the admonishment had held a distinct twinkle in her eye. So, smiling, he tossed the clothes on the bed and followed to join her.

* * * * *

"Good evening. My name is Leila Sutton, most of you know me as Lady Tsoukalous." She smiled at the audience in the ballroom, meeting first Esmerelda's and Iris's excited eyes in the front row, then meeting Nichola's, Rom's, Aleksei's, and the rest of the Small Council, who stood in the back leaning against the wall. "I'd like to take this time to thank you for allowing me to address this council on an important matter that affects our community as a whole. As most of you know, we had a tragic loss to our community at the end of August." Leila began somberly from the podium, speaking to the seated vampires in the ballroom. "So, before I get into the details of my talk with you this evening, I have a video presentation to show you." She nodded to Devin who pushed a button on the control panel.

She moved to the side as the room darkened and the video screen behind her lit up showing Burke's smiling face sitting comfortably behind his desk.Some of the vampires, mostly made vampires, in the audience gasped because of the clarity of his image.

"Howdy! For those of you who don't know me, my name is William Lionel Burke, and if you are watching this instead of hearing my words in person, it is because I am dead."He smiled good naturedly at the camera and his chocolate brown eyes twinkled. "I gave my life in the pursuit of stopping a monster whose actions were threatening the existence of our community.

So, I am here basically posthumously," Burke smiled charmingly, "to talk to you today about a subject that in my opinion is long overdue for discussion amongst us. That subject is Companion Rights. You see, I was born in 1803 in New Orleans, moved to the Texas territory when I was a young boy, and marched with Sam Houston to fight for Texas Independence! I transitioned into a vampire in 1841 on my own, having no idea what I was. In 1860, I met and befriended a good man, Fred, and because I was a young vampire, I accidentally turned him into my companion. He and I became Union spies in the war to free the slaves. Through our efforts, Lincoln's Union Army was successful, and Fred and I received commendation's from the President."There was a murmur amongst the seated vampires.

"I tell you this because I want you to know that I am no stranger to the fight for independence and freedom. We vampires value our independence and autonomy, even from each other! Hell, this governing body has only been in existence since the end of the Vampire-Shifter war in the late thirteenth century and only continues to operate through our cooperation with each other! We are a society made up of all nationalities, all races, and all creeds.So, why do we cooperate with each other? It's for our survival!

Now ask yourself some questions. Who here would struggle to survive without our Companions?" Burke paused briefly and the vampires muttered to themselves."Who do we make into our companions? Our friends, family, and sometimes lovers. We make companions from the people that we care for. Sometimes if we are lucky they serve us and protect us for centuries! They do this without ever being able to have families of their own. Why? Because as far as they are concerned, we, their makers, are their family.

And what is the first thing that happens after a vampire is killed? Well, if we haven't made a provision for them to be bonded by another vampire (which is an extremely rare occurrence, and actually a work around of vampire law), we kill them. I ask you is this the way we should treat our family?" Burke paused again, and the vampires in the room whispered amongst themselves.

"During this special meeting of the Large Council, you will have the opportunity to provide a blood sample to Dr. Lambert so you can possibly match up with family members amongst our community. In the twenty-first century, we vampires are finally seeing that family is an integral part of our society and the first step in the survival of our species.

I didn't live long enough to find my vampire family. But it didn't matter, I had a family in my companion, Fred, and I made some great friends who I could trust to provide a purpose and a home for him after my death. So, what I ask this body to do is provide hard and fast protections for our companions, because companions are not our slaves, they are our family. At a minimum, they have a right to not be abused at our hands and they have a right to live on after our deaths.

My good friend, Klaus Tsoukalous, and his mate Leila Sutton will be handing out a proposal for your review, discussion, and vote. I hope this council decides to do the right thing and take the just action of protecting our companions. Thank you for listening to my words today."

As the video stopped and the lights came back on, Leila stood in front of the podium once more to a room full of murmuring vampires. "If I could have your attention, please." She asked and the audience stopped speaking. "In the packets beneath your chairs, you will find the William Lionel Burke

Companion Protection Act for your review..."

Epilogue

January 2022

"So, you are leaving for Toronto in a few days, my friend?" Aleksei Ostrovsky's, Eastern European accent flowed in the room as he sat with Nichola at the table in front of the bar in Nichola's family suite. Ever since the old vampire had received the results back that he and Nichola shared DNA markers that meant that they had a common ancestor, the old vampire had been making more alone time with Nichola than ever before. They watched as Mansuetus, and Cassie scrambled throughout the suite to pack everything for the trip.

"Yes, we are stopping over in San Antonio to collect Devin, Fred, Dene and Zachary, Leila's oldest son. He has resigned his position with the San Antonio Police Department. I am hoping to convince him to become an investigator for the small council." Nichola pet Princess's soft fur, who had perched herself on his lap to watch the packing activity with interest.

"Ah, I look forward to meeting her oldest son! Rom tells me that he was a very good detective and though still human, has some amazing abilities. That is high praise from him. Devin and the companions went a head last week, Iris tells me. I was surprised to hear that." Aleksei responded.

"Well, Devin has shown no sign of fang as of yet, and William's plane was here and needed to be moved, so they took it back to San Antonio. Also, Devin wanted to assist Zachary in overseeing the construction of a spray booth on the ranch, so the good doctor went to assist. I heard something from Leila about updates to the pack house and adding of some single-family homes for families with children." Nichola murmured hearing Cassie and Leila speaking in the bedroom.

"Ah, yes, Iris told me that he had left all of his holdings to your sons." Aleksei remarked.

Nichola smiled at the term 'your sons'. "Yes, after his death and I had bonded Fred, he told us of the package that William had created and addressed to me, the first night that we had arrived in San Antonio. He had changed his will, making the boys his heirs and provided the video that we presented to the Large Council."

"How did Leila take the decision about the changes to the companion act? Iris says that she has been unusually quiet about it." Aleksei asked.

"Well, at first she was unhappy. But, as I explained to her, our society moves slowly, and for us wholesale change can be concerning and disruptive. Partial rights is better than no rights. The fact that the small council will take immediate action against any vampire that abuses, or arbitrarily kills companions was comforting for her. Also, provisions being fully allowed for a vampire to voluntarily bond the companion of another who dies without a will, also pleased her. What really made her angry I believe was that Rom and Beutel sided with each other and argued against the full act itself. She felt betrayed by Rom, I believe. But the fact that Charles and the Prince argued on behalf of the act was satisfying and of course your support and vote in favor of it helped to offset the disappointment of only a partial victory. Es supporting the act despite Rom's arguing against it helped to fully smooth her feathers. After Es won the vote to change the Large Council meetings from once every two-hundred years, except for special sessions, to once every one-hundred years, Leila was extremely happy." Nichola smiled.

"Yes, the Lady Esmerelda surprisingly taking part for the first time in Large Council activities is definitely due to your mate's influence. Rom was not happy I am told." Aleksei laughed.

Nichola chuckled. "Yes, with his mate and his daughter totally against his actions he felt very put upon! I am not sure that he was quite prepared for the uproar."

Aleksei laughed heartily. "Well, your mate is young and as with all younglings impatient! But she has some first-rate ideas. I believe that she will make an excellent addition to our community."

"I personally didn't realize that she had such a political streak, but it seems to make her happy, and of course if it makes her happy..." Nichola trailed off smiling again, stroking Princess's soft fur as the small dog snuggled against his chest.

"I am glad that we are speaking of Leila. I've wanted to ask you, but didn't want to intrude..." Aleksei started hesitantly.

"Ask away, Aleksei." Nichola smiled. "After all we are now family."

"Yes." The ancient vampire smiled happily. "I wanted to ask are you breeding?"

Nichola looked at him quizzically, then looked down at the dog. "I don't believe that Leila intends to breed her, at least I am hoping that she isn't. One is definitely enough. I am sure that she can give you the information on her breeder though if you are interested in obtaining a pup. They are located somewhere in Texas."

"No, son." Aleksei chuckled. "I am not interested in a dog, as cute as they may be." He leaned over to pet Princess. "You are now fully mated vampires. I am asking if Leila finds herself pregnant as of yet." He looked up from the dog into Nichola's eyes.

Nichola blinked at him stunned for a moment, thinking that age had finally caught up with the old vampire. "Aleksei, that is not possible. Take Rom and Es. Es has never been pregnant, and vampire women do not menstruate."

"It is not possible for the Lady Esmerelda to become pregnant. Though mated, she is a made vampire. You and Leila are both pure blood mates. Though very rare it is not unheard of. I myself am a product of such a union." He smiled at Nichola gently as his eyes widened in shock.

They heard a sudden clatter, and both looked to see Cassie who had dropped a suitcase, staring at them. She stood there with a surprised look on her face and her hands over her mouth, then she went sprinting for the bedroom, yelling, "Lady Tsoukalous!"

"Cassie!" Nichola called after her, quickly handing the dog to Aleksei and moving to follow.

The door to the suite was suddenly thrown open and an enraged Rom, followed closely by Es, entered to yell, "Nikolaos! I have just found out that my daughter boarded a commercial flight this morning to chase after your son! She insists that he is her mate, though he insists that he is not! We need to talk about this!"

Nichola half turned to look at Rom, then ignored him as he heard Leila yell, "Impossible! He said it was impossible!" and smiling happily, quickly went to take care of the most important person in his life. The only one who truly mattered now, the one who would always be with him, the one that he would love forever.

Now, Always, Forever – Foreign Language Glossary

※

agápi mou - my love

awki – prince (quechuan)

i allagí mou – my changeling

allaxiéra – changeling

ángixe me – touch me

agapitós - beloved

áse me na se agapíso – let me love you

áse me na se agapó gia pánta – let me love you forever

Château les Ténèbres – Dark Castle

Despótis - Lord or Master

Déspoina - lady or mistress

Dóxa to theó! - Thank God!

efcharistó – thank you

efcharistó, glykó mou, Se agapó – thank you, my sweet, I love you

éla gia ména – come for me

éla na to párei – come on pick it up

epitrépste mou na sas dóso efcharístisi – allow me to give you pleasure

fíla me – kiss me

glukó mou - my sweet

Glykó – sweet one

i psychí mou – my soul

i theá tis omorfiás mou – my goddess of beauty

Kyría - Lady, madam, mistress

Kýrios - Mister, main, lord, master, sir

Le violeur vampire déchirant – The Ripping Vampire Rapist

lígo vampír – little vampire

maman - mama

mikró – little one

Mírame. Mirame ahora. - Look at me.Look at me now.

moró – baby

moy golub' – my dove

Naí – yes

No más oraciones, mi belleza oscura. Eres mía. - No more prayers, my dark beauty. You are mine.

Ñusta – Princess (Quechua)

nóstimo – delicious

Ochi agápi mou – no my love

Oh Dios, por favor, sálvame de este demonio - Oh God please save me from this demon.

o ómorfos ángelos mou - my beautiful angel

ómorfi adelfí psychí mou – my beautiful soulmate

O Theé mou – Oh my God

Panemorfi – beautiful

Parakaló agápi mou, Lypámai – Please my love, I am sorry.

páre me sto glykó sou sóma – take me into your sweet body

pio agapiméni mou – my most beloved one

pouliche fougueuse – spirited filly

Prépei na eímai mésa sou me ton éna í ton állo trópo - I need to be inside of you one way or the other.

Se agapó – I love you

se parakaló agápi mou – please my love

Se parakaló voíthisé me – please help me

Sulpayki – thank you (Quechua, pronounced: sool-pay-ki)

Sumag – beautiful (Quechua)

sýnchrones gynaíkes – modern women
thélo na eímai mésa sou – I want to be inside of you
Ypóschomai – I promise

About the Author

A realist that started writing her first manuscript and creating other worlds and characters in elementary school, V. P. Nightshade, when not running her two businesses, can be found absorbed in a gripping, bodice-ripping, novel which usually has fangs or claws. She has spent her life reading and writing paranormal and romance novels and short stories with an eye to how otherworldly creatures would truly function in the real world and publishing was always on her bucket list.

V. P. has an MBA, is wife to a man who is so grouchy it is actually funny, mother to two wickedly handsome sons, and would love to be a grandmother one day, but her children seem to be stubbornly against it.

You can reach her at vpnightshade@gmail. com.

Now, Always, Forever is her second published novel.

You can connect with me on:
f https://www.facebook.com/VPNightshade.Author

Also by V.P. Nightshade

Vampiris Bloodline - A Paranormal Vampire Romance Series

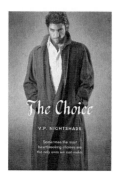

The Choice: A Paranormal Vampire Romance (Vampiris Bloodline - A Paranormal Vampire Romance Series Book 1)
Readers of paranormal romance will love this contemporary story about the struggle over who we love, what we choose, and the things that are chosen for us.

https://www.amazon.com/dp/B0984RWZXH

Made in United States
North Haven, CT
29 March 2022

17642276R10137